PRAISE FOR PAUL LEVINE

TO SPEAK FOR THE DEAD

"Move over Scott Turow. *To Speak for the Dead* is courtroom drama at its very best."
—Larry King

"An assured and exciting piece of work. Jake Lassiter is Travis McGee with a law degree . . . One of the best mysteries of the year."
—*Los Angeles Times*

"Paul Levine is guilty of master storytelling in the first degree. *To Speak for the Dead* is a fast, wry, and thoroughly engrossing thriller."
—Carl Hiaasen

NIGHT VISION

"Levine's fiendish ability to create twenty patterns from the same set of clues will have you waiting impatiently for his next novel."
—*Kirkus Reviews*

"Sparkles with wit and subtlety."
—*Toronto Star*

"Breathlessly exciting."
—*Cleveland Plain Dealer*

FALSE DAWN

"Realistic, gritty, fun."
—*New York Times Book Review*

"One of the best mystery writers in the business today. The story fairly leaps with enthusiasm toward the finale. *Riptide* is Paul Levine's finest work."
—*Ocala (FL) Star Banner*

FOOL ME TWICE

"You'll like listening to Jake's beguiling first-person tale-telling so much that you won't mind being fooled thrice."
—*Philadelphia Inquirer*

"A fast-paced thriller filled with action, humor, mystery and suspense."
—*Miami Herald*

"Blend the spicy characters created by Elmore Leonard with the legal expertise and suspense made famous by John Grisham and you have Paul Levine's *Fool Me Twice*."
—*Lake Worth (FL) Herald*

FLESH & BONES

"The author keeps the suspense high with innovative twists and touches of humor that spice up the courtroom scenes."
—*Chicago Tribune*

"Filled with smart writing and smart remarks. Jake is well on his way to becoming a star in the field of detective fiction."
—*Dallas Morning News*

"A well-focused plot that stresses in-depth characterization and action that is more psychological than macho. The author keeps the suspense high with innovative twists."
—*Atlanta Journal Constitution*

LASSITER

"Since Robert Parker is no longer with us, I'm nominating Levine for an award as best writer of dialogue in the grit-lit genre."
—*San Jose Mercury News*

"Lassiter is back after fourteen long years—and better than ever. Moving fast, cracking wise, butting heads, he's the lawyer we all want on our side—and on the page."
—Lee Child

"Few writers can deliver tales about sex and drugs in South Florida better than Levine."
—*Booklist*

SOLOMON VS. LORD

"A funny, fast-paced legal thriller. The barbed dialogue makes for some genuine laugh-out-loud moments. Fans of Carl Hiaasen and Dave Barry will enjoy this humorous Florida crime romp."
—*Publishers Weekly*

"The writing makes me think of Janet Evanovich out to dinner with John Grisham."
—Mysterylovers.com

"Hiaasen meets Grisham in the court of last retort. A sexy, wacky, wonderful thriller with humor and heart."
—Harlan Coben

THE DEEP BLUE ALIBI

"An entertaining, witty comedy caper with legal implications . . . sparkles with promise, humor, and more than a dash of suspense."
—Blogcritics.com

"A cross between *Moonlighting* and *Night Court* . . . courtroom drama has never been this much fun."
—Freshfiction.com

"As hilarious as *The Deep Blue Alibi* is, it is almost possible between the cleverly molded characters and sharp dialogue to overlook that the novel contains a terrific mystery, one that will keep you guessing."
—Bookreporter.com

KILL ALL THE LAWYERS

"A clever, colorful thriller . . . with characters drawn with a fine hand, making them feel more like friends than figments of the author's imagination. Levine ratchets up the tension with each development but never neglects the heart of the story—his characters."
—*Publishers Weekly* (starred review)

"Levine skillfully blends humor, a view of Miami, and the legal system into tidy plots."
—*South Florida Sun-Sentinel*

"Another successful fast-moving, highly entertaining mystery. Irreverent to juveniles, judges, and the judicial system, but does it all with a wink. Encore . . . encore."
—*ReviewingTheEvidence.com*

HABEAS PORPOISE

"Steve Solomon and Victoria Lord are smart and funny and sexy in a way that Hollywood movies were before comedies became crass and teen-oriented."
—*Connecticut Post*

"A *Moonlighting* crime novel. Great fun."
—*Lansing State Journal*

"Entertaining and witty with lots of laughs."
—MysteriousReviews.com

IMPACT (ORIGINALLY PUBLISHED IN HARDCOVER AS 9 SCORPIONS)

"A breakout book, highly readable and fun with an irresistible momentum, helped along by Levine's knowledge of the Supreme Court and how it works."
—*USA TODAY*

"Sizzles the Supreme Court as it has never been sizzled before, even by Grisham."
—F. Lee Bailey

"A masterfully written thriller, coiled spring tight. The plot is relentless. I loved it!"
—Michael Palmer

BALLISTIC

"*Ballistic* is *Die Hard* in a missile silo. Terrific!"
—Stephen J. Cannell

"It's easy to compare Levine to Tom Clancy but I think he's better for two simple reasons—he's a better storyteller and his characters are more believable, good guys and bad guys alike."
—Ed Gorman

ILLEGAL

"Levine is one of the few thriller authors who can craft a plot filled with suspense while still making the readers smile at the characters' antics."
—*Chicago Sun-Times*

"The seamy side of smuggling human cargo is deftly exposed by the clear and concise writing of the Edgar Award–nominated author. *Illegal* is highly recommended."
—*Midwest Book Review*

"Timely, tumultuous, and in a word, terrific."
—*Providence Journal*

BUM
LUCK

BOOKS BY PAUL LEVINE

THE JAKE LASSITER SERIES

To Speak for the Dead

Night Vision

False Dawn

Mortal Sin

Riptide

Fool Me Twice

Flesh & Bones

Lassiter

Last Chance Lassiter

State vs. Lassiter

THE SOLOMON & LORD SERIES

Solomon vs. Lord

The Deep Blue Alibi

Kill All the Lawyers

Habeas Porpoise

LASSITER, SOLOMON & LORD SERIES

Bum Rap

Bum Luck

Stand-Alone Thrillers

Impact

Ballistic

Illegal

Paydirt

BUM LUCK

PAUL LEVINE

 THOMAS & MERCER

Text copyright © 2017 by Nittany Valley Productions, Inc.

Published by Thomas & Mercer, Seattle

www.apub.com

Amazon, the Amazon logo, and Thomas & Mercer are trademarks of Amazon.com, Inc., or its affiliates.

ISBN-13: 9781477823101
ISBN-10: 1477823107

Cover design by Cyanotype Book Architects

Printed in the United States of America

For Marcia
from here to eternity
and
for Don Russo (1946–2014)
football player, rugby player, trial lawyer, friend

PART ONE

"Lawyers spend a great deal of their time shoveling smoke."

—Oliver Wendell Holmes Jr.

-1-

Dead Lawyer Walking

Thirty seconds after the jury announced its verdict, I decided to kill my client.

Or maybe it was quicker than that. Maybe there was an instantaneous firing of neurons and synapses, or whatever ignites sparks in my bourbon-pickled brain.

Did I mention the pounding headache? The thud of a pile driver ramming caissons into my cranium? I could barely hear the judge over the echoes.

"Has the jury reached a verdict?"

"We have, Your Honor."

"The clerk will publish the verdict."

"We, the jury, find the defendant, Marcus Thurston, not guilty of murder in the second degree."

Yeah, him. Marcus "Thunder" Thurston, All-Pro running back for the Miami Dolphins. Charged with pumping five bullets into his wife. Now free to carry a football . . . and a nine-millimeter Glock, if he so desired. Hearing the verdict, and perhaps a chorus of cheerleaders singing, Thurston clopped me on the shoulder. An affectionate but hearty clop you might use for chopping wood. If I didn't tip the scales at 240 pounds, I might have toppled face-first onto the defense table.

"Way to go, bro!" Thunder smacked me again.

"Don't 'bro' me, and don't touch me."

"Whassup with that, Jake?"

"I don't mind getting my hands dirty. I just need a minute to get the stains out."

"Hey, lose the 'tude, dude."

My headache was approaching the red line. On a scale of one to ten, we're going to need more digits. The thud-thud-thud of the pile driver subsided just long enough for an ice pick to stab deep into my skull.

"You're a narcissist, Thunder. With a Hall of Fame ego and a total lack of empathy."

A storm cloud hooded his eyes, and for the briefest moment, there was the same fearsome look Eva Thurston must have seen in the last seconds of her life. Then Thunder barked out a laugh and grinned. It was the thousand-watt smile he flashed on cue for his Nike commercial. The one where he jitterbugs the length of the football field, dodging mammoth defenders, then sprouts wings and soars skyward.

Like a god.

Or a demon.

I wanted to rip off those wings, watch him fall to earth.

Splat.

Bones splintered, organs crushed, arteries spurting.

Killing my client would be an act of justice, I told myself. Justice rooted in truth and fairness. Not justice bought and sold, bartered and compromised. A courtroom should be a holy place, our secular church. A palace of integrity and morality. But the palace has been sacked by the Huns.

Call me Attila.

Already reporters spilled out of the gallery and crowded the bar, firing questions.

"Thunder, will the NFL lift your suspension?"

"If you had it to do over again, would you still shoot your wife?"

"Lassiter, did you trick the jury with the Stand Your Ground law?"

I hadn't expected to win. And now that I had, victory tasted like swill. "Head straight to your limo," I ordered Thurston. "No talking to the press."

"Why not, bro? We won. Nothing I say can mess that up."

My eyes squinted through the pain, interfering with my ability to pack my trial bag, much less plan a murder. I could kill Thurston right now. Grab my fountain pen—a Montblanc Skeleton, a gift from an ex-lover whose name escaped me—and jam it straight through his left eye and into his brain. Sure, I could easily kill him. I just needed to figure out how to get away with it . . . the way Thurston did.

Of course, he had a damn good lawyer.

Me.

Jake Lassiter. Defender of the Bill of Rights, or at least a few of them. Purveyor of justice, or a reasonable facsimile thereof. Last bastion between freedom and forty years in a steel cage. In other words, the guy you call when you're guilty as hell.

I never intended to be a hero . . . and I succeeded. But all the trickery, all the gamesmanship had caught up with me. Thurston was the tipping point. How far had I fallen? Surely not from the mountaintop. More like the curb to the gutter.

Back in night law school, they taught us right from wrong, black from white. But they didn't teach us shades of gray. For twenty years I've made my living in the gray. Now I felt blanketed by a poisonous fog, a shroud that protected the guilty and shielded evil and cruelty from view.

A deep baritone startled me. "Gonna kill you, Thurston! Kill you hard and slow."

I turned to find Clyde Garner waving a thick index finger under my client's nose. A ruddy-faced man in his sixties, built like an oil drum, Garner owned a tree farm in Homestead. His daughter, Eva, had been a Junior Orange Bowl Princess, then Citrus Queen, and more recently the wife of Thunder Thurston. A thousand people attended her funeral, but Thunder wasn't one of them.

"Back off, old man." Thurston glared at Garner, menace in his eyes. "Only did what I had to do."

"Feed you to the wood chipper," Garner said, "one leg at a time."

So now there were at least two of us who wanted Thurston dead. If I didn't leave my business card at the murder scene, maybe I could get away with it. Who knows how many folks in Miami—other than Dolphins season-ticket holders—thought Thurston should be chopped into bite-size pieces?

"Mr. Garner," I said. "Please don't make things worse."

He swiveled toward me, his neck overflowing the collar of his white dress shirt. "Worse, shyster? What do you know about worse?"

"When I look at you, Mr. Garner, I see a good man."

"Don't kiss up to me, sleazebag."

"Please don't do anything that will come back to haunt you."

"You have no idea what haunts me, shyster." His eyes narrowed; his cheeks flushed. His hatred washed over me, a toxic tide. He leaned closer, gave me a whiff of boozy breath. "Gonna kill you, too. Maybe first, I dunno."

"The last thing Eva would want would be for you to—"

"Don't you mention her name, bloodsucker!"

His burning anger had shifted to me.

"All I'm saying, Mr. Garner—"

"You had your say! You know what you are, Lassiter?"

I didn't, though the words *shyster*, *sleazebag*, and *bloodsucker* still hung in the air.

"Dead lawyer walking. That's what you are. You're a dead lawyer walking."

Vigilante Justice Is an Oxymoron

My first shot was high and to the left, just above his ear. I adjusted my aim, relaxed my shoulders, tightened my two-hand grip, eased the barrel of the Beretta a smidgen to the right, and squeezed off another round.

The gunshot plunked just below his collarbone. The third shot caught him squarely between the eyes.

"You nailed him!" Steve Solomon whooped just as the horn beeped.

"Die, Thurston, die," I whispered.

"Cease all fire," a voice announced over the speakers. "Place your weapons down and move behind the red line."

We were outdoors at the Glades Trail Range on the edge of the Everglades. It was another day of steam-room, shirt-sticky, withering heat. Summer in Miami. The only relief would be the afternoon thunderstorms that slicked the highways and caused multicar collisions, often with roadside gun battles. Already smoky-gray storm clouds had gathered to the west over the shallow slough. If it rained in hell, the place might be mistaken for Miami.

I was with Steve Solomon and Victoria Lord. Law partners and lovers, they shared a house on Kumquat in Coconut Grove. You could almost toss a mango from their yard and hit my little coral rock house on Poinciana. Solomon and Lord were my pals and competitors for clients, those presumably innocent souls—cue the laughter—who could pay handsome fees.

Solomon and Lord were each in their midthirties. Even though I'm fifteen years older, somehow the three of us became best buds. Every few weeks we take target practice. Handguns at twenty-five yards. Loser buys lunch and accepts all manner of insults.

They were shooting at conventional bull's-eye targets. Ten points in the middle, declining values toward the outside of the circle. I had a different target. An assistant range master was a former client—he'd been arrested for toting a concealed firearm to church—and let me use police perp targets. You know the ones, silhouettes of bad guys. Anonymous on paper, but Thunder Thurston in my brain.

"Victoria wins," Solomon said as we took seats on the bench behind the firing line and removed our ear protectors. "I'm second. Jake, you're last, so you're buying lunch, and not at a taco stand."

"Vic always wins," I complained.

"Women make the best snipers," Solomon said.

I nodded my agreement. "In my experience, that's a fact."

"Is that a sexist remark, Jake?" Victoria demanded.

"Only if I were talking about women in general, but I mean the ones in my life," I said.

Solomon punched me on the shoulder. "Smooth recovery, pal."

"Experts at kill shots," I continued. "Break a man's heart at a hundred yards."

"Quit while you're ahead!" Solomon warned.

Steve Solomon was a wiry, dark-haired guy who had played some baseball at the University of Miami. Lousy hitter, lazy fielder, savvy base stealer. Victoria was tall, slender, blonde. Perfect posture. Poised and proper and Ivy League smart. They squabbled a bit, and at first I thought they made an odd couple. But there's something about opposites attracting. In court Solomon could be reckless and unprepared, always shooting from the hip. Victoria's files were cross indexed and color coded, and her research was updated daily. Together they made a formidable team.

And me, Jake Lassiter? Before I started earning my living stomping back and forth in front of the judge's bench, I was warming the bench for the Miami Dolphins. I played a little linebacker when a starter was hurt, but more often, I only got my uniform dirty on the suicide squads, banging heads and making (or missing) tackles on the kickoff and punt teams.

After a few years, the NFL decided it could sell beer without me. The Saskatchewan Roughriders of the CFL offered me a contract at essentially minimum wage, but instead I enrolled in law school at the University of Miami, night division, where I proudly graduated, *no cum laude*, top half of the bottom third of my class.

For the past twenty years, I've been stalking the halls of Miami's comically named Justice Building. It should be called "the Law Factory," the place we grind the cheap meat, jam it into hog intestines, and sell it to the public as tasty treats. Truth be told, the relationship of "law" to "justice" is roughly that of roadkill possum to filet mignon.

During these two decades, I've won some cases, lost a bunch more, occasionally spending a night in jail for arguing too vigorously with judges. My shaggy hair, once the color of Everglades saw grass bleached by the sun, is going gray. Not the distinctive silver-fox gray of those handsome, crinkly-eyed dudes in Viagra commercials. More like cigar-ash gray. My face, now as craggy as Mount Rushmore, had once attracted fishnet-stockinged groupies in low-end cities of the AFC, primarily Cleveland and Buffalo. I've never been married, and with slim prospects these days, I sleep alone.

The horn blared over the speakers. The range master announced that shooters could retrieve their targets, and no one was allowed at the shooting stands. We stayed put on the bench. No need for souvenirs.

"This is the worst you've ever shot," Solomon reminded me, in case I'd forgotten.

"I've had a headache for a couple days."

Victoria fixed me with a concerned look. "Are you taking anything for it?"

"The usual. Aspirin and tequila."

"You were squinting as you shot," she said.

"The target was moving on me a little bit."

Victoria the Nurturer pursed her lips with even more concern. "Double vision, Jake?"

"It'll go away."

"So this has happened before?"

"Jeez, Vic. No more cross-exam. Let's have lunch. Calle Ocho. Palomilla and guava shakes."

She was trying to make eye contact, but I busied myself slipping nine-millimeter shells into a magazine. It requires some dexterity, especially when your hands are the size of catchers' mitts. I was having trouble, and Victoria noticed.

"Jake, what's going on?"

I took a second. At the adjacent skeet and trap range, shotgun blasts echoed like distant thunder. "Thunder Thurston was guilty."

"Aren't they all?" Solomon asked.

That was quite nearly true. I usually assume my clients are guilty. It saves time. But not a lawyer's soul. With Thurston, I had violated my own rule. Hoping he was innocent, I'd dropped my skepticism, and, for a while, I believed his story.

"Thurston's worse than most," I said. "He's a cold-blooded, heartless murderer. Probably a sociopath. And he got away with killing his wife, thanks to me."

Victoria said, "You were just doing your job."

"Which happens to be trying cases," Solomon said. "Not seeking justice."

"I hate that tired old excuse. It makes me want to tear down the pillars of the courthouse."

"Jake, my friend," Solomon said. "Your job is to jiggle the pinball machine, hit the flippers, and drop the ball into the hole without lighting up the 'Tilt' button."

I pressed my knuckles into my forehead, trying to knead away the pain. "What the hell's that mean?"

"It's all a game."

"You might have a different point of view if I'd lost your trial."

"What if you had, big guy?" Solomon said, in a mocking tone that always aggravated me. "Would you have busted me out of jail to do justice?"

"Hell, no. I would have sent you a card every year on your birthday and spent as much time as possible soothing your fiancée's broken heart."

Solomon laughed. "Truth! My best man speaks the truth."

Best man. That would be me.

Technically, Solomon and Lord were engaged, but neither seemed in a hurry to walk down the aisle. There had been a moment in the past when Victoria had taken a fleeting interest in me, but equal quantities of whiskey and angst had been involved.

Victoria clasped one of my hands with both of her own. "Your client's wife attacked him with a knife."

"Sliced him open!" Solomon joined in.

"So maybe you shouldn't second-guess the jury," Victoria added.

"Your client stood his ground under Florida law," Solomon piled on after the whistle, just like the Dolphins' Ndamukong Suh. "Blame the legislature for passing the statute. Or the governor for signing it. But you didn't do anything wrong."

9

Overhead the gray clouds grew darker and heavier. To the west, over the Everglades, lightning flashed.

"That knife wound," I said, barely above a whisper.

"What about it?"

I bought a moment of time by exhaling a long breath. "It might have been self-inflicted. After the shooting."

"What!" Victoria's eyes went wide. "Thurston admitted that?"

I shook my head. "If he had, I wouldn't have put him on the stand to say Eva stabbed him. I've never knowingly used perjured testimony. But this time I came close."

They waited for me to tell more, so I did.

"I asked Doc Riggs to study photos of the wound, the blood splatter, the ER report. He said he couldn't be certain, but given the size and shape of the blade, the superficial nature of the wound, and its location, it seemed likely that Thurston stabbed himself."

"Holy . . . ," Solomon said.

"Moley," Victoria said.

Sometimes the kids are so damn cute.

"I confronted Thurston," I said. "Told him I wanted to work out a manslaughter plea before the state blew his defense out of the water. He stuck to his story. Eva came at him like a ninja. He feared for his life and shot her in self-defense."

"Five times," Victoria said, as if I didn't know.

"Thurston said I could either quit the case or take it to trial and put him on the stand. The state never questioned the knife wound. The jury bought his story, and here we are."

They were both silent a moment. Then Solomon said, "That doesn't change anything. You did nothing wrong."

"The result was wrong. But I could right it."

They both waited for me to continue. The storm clouds had turned angry. A jagged lightning bolt creased the sky, and thunder clapped in the distance.

Finally Victoria said, "How could you right it, Jake?"

"I could kill the bastard."

Solomon cackled. "Good marketing plan, Jake. I can picture your TV commercials. 'If I lose your case, you go to jail. If I win, I kill you.'"

"Rough justice is better than none. So is vigilante justice."

"Vigilante justice is an oxymoron," Victoria said. "You can't kill a client."

"She's right," Solomon said. "You gotta hire someone to do it."

"Steve!" Victoria shot her partner a look somewhere between scolding and skinning alive.

"I could get away with it," I said. "Who knows more about evidence and proof than we do?"

Victoria wrinkled her forehead. "We?"

"I might need alibi witnesses."

"That's not happening," Victoria shot back.

"I think you played football too long without a helmet," Solomon added.

"Jake, I've never known you to be so consumed with talk of violence." Victoria again. "Are you feeling okay?"

"Just peachy."

"How do you go twenty years being a respectable lawyer—"

"That's a stretch," Solomon chimed in.

"And suddenly become an agent of vengeance?" Victoria continued.

"Agent of justice," I said. "It's not like this would be my maiden voyage."

They both looked at me dubiously.

"Before your time," I said.

"You killed a client?" Solomon asked.

"Nope. If I'd killed him, there wouldn't have been anyone to file a complaint with the Florida Bar."

In unison the cute kids said, "What complaint?"

So I told them.

-3-

Spanked

Fifteen years earlier . . .

Florida Supreme Court, Tallahassee, Florida

The chief justice stares down at me from the stately mahogany bench. Trim and fit under his black robes, he has a fine head of judicial white hair and wears rimless bifocals. Over the years I've read—okay, skimmed—hundreds of his written opinions, which are generally smart, focused, and fair.

I respect the guy. The feeling is not mutual.

"Mr. Lassiter, how did you get here today?"

"American Airlines, Your Honor. Nonstop from Miami."

He grimaces. "You got here through your own disgraceful misconduct. You egregiously violated your oath."

There are three justices to his left and three to his right, perched like ospreys on a wire, studying the field mouse who will shortly become a mid-morning snack.

The justice to the chief's right is a woman in her seventies who wears a white silk jabot that peeks daintily out of her robes. She gives me the evil eye, or really two evil eyes that are magnified by her thick glasses.

This full-court press has been convened for a flogging. Or, more precisely, a "public reprimand." It's pretty much the most humiliating moment of any lawyer's life . . . even worse than cutting loose a nuclear fart during closing argument.

In the gallery a dozen lawyers await their own cases. Real cases, civil and criminal, not the staged shaming of one of their brethren. Some of the lawyers squirm in their seats, feeling for me. They could be standing at the podium, sweat trickling down their backs.

"You admit striking your client and breaking his jaw?" the chief justice demands.

"I'd just won a date-rape case by suppressing the only physical evidence, a bottle of roofies. My client laughed when the verdict came in. He asked if he could pay my retainer now for next time, because he figured I was his get-out-of-jail-free card."

"So, angered by his insouciance, you resorted to violence?" the chief says.

"I don't know what *insouciance* means. But I wasn't angry at him, Your Honor. He is who he is. A rich man's spoiled dipshit son who does what he wants. What I was furious about was me. I'm the latest one to enable him."

"Did you handle the trial ethically?"

"I did everything by the book. But the result was injustice. That's what I can't live with."

The chief shoots a sideways glance at Justice Evil Eyes, who shrugs and emits a scoffing sound from her throat without moving her lips. The chief turns back to me.

"Perhaps, Mr. Lassiter," the chief says, "you should consider whether you have chosen the right profession."

-4-

Inhaling the Devil

When I had finished telling my pals about my public censure and court-imposed anger management therapy, Solomon was the first to speak. "The way I see it, you've set a precedent. Go punch out Thunder Thurston."

"Thunder killed a woman," I said. "He deserves to die."

Victoria's brow furrowed into little worry lines. "Jake, you're just speaking theoretically, aren't you? This isn't real. You're simply philosophically inclined toward retribution."

"I'm philosophically inclined toward a nine-millimeter Beretta." Fat raindrops, surprisingly cold, began pelting us, and a thunderclap rattled the windows on the range master's shed.

"Not a good career move," Solomon said. "Thurston's about to sign a new contract. You'll make a bundle repping him."

"I don't care about the money."

"Let me amend my earlier statement," Solomon said. "Did you even wear a helmet playing football?"

"Why can't you understand what I'm saying?"

Solomon threw up his hands. "Because you're the guy who used to say, 'They don't call us sharks for our ability to swim.'"

"I said and did a lot of stupid things when I was young."

"The Thurston verdict will bring you business, and your bosses at Harman and Fox will be loving it. You don't get a murderer off the hook every day."

"That's great, Solomon. Maybe that will be in my obit. 'Miami lawyer Jake Lassiter, who got murderers off the hook, died yesterday of regret.'"

"Jake's suffering from existential angst," Victoria diagnosed.

"He's a shark who's lost his teeth," Solomon said. "He's forgotten we're just hired guns."

The horn blared, and the range master announced that all us trigger-happy citizens could once again approach the firing line, if we felt like shooting in the rain. My pals and I stayed put on the bench.

"Be rational, Jake," Victoria said. "What purpose would killing Thurston serve?"

"He'd never harm a woman again."

"There's another way to accomplish that."

"Yeah?" I gave her my big-dumb-guy look. It comes naturally.

"Identify Thurston's weaknesses."

I thought about it a moment. "Drugs. Prescription and otherwise."

"Such as?"

"OxyContin and Percocet. Gets them from the team doc."

"That won't help."

"One time at his condo, he handed me a big-ass syringe and a bottle of Toradol. Asked me to inject him in the butt."

Victoria wrinkled her nose. "Did you do it?"

"No, but one of his posse did. A lot of players get swag bags of medication from kiss-ass quacks who want signed jerseys to hang in their offices."

"Anything else?"

"Amphetamines. I've seen him snort Adderall. Says it makes him faster."

"Inhaling the devil," Solomon said. "That's what meth is called on the street."

"How's he get it?" Victoria asked.

"From one of his posse. Big dude, muscle gone to fat. Goes by Jelly Bean."

"Jelly Bean is a street name for meth," Solomon said.

Victoria shot a sideways glance toward her lover and law partner.

"What?" he said.

"Inhaling the devil? Jelly Bean?"

"C'mon, Vic. You know I got street cred."

"Only if the street's Ocean Drive. You grew up on Miami Beach, for crying out loud."

"Hey Nick and Nora," I said. "Let's get back on track."

"Do you know how to find Jelly Bean?" Victoria asked.

"He hangs out in Thurston's condo, acts as chauffeur, rounds up his groupies. They've been tight since high school in Belle Glade."

"Dirt-poor town," Solomon said. "Nothing but sugarcane fields."

"And now Thurston is a multimillionaire about to score a huge contract," I said.

"Is it possible Jelly Bean resents his old buddy?" Victoria asked.

I shrugged, and pain flared in my right shoulder. Long-ago rotator cuff surgery left me with a rusty joint. "Where you headed with this?"

"I get it," Solomon said. "When they were kids, they're swinging machetes in the cane fields every summer instead of going to camp at Weeki Wachee Springs. They're wearing hand-me-down clothes, hanging on street corners, maybe breaking into parking meters. Flash forward, Thunder is rich and famous, and Jelly Bean is his bitch."

"I was going to say valet," Victoria said.

It was becoming clear. "So if Jelly Bean gets busted," I said, "he's got something to trade."

"Victoria's nailed it," Solomon said. "You shouldn't kill Thurston. You should frame him."

-5-

Muck Is a State of Mind

That evening, on the back porch at home, I celebrated my friend Jack's birthday. Jack Daniel's, that is. The smoky Tennessee whiskey just turned 150 . . . an even century older than me.

As I sipped, I savored.

As I savored, I planned.

I would follow Solomon and Lord's advice. I would get dirt on Thurston and take it to the State Attorney. Tomorrow.

Tonight, drinking the liquid gold, I looked back.

I had taken Thunder Thurston's case because I'd thought he was innocent.

I'd thought he was innocent because Johnnie Duncan had said he was.

I respect and trust Duncan, and that was what buried me deep in the crud of *State of Florida vs. Marcus Thurston*.

Ten years ago Duncan was head football coach at Glades Central High School in poverty-stricken Belle Glade. At the time, Florida State's coaches were salivating over Thunder Thurston, a five-star running back who was considered the nation's number one recruit.

Rumors circulated that a package deal was in the works. A recruiting website ran a piece saying Duncan had demanded a coaching job at FSU, plus a cash bonus for delivering Thurston to Tallahassee. Enraged, Duncan looked for a lawyer to sue the website and found me, an ex-jock, ex-public defender, ex-a lot of things.

"I'm a deacon in my church, and I take the teachings seriously," the coach said on the phone. "I instill in my players the concept of integrity, and that's the way I live."

"From what I hear, you do a great job as a coach and a deacon," I said.

"Do you know what they call Belle Glade?"

"Muck City," I said, "because of the sugarcane."

"Not just that. Muck is a state of mind. The boys can cut cane, play football, or sell drugs. I teach them to live clean and go to church. Several have made it in the NFL, and I expect Marcus Thurston will be the next big one. Even more important, he's a fine young man. I would never try to profit from his labors."

I talked Duncan out of suing the website on the grounds it didn't own anything except a laptop and a cappuccino machine. Instead I wrote a lawyer's letter demanding a retraction and an apology and got both. Then Duncan told me a secret. Florida State really had offered him a position when the school was romancing Thurston. Offended by the obvious quid pro quo, Duncan had turned it down.

In stepped karma. The good kind. The Atlanta Falcons offered Duncan a job coaching running backs. It was a startling leap, from high school to the NFL without an intermediate stop in the college ranks. Once he was assured that his Glades Central chief assistant—another church deacon—would take over the head coaching job, Duncan headed to Atlanta.

Coach and former player stayed close. Duncan took pride in Thurston's achievements. All-American at Florida State. First-round draft choice of the Dolphins, All-Pro in his third season.

Six months ago Coach Duncan called me again.

"You must have forgotten all about me," he said when I answered the phone.

"No way, Coach. Why would you say that?"

"You never sent me a bill."

"Never intended to. It was an honor getting to know you."

"I guess you heard Marcus was arrested for killing his wife."

"It's all over the news."

"You're an honest lawyer and a tough lawyer, Lassiter, and that's what Marcus needs. He's innocent."

"How would you know?"

"He told me so, and Marcus doesn't lie. I'd trust that young man with my sister or my bank account. If you represent him, I'll be a character witness, and a darn good one."

And that's how Thunder Thurston came into my life. Not that it's Coach Duncan's fault. That would be like General Custer blaming Bloody Knife, his trusted Sioux scout, for the massacre at Little Big Horn. I believe in taking personal responsibility. As Jimmy Buffett, the troubadour of the Florida Keys, told us in "Margaritaville," "it's my own damn fault."

Those were my thoughts as I finished the whiskey and my eyes grew heavy. Then one last little sentiment just before I dozed off, sprawled in the porch chair.

Thunder, you betrayed Coach Duncan. My only regret in destroying you is the suffering it will cause to that good man.

-6-

The North Star, the Burning Bush, the Holy Virgin

I spent the next morning sparring with State Attorney Ray Pincher. Not in court. Not metaphorically.

Really *sparring*.

In the ring at the Riverfront Athletic Club. Wearing red leather headgear with foam padding to shield my weary brain. Down below, my groin protector, the banana pouch model, to protect an even more important part of the body. We opted for the lighter gloves—twelve ounces instead of sixteen—because we both enjoyed the solid *thwomp* when a punch landed. Of course, we inflicted more damage on each other, but that was part of the fun.

A few lawyers and bankers stopped to watch us. Sweat beading on his shaved head, Pincher danced around the ring on his toes, flicking jabs, as if zapping insects with an electric wand. I kept both elbows tight against my ribs and plowed forward, always forward, cutting off the angles, muscling Pincher against the ropes, where I would try to shatter his ribs into shards and splinters.

Did I mention we're friends?

Which was strange because we were frequently opponents in court, where our competitive natures overcame our legal training, to say nothing of ethics, etiquette, and plain common sense. In the courtroom, just as in the boxing ring, Sugar Ray Pincher would jab, jab, jab, seldom knocking me down but often drawing blood.

I was bigger, stronger. He was quicker, meaner.

Ray Pincher was also a damn fine prosecutor. "Jake Lassiter! The Jakester!" he would greet me each morning of trial. "The lawyer who took the *shy* out of *shyster* and put the *fog* into *pettifogger*."

"Screw you, Sugar Ray," was my witty reply.

Okay, he was a more eloquent orator, probably from his training at a Baptist seminary, back when he intended to be a preacher instead of a prosecutor. Of course, he still believed he was doing the Lord's work. He was also a helluva politician. His billboards showed him bare chested in boxing gear, gloves raised. The tagline: "Elect a Fighter!" With broad support from every ethnic group in this diverse and fractured community, he became one of the few African-Americans to win a countywide office.

As a teenager, Pincher boxed Golden Gloves, which explained the "Sugar Ray" sobriquet and his ability to dance circles around me while blackening my eyes with quick little flurries. Just now he snapped two jabs that caught me on the right cheekbone.

Pop-pop.

I lowered my head and bulldozed forward. Tossed a left that was too slow arriving. Pincher slipped his head sideways and came back with a combo, left jab to the face, right hook into my gut. Thankfully, I have a hard head and my midsection is still reasonably taut, though the washboards are hiding under an extra ten pounds of blubber.

Pincher grinned at me around his mouthpiece and lowered his gloves to waist level. Muhammad Ali taunting Chuck Wepner.

Try to hit me, he seemed to be saying.

My left hook surprised him. Caught him on the side of the jaw. His legs hippity-hopped; his knees wobbled. My follow-up right dug into his solar plexus, and his mouthpiece flew out.

But he never fell. He just formed a *T* with both gloves, our mutually agreed way of calling a time-out. The idea was to spare each other hard feelings and brain damage.

"I can't believe you're still on your feet," I said. "My balls weigh more than you, but I can never knock you down."

"Twice. You knocked me down twice last year." Pincher's breaths came in short gasps.

"Low blow the first time, head butt the second," I confessed.

I tried untying my glove laces with my teeth, and Pincher said, "So why'd you want to see me so urgently?"

"Thunder Thurston."

"You here to gloat?"

I let the laces go, gloves still on. "Nothing to brag about. I wish I'd lost."

"Bull!"

"I mean it. I wish you'd prosecuted instead of Strychnine. She's so ferocious she turns off jurors. With that devilish charm of yours, you'd have gotten a big, fat guilty verdict."

Pincher was one of the rare elected state attorneys who still tried cases himself. I respected him for that. But he'd turned over *State vs. Thurston* to Stacy Strickstein, head of his homicide division, known to the defense bar as Stacy Strychnine.

She was a savage prosecutor who played it so close to the ethical line that her Prada pumps sometimes stepped out of bounds. She could eviscerate a witness on cross, and her closing arguments were emotional and vicious. Needless to say, she did not congratulate me when the jury returned its verdict.

Instead she insisted the judge poll the jury. She then leaned on the jury box railing, drilling the jurors with an executioner's glare, as each one affirmed his or her verdict. On the way out of the courtroom, she turned to me and said, "This isn't over, Lassiter."

"Actually," I said, "the fat lady has sung," an unfortunate reference to the overweight woman who'd turned out to be the foreperson.

Now Pincher said, "If you wanted to lose, why'd you fight so hard?"

"Reflexes. Instincts. Like in the ring. You hit me, I hit you back. Strychnine played dirty in opening statement, blowing smoke about some incendiary evidence she could never get admitted. Consciously, I wanted to lose, but my subconscious wouldn't let me. I fought back hard, and now I regret it."

He studied me, maybe trying to determine if I was being truthful or just peeing on his leg. After a moment, I said, "I guess you were afraid to take me on in court."

He laughed and spittle flew. "I *love* trying cases against you. It's like wrestling a rhinoceros. But if I'd convicted Thurston, all the Dolphins fans would hate me, and if I lost, I'd look like a fool. Not good in an election year." He fixed me with a quizzical look. "You still haven't told me. Why'd you want to see me?"

"I can help you nail Thurston."

"Whoa, whoa, whoa!" Pincher took a step back and raised his arms as if I were pointing a gun at his chest.

"I know who sells Thurston his drugs."

"I'm not listening, Jake."

"His name is Rashan Drexler. Goes by Jelly Bean."

"I can't hear you."

"You nail Drexler, you'll flip him like a pancake. Get him to wear a wire when he makes the delivery and Thurston pays him."

"I know you consider the Ethical Rules as mere suggestions—"

"Amusing suggestions," I clarified.

"Even so, Jake, you can't squeal on your own client."

"I didn't learn about the drug dealer in a privileged conversation."

"Doesn't matter. Don't be talking sleaze around me. I'll report you to the Florida Bar."

"Ah, get in line. They don't scare me."

"You been hit in the head too many times. They could pull your ticket."

"Maybe I don't care, Sugar Ray."

"Shut your stupid white-ass mouth."

I did as I was told. For a moment, the only sound was the clang of weights on the other side of the gym and music blaring from the spinning class. Finally, I said, "I'm a fallen priest."

"What the hell does that mean?"

"I used to believe justice was the North Star, the burning bush, the holy virgin."

"And now?"

"Just fairy tales."

"You don't even see the other side, Jake."

"What side is that?"

"Mine! You know how many cops bring me cases I can't prosecute? Even when I know the dirtbag did it, I can't file without the evidence. You think I get all weepy every time it happens?"

"I think you just powder your nose and hold a press conference about how many penny-ante drug dealers you've convicted."

Without warning or preamble, he pivoted and hit me.

Twice. *Pop-pop.*

Left jabs, one to the forehead and one to the nose. Not hard, but not love taps, either.

"What's that for?" I brought my hands up, elbows in, not knowing what to expect.

"Gonna whup your ass."

"Why?"

"You've been gaming me."

24

"How?"

"Damn it, Jake. I always trusted you."

"What? What did I do?"

He bobbed. He weaved. He jabbed.

He uncorked a straight left that landed flush on my mouth. "Fight now. Talk later," he said.

Indicting a *Sandwich de Jamón*

On his toes, Pincher spun gracefully around me, snapping jabs at my kisser. He kept circling to his left, forcing me to circle to my right. After five revolutions, I started feeling dizzy.

"What's going on, Sugar Ray?"

"What's that rap of yours, Jake? 'Buckle your chin strap. Law is a contact sport.'"

"Yeah, so what?"

"So's boxing!" He came closer, fired a short left hook into my ribs, then backed away, keeping up his patter. "I hope I'm wrong, but I think I just figured out your game."

"Whadaya mean?"

"You got wind of Stacy Strickstein's investigation."

I tossed a looping left hook that grazed the top of his head. "What's she supposedly investigating?"

"As if you didn't know."

Pop-pop-pop. Three jabs, harmless, except my ears were starting to ring.

"No idea, Ray. I can't relate to Strychnine. She's got no human DNA."

"Which makes her a bulldog prosecutor."

"So what's she sniffing?"

"Jury tampering. Bribery."

"By who? Or is it whom?"

"You! The Jakester. She seems to think you bribed a juror in the Thurston trial."

"Stacy Strychnine is crazy—you know that, right? She sees conspiracies in her dreams, thinks all defense lawyers are scum."

"The woman does lack nuance. I'll grant you that."

"The word downtown is she's gonna run against you in the next election."

"It's the truth. She's already raising money."

"I wouldn't bribe a juror, Sugar Ray."

"I told her that."

"Thank you."

"The Jakester will cut corners, I said. He'll break all the china in the shop. He'll bend the rules to their breaking point. But in his heart there's light, not darkness."

"But you didn't convince her?"

Pincher did the Ali shuffle, the laces on his white shoes twirling. He came out of the dance with a left-right combo that I blocked with a glove and a forearm.

Skipping away, Pincher said, "She thinks I can't be objective because you and I are close friends."

"Not that close."

"Stacy's working with the grand jury."

"Ah, jeez, the grand jury will indict a ham sandwich."

"In these parts, a *sandwich de jamón*." He danced another revolution around me, staying away from my left. "I won't prejudge. But you're behaving oddly, coming over here trying to frame your own client."

"Trying to do justice, Ray."

"You don't get to decide what's just. You just follow the law."

"Yeah, and look where that's gotten me."

"You need to change your path, Jake. You're on the road to Damascus. Do you remember Saul of Tarsus?"

"Sure, I went to Sunday school. Saul used an alias. The apostle Paul."

"Hardly the way I would put it, but not wrong, either. Saul was a Pharisee whose life work was persecuting the early Christians."

"That's some job description."

We both kept our distance. Talking and dancing.

"Saul was on the road to Damascus when he was visited by divine revelation," Pincher said. "Jesus spoke to him, and Saul underwent redemption and became the apostle Paul."

"Unless you're the divine one, I'm missing the point here, Ray."

He moved closer, threw a punch that missed. "You need redemption, Jake. You need to believe in the good book, which in our case is the law."

"I believe in the big print, but the footnotes give me trouble."

"Jury tampering is in capital letters."

"This is crap, Ray. I didn't bribe a juror. I didn't even want to win."

"Which is starting to sound like your cover story. Like maybe you got wind of the investigation. So now you come to me and say, 'Oh, my bad. I got a guilty man off. Let me help you nail him.'"

"C'mon, Ray. You said yourself I'd never—"

He thwacked me with a straight left jab, flush on the nose, and my eyes watered.

"I might have been wrong about you, not-so-close friend."

That stopped me. Was he serious?

I was standing flat-footed, openmouthed, arms down when he launched a left hook from somewhere west of Hialeah. The punch was thrown with anger; Pincher apparently believed Strychnine instead of me. Thinking I'd tricked him all these years, that my heart really was filled with darkness.

The punch landed squarely on my right temple, or rather on the headgear over my temple. Without the padding, my skull might have splintered like a walnut crushed by a mallet. Still I felt a shock wave from ear to ear. I toppled sideways, knees buckling, arms flailing.

I hit the canvas with a thud, wondering for the briefest moment why the lights had gone dim and I was so damn sleepy.

IN THE ELEVENTH JUDICIAL CIRCUIT IN AND FOR

MIAMI-DADE COUNTY, FLORIDA

In re: Investigation of Jacob Lassiter, Esq.

Pursuant to Florida State Section 918.12, to wit, Jury Tampering.

Investigation No. 2016-MDC-GJ-149

Partial Transcript of Grand Jury Proceedings

Q: [By ASA Strickstein] Mr. Gutierrez, before we begin, do you have any questions?

A: [By Manuel Gutierrez] Where's the judge?

Q: There is no judge during grand jury testimony, Mr. Gutierrez. It's just you, me, and the twenty-one citizens on the panel.

A: [Witness waves] Hola. Hello there.

Q: You have been granted immunity, sir. Do you understand what that means?

A: Si yo le dijera la verdad. If I tell the truth, you won't put me in jail, even if I committed a crime.

Q: Now, sir. Do you know a man named Jake Lassiter?

A: Sí. I was on the Thunder Thurston jury. Número tres. That was me.

Q: Did there come a time that Mr. Lassiter spoke to you outside the courtroom?

A: The end of the first day. I was walking to the juror parking lot. Mr. Lassiter came up behind me as I was getting into my car.

Q: What did he say?
A: [No answer]

Q: Mr. Gutierrez . . .
A: Isn't that hearsay? On *The Good Wife*, that would be hearsay.

Q: It's perfectly fine in the grand jury, Mr. Gutierrez. Our rules are different. Now, what did Mr. Lassiter say?
A: He said, "Nice 'Cuda."

Q: Meaning what?
A: I drive a Barracuda I restored myself. Mr. Lassiter says, "What is it, '71?" And I say, "You nailed it, but you won't believe what's under the hood."

Q: Then what happened?
A: I open the hood, and Mr. Lassiter says, "What the hell is that, a jet engine?" And I tell him, "It's a Dodge Viper four-hundred-fifty-cubic-inch V-10 with a six-speed stick. It'll go one forty-five without breaking a sweat."

Q: And then?
A: Mr. Lassiter laughs and says, "Number three, you've got yourself a Vipercuda."

Q: So by saying "number three," he recognized you as being on the jury in the Thurston case?

A: Sure. He'd picked the jury that morning. Then he tells me he drives an '84 Eldo convertible, maybe I'd be interested in doing some restoration work.

Q: And what did you say?
A: Nada. I was, you know, uncomfortable.

Q: Then what happened?
A: Mr. Lassiter gets into the passenger seat of my 'Cuda, opens the glove compartment, and puts an envelope inside. Says to me, "Here's my contact information."

Q: Did you open the envelope?
A: After he got out, sure.

Q: What did you find, Mr. Gutierrez?
A: A phone number written on the envelope. And inside, el dinero. One thousand dollars in hundreds.

PART TWO

"Have you a criminal lawyer in this burg?"

"We think so but we haven't been able to prove it on him."

—Carl Sandburg, *The People, Yes*

-8-

Manure Is a Metaphor

The lights behind my eyes flickered back on, and my headache cranked up a few notches on the Richter scale. I was alone in the ring. Ray Pincher never apologized for rattling my brain. He just headed out without showering or saying good-bye.

It took several minutes for the cobwebs to clear. Then I remembered the headline of the day. Stacy Strickstein wanted to indict me.

What the hell is her evidence?

I didn't bribe a juror. So she had no case, right?

Wrong!

She had something, or she wouldn't have taken the case to the grand jury. Meaning she had flawed, fabricated, possibly perjurious evidence. Her proof might be a steaming pile of turds, but it could still support an indictment. Such are the ways of our so-called justice system.

I needed fresh air. But after showering and changing clothes, as I walked to my car, all I got was the dank, oily blast of a Miami River breeze. Fifty yards away, a rust bucket freighter with a Panamanian flag sputtered east toward open water.

The day had turned crotch-rot, soggy hot. Miami in the summer is basically uninhabitable except for insects and reptiles . . . and lawyers, if that's not redundant.

Along North River Drive, the fronds of a bottle palm tree waved in the weak morning breeze. As palm fronds are inclined to do.

A black-and-white skimmer fluttered its wings and flew out of the tree, headed toward the ocean. As seabirds are inclined to do.

My Biarritz Eldorado convertible, vintage 1984, cream colored with red velour pillowed upholstery, was illegally parked next to a fire hydrant alongside the river. As I am inclined to do.

I wasn't paying attention to much of the surroundings. My ice-pick headache now had company. Somewhere inside my skull, Quasimodo was yanking the ropes, and the bells of Notre Dame were pealing a cacophonous song. Tinnitus. A frequent guest after every concussion. Other than my ailments, all was normal alongside the river, except . . .

That bottle palm tree wasn't planted in the ground. It seemed to be growing out of the passenger seat of my Eldo. Its feathery fronds poked out of a tear in the canvas top.

What the hell! Was I hallucinating after being battered by the State Attorney?

No, the tree was real. But surely something was amiss. Either Jack of beanstalk fame had tossed genetically modified seeds into my car, or some idiot had vandalized my tail-finned beauty.

I unlocked the door and slid into the driver's seat. The car was ripe with a mulchy, moist plant aroma. Sure enough, the tree was riding shotgun. Dirt trickled through the torn top and into my shirt collar. Who would desecrate my ancient but amiable chariot? Who had a grievance against me?

Angry ex-clients, of course.

Disgruntled opposing litigants.

A former lady friend or two.

The past, I learned long ago, clings to us like mud on rusty cleats.

But I didn't think this was an old ghost returning to haunt me. Not with a recent threat still rattling in my brain: *"Dead lawyer walking. That's what you are. You're a dead lawyer walking."*

Clyde Garner. Father of Eva, recently deceased at the hand of my client. Garner owned a tree farm just off the turnpike in Homestead. Take that, Sherlock Holmes.

I sat there a moment, as more dirt cascaded through the torn canvas. Getting riled, feeling my heart rate accelerate until I heard it pound in my ears, competing for attention with the pealing bells. I didn't deserve this. And if I didn't do something about it, Garner would just come back at me again, harder. The man was due a visit.

I turned the key in the ignition, and nothing blew up. Gunned the engine and pulled onto North River Drive. I drove two blocks and hung a left on Northwest Second Street, which took me onto the entrance ramp of I-95, heading south. I could be at Garner's farm in an hour. I had a palm tree I intended to shove up his ass.

Just then my cell phone rang. The Penn State fight song with its quaint hundred-year-old lyrics, "Victory we predict for thee."

I said howdy, and Thunder Thurston growled at me, "Lassiter, I need your ass over here, now."

"Why? You kill somebody else?"

"Tired of your negative vibe, dude. Meet me at the PBC."

Meaning the *Pro Bowl Clipper*, the 104-foot motor yacht Thurston used for cruising, partying, and whoring. A more accurate name for the yacht might have been *Pro Bimbo Clipper*.

I said, "No time for a cooze cruise."

"It ain't that. You know the Jacuzzi on the aft deck."

"If it's broken again, call a plumber. And tell your strippers not to toss their thongs in the water. Fouls the motor."

"There's three feet of horseshit in the tub," he said.

"What?"

"Or maybe cow shit. I ain't a farmer."

But Clyde Garner is.

"You know how I keep the deck all shiny and polished," Thurston continued.

"Yeah. Yeah. The best Brazilian teak."

"The best *Burmese* teak. Covered in shit, too. You know who did this?"

"I've got a pretty good idea."

Garner was getting around, I thought. The yacht was docked at the Miami Beach Marina, across the bay. I pictured Garner with a crew of undocumented workers, shoveling shit from the back of a dump truck. I liked the picture. He'd gotten to Thunder. Pissed him off. And suddenly I wasn't so angry at Garner for messing up my car. Even before today, the canvas top leaked in summer storms and needed replacing. Maybe now insurance would cover the cost.

"That fat-ass cracker!" Thunder exploded. "Does he think he can shit on me?"

"You're being too literal."

"Meaning what, law man?"

"The manure is a metaphor."

"If you're thinking I don't know what that is, you're wrong. I took English 101 three times. I know metaphors and I know silly-mees."

"Similes," I said. "But you're jerking my chain, Thunder. You graduated college a semester early, and your GPA was just under three point five, even though you barely studied."

"So what?"

"So save your badass gangsta rap for your homies. You're smart as hell. It wouldn't surprise me if you'd researched the Stand Your Ground law before you shot Eva."

"What if I did?"

"You learned how to get away with murder."

"She threatened me with the knife, dude."

"Odd the way you said that. 'Threatened.' Why didn't you say 'stabbed'?"

"She did both. Threatened, then stabbed. You saw the blood."

"A cute little paring knife with a three-inch blade. Good for slicing cucumbers."

"She swung at my neck. If I hadn't stepped back, I'd be dead."

"With your eye-hand coordination, your fast-twitch muscle fibers, your hundred-pound weight advantage, I'm surprised she nicked you at all."

"Ain't doing this, Lassiter. She stabbed me. I shot her. End of story."

"You know what I think happened?"

"I don't care."

"You intentionally provoked Eva. Once she picked up the knife, you had no fear because you had the gun within reach. You shot her five times, put on gloves, grabbed the knife, and oh so gently ran the blade across your abdomen. The cut was three inches long and a quarter-inch deep. It wouldn't have wounded a piece of sushi."

He made a scoffing sound through the phone line. "If I'd told you that's what happened, would you have put me on the stand to say how I feared for my life?"

"Hell, no. I told you that after Coach Duncan introduced us. I don't use perjured testimony."

"So much for your rep as a street fighter."

"Even a whore's got rules," I said.

"You are one self-righteous dude for someone who coached my testimony."

"That's bull. I told you to tell the truth."

"Sure, you used those words. But what you meant was to tell a story that *sounded* like the truth, a story you could sell to the jury."

"How the hell do you know what I meant?"

"That's how I read it, and like you said, I'm damn smart. So you better examine your own motives before pointing a finger at me."

I let that sink in a moment. Was he right? When I'd thought Thurston was innocent—hoped he was innocent—had I unconsciously coached him to tell a better story?

No! If Thurston had planned the killing, he had his "I-feared-for-my-life" speech ready as soon as he pulled the trigger.

For no apparent reason, Thurston chuckled. The same practiced little chortle he used in his Burger King commercial when he extolled the virtues of crispy spicy onion petals.

"C'mon Lassiter, I'm just playing you. I was innocent, and you did a helluva job proving it. Now, what about my ex-father-in-law and his manure?"

I tried to let my angst go, at least for the moment. "I think Clyde Garner is saying he's going to bury you."

"Bury me? I'm gonna mess him up good."

"No, you're not."

"You get me off if I hammer Garner?"

"Not a chance."

"Then what you gonna do, lawyer? What you gonna do for the Thunder?"

Dishing in that urban patois that we both know is bullshit.

Thunder majored in speech at Florida State, then hired an elocution coach to enhance his chances of landing national television spots. It had worked. His diction was better than mine, and when the cameras were rolling, his voice was as friendly and melodious as Samuel L. Jackson pitching credit cards on television.

And what about Thunder referring to himself in the third person?

"What you gonna do for the Thunder?"

It was revealing. His lack of humility and self-awareness. His narcissism, which, after all, was the hard currency of the All-Pro ego. Thurston had to be the center of attention, the planets revolving around him, as if he were Earth in a pre-Copernican universe. This could be the flaw Victoria Lord had told me to find . . . and exploit. But how? I had no idea.

"I'll take care of Garner myself," I told my egomaniacal client.

"What are you gonna do?"

"You don't want to know."

"Okay. Just do it." Sounding like his Nike commercial.

The line went dead. A new thought came to me, not fully formed. Just a glimmer of an idea, swimming alongside the flotsam and jetsam in my brain. I would now operate on the classic principle that the enemy of my enemy is my friend.

Clyde Garner, you and I have some conspiring to do.

-9-

Touch My Chedda, Feel My Beretta

I took I-95 south until it ended, ingloriously dumping traffic onto overcrowded US 1, regarded as Useless 1 by drivers up and down the Eastern Seaboard. It was stop-and-go through the outskirts of Coconut Grove, past the University of Miami, where young scholars were hard at work catching rays on the pool deck. Then gridlock at the Red Road traffic light in South Miami.

Before setting out, I had manhandled the canvas top open, prying out the palm tree and tossing it into the backseat. My anger with Clyde Garner had subsided, and I now felt empathy for him. The man was still mourning the loss of his daughter. What had I lost, a leaky convertible top?

My drive had become a mission of mercy. I didn't want Garner to get hurt—or worse—go after Thurston. The thought occurred to me that he might succeed in killing Thurston. That would satisfy my eye-for-an-eye urge, but Garner would likely spend the rest of his life in prison, and that—like Eva's death—would haunt me. I'm the one who triggered the injustice that led to this dark and dangerous place. I'm the one who needed to correct it. Which is why this was also a mission of another kind. Together, Garner and I could go after Thurston. With my criminal law expertise and his wood chipper, who knows what we might accomplish?

Getting him to trust me, though, would not be easy. I hadn't forgotten what he'd said: *"You're a dead lawyer walking."*

As opposed to my usual state: *live lawyer talking.*

I hoped that the palm tree prank satisfied Garner's beef with me, but I doubted it. He surely would not greet me with a fruit basket and chocolate-dipped pineapple slices.

By the time I reached the Snapper Creek Expressway, I was beginning to regret having put the top down. The sun's glare intensified my headache. I also tasted blood from the busted lip Pincher gave me in the ring. Even with the sun out, a light rain started to fall. No, I don't know how that happens, but it does. Not that we needed the rain. Last winter was the warmest, wettest anyone in South Florida could remember. Art Basel—a gathering of thousands of people who pretend they love art as an excuse for partying—had nearly been washed out to sea. On Miami Beach, every high tide backwashed ocean water onto Alton Drive. On this side of the bay, water bubbled up through the limestone, flooding low-lying neighborhoods. With the polar ice caps melting faster than 7-Eleven Slurpees, Miami could soon rename itself Atlantis.

Traffic eased and the rain stopped as I headed southwest across the sprawling suburbs of Kendall. The road soon merged with the Don Shula Expressway, which then blended into the Ronald Reagan Turnpike. As far as I knew, neither my old football coach nor the Gipper had anything to do with pouring asphalt, but our politicians love to name highways after celebrities, Latin American heroes, and campaign contributors.

An hour after leaving downtown Miami, I was pulling through the coral rock gates of Garner Tree Farm. My old Caddy purred contentedly along a winding gravel road lined with royal palms perhaps eighty feet high. The palms appeared to be precisely fifty feet apart. It was a damn impressive gravel road.

Behind the towering rows of palms were endless acres of trees, shrubs, and even more palms. Dwarf dates, tiny Chinese fan palms, larger queen palms, coconut and Bismarck palms, and others I couldn't recognize or name. Palms to the horizon, maybe distant cousins of the one in my backseat.

With my top down, I could hear the whirring of irrigation pumps, and the air was filled with earthy scents. It took another ten minutes and perhaps a thousand royal palm sentinels to reach Garner's farmhouse headquarters.

It was a sprawling one-story ranch house of Dade County pine with a metal roof and rain barrels under the drain spouts. Two Hispanic men in work clothes were spreading mulch from a wheelbarrow onto a flower bed when I pulled up. They eyed my Caddy with the palm in the backseat, then resumed their work.

I got out of the car and immediately got socked in the face by the moist heat. No ocean breeze this far inland, and with all the irrigation ponds and lakes, the humidity was roughly one zillion percent. And breathing? It was like trying to catch a breath through a sumo wrestler's loincloth. Not that I know from experience, but I have a good imagination.

I used my workable Spanish to ask a few questions of the two workers. They told me that Clyde Garner was in the thatch palm orchard about a half mile from the farmhouse. Just walk straight through the frangipani field; turn left at the mahogany trees. Take the wooden footbridge over the irrigation canal, follow the curving path past a sixty-foot-tall live oak tree, and then, just past a stand of black olive trees, well, that's where Garner was checking on his thatch palms.

Okay, I can do that.

* * *

"You got balls coming here—I'll give you that," Clyde Garner said.

"I'm hoping to still have 'em when I leave," I said.

Garner snorted a mirthless laugh. He wore muddy work boots, green pants, a long-sleeve denim shirt, and a long-billed camo cap with a sun-shade neck protector. He sat astride a four-wheel ATV, towing a small trailer equipped with a metal tank. Fertilizer or pesticide, I figured.

"You were a lousy linebacker, and now you're a shyster lawyer."

I didn't disagree with either end of that proposition.

"What the hell are you doing here, Lassiter?"

"Returning a palm tree. It's in the car."

"My boys' idea. Brick and Slade."

"So you knew about it in advance?"

"I didn't mind if they messed you up a little. You gonna sue me?"

"I just want to ask you—plead with you, really—to stay away from Thurston. I know you want to make him pay for what he did, but you can't do it alone."

"Who's gonna help? You, Lassiter?"

"Yeah, me."

He sized me up a moment, probably gauging my sincerity. "I don't believe a word you say."

"Can't blame you, but will you hear me out?"

He spent another moment considering, then said, "My daddy taught me what he called the courtesy of listening." He got off the ATV, mopped his face with a kerchief from his shirt pocket, and said, "Let's talk in the shade. You don't want to get the skin cancers I been fighting."

We found a red maple tree by the irrigation canal and stood there, awkwardly, neither of us saying a word. A pair of ducks with mottled-brown feathers floated in the water. Overhead a pair of white egrets flew in the general direction of the Everglades.

Before I could start my pitch, Garner said, "You know why you make my blood boil?"

"Because I got your daughter's killer off."

"Because you fought so damn hard for him."

"That's the only way I know."

"You kept out the evidence of Thurston assaulting those other women."

"The *judge* kept it out. All I did was argue that the pattern wasn't sufficiently similar. He'd never used a gun before, and the other incidents never involved serious injuries."

Garner brushed at his face, where a gnat was buzzing. "Why didn't the damn prosecutor fight you on it?"

"That was Strickstein's strategy. She was afraid that if the judge let the evidence in and she got a conviction, it would be reversed on appeal. She played it safe."

"Is that what you would have done in her shoes?"

I paused a moment, and he coughed out another humorless laugh. "I didn't think so. You're balls to the walls—aren't you, Lassiter?"

"Like I said, I don't know any other way to do it."

"So now you claim to have some regrets about getting a murderer off?"

"I do."

"And you want to help me nail Thurston."

"Yes."

"By any means, Lassiter? Even illegal ones?"

"They're the only means available, so yes."

He hawked up a wad of phlegm and spat toward the canal bank. "You're as full of shit as Thurston's Jacuzzi."

"Give me a chance, Mr. Garner. Tell me about Thurston and Eva."

He leaned against the trunk of the maple tree and looked into the distance. I can't read minds, but I knew he was thinking about his daughter.

"She was a tomboy growing up," he said. "How could she not have been, a kid out here?"

46

He spread his arms in a gesture, taking in the tree farm. He told me his family's story, some of which I already knew. From a ten-acre plot bought by his grandfather in the 1950s, the next two generations of Garners kept buying land and growing trees. Now the farm was nearly six thousand acres, and the trees were uncountable. Clyde Garner and his wife had three children. Eva, of course. And twin boys, Brick and Slade. Like their father, barrel-chested, thick-necked, and hands the size of ham hocks.

The twins never played sports at Homestead High, despite pleas from the football coach, who saw a pair of defensive tackles, and the track coach, who envisioned shot-putters and discus throwers. Instead they worked the fields after school, and when they graduated with agriculture degrees from the University of Florida, to the fields they returned. The fragrant grime of moist earth was part of their DNA.

Eva was the rose among the thornbushes. She was the beauty-pageant queen and the athlete, running track in high school, making friends with—in Garner's term—the "Afro-Americans."

"My great-great-great-grandfather fought in the Civil War," Garner said, "and not on the winning side. Most people probably think I'm a redneck. But I never had problems with the Afro-Americans Eva brought over to the house." He let out a long sigh. "And then, of course, she met that son of a bitch Thurston."

Fresh out of the University of Miami with a degree in public relations, Eva got a job downtown with the Miami Heat. She handled celebrity ticket requests. If Alex Rodriguez or Spike Lee or Scottie Pippen wanted to sit next to the Heat bench, Eva Garner was the one to ask.

"Thurston showed up in person, demanding six tickets courtside for his posse," Garner told me. "Not the usual two seats. It was the day of the game. The Spurs."

"Tough ticket," I said.

"Right. She didn't have them. So Thurston causes a ruckus, saying he gained sixteen hundred yards for the Dolphins. 'Thunder don't sit in no second row. Thunder ain't no benchwarmer.'"

I could hear him saying it. Slathering some Muck City into his voice, referring to himself in the third person, demanding to be treated as a potentate of South Beach.

"And that's the man she married," Garner said with resignation.

We stood in silence another moment, and Garner leveled his gaze at me. "I know my Eva. She never stabbed that bastard."

"Her prints were on the knife handle."

"Why wouldn't they be? She did the cooking. I told the prosecutor my guess was that Thurston shot her, put on gloves, then cut himself."

Great minds think alike, I thought. *But then, so do addled ones.*

"What did Strickstein say?" I asked.

"That she couldn't try a case based on a grieving father's guesswork. That she had to play the cards she was dealt."

Standard prosecutorial fare, I thought, though it must have sounded cold coming from the reptilian Strychnine. Empathy was not her strong suit.

"The prosecutor did something else I could never understand," Garner said.

My look asked a question, so he continued. "She never told the jury about Thurston's threats."

"What threats?"

"Text messages between Thurston and that thug friend of his."

There were a few thug friends from which to choose, but I thought I knew who Garner meant. "Drexler. The guy they call Jelly Bean."

"Yeah, him. It all had to do with Thurston looking at a big contract next year."

I knew about that, of course. Thurston was in the fifth year—the option year—of his rookie contract and stood to sign for $55 to $60 million for the next five seasons. I was the one who was supposed to negotiate the best deal with the Dolphins or, failing an agreement, shop his talents around the league.

"Thurston would lose a ton in a divorce," Garner said. "That's why he wanted Eva dead."

"He texted that to Drexler?"

"Not in those words. You want it verbatim?"

"Preferably."

"Not hard to remember. 'Bitch touch my chedda, feel my Beretta.' Eva told me that's from some dumb-ass hip-hop song."

"Pretty famous song," I said. "Notorious B.I.G.'s 'Warning.'"

Garner gave me a look, and I said, "My secretary loves hip-hop. I'm the unintended audience."

"Then you'd know that chedda is cheddar," he said. "Like cheese. Meaning money. You understand the rest of the lyric, Lassiter?"

"Touch my money, I'll kill you."

"Exactly. Now, why did the prosecutor keep this away from the jury?"

I shrugged. "I don't know. I'd like to see the texts."

"You and me both, Lassiter. But the thing is, they've disappeared."

-10-

A Trespasser and Troublemaker

Naturally I got lost finding my way back to the farmhouse and my car. My mind was trying to make sense of everything Garner had told me, and I must not have been paying attention to directions. Within minutes my black leather shoes were sinking into the mud in a freshly irrigated stand of sea grape trees. No, I hadn't come this way.

Nothing Garner told me made sense. In court Stacy Strickstein had busted her ass and my chops trying to convict Thurston. At least that's the way it had seemed to me. Sure, she'd failed to come up with expert testimony that the knife wound might have been self-inflicted, but then again, Doc Charlie Riggs had been far from certain. There was no way to know if Strickstein had even suspected that Thurston stabbed himself. Or if she had, whether in trial preparation, an expert witness disabused her of the notion.

Garner had attended court every day of the trial. He'd written notes of all the prosecutor's deficiencies. Families of murder victims are like that. Overwhelmed by grief, they latch on to the criminal case as a path to salvation, which it never is, even when the defendant is convicted. The families focus on the minutiae of trials, misunderstanding the law, and making suggestions based on their own ungovernable emotions. It's human nature, and they can't help themselves. But family involvement drives prosecutors crazy.

Garner had told me that Strickstein didn't pick a jury to his liking. She didn't fight hard enough to get in evidence of prior assaults. She didn't object to several lines of my questioning. And worst of all, in Garner's eyes, she couldn't locate the threatening texts. Under subpoena Thurston's cell phone carrier came up empty. No such texts existed. That intrigued me.

"Did you ever see the texts yourself?" I'd asked Garner.

He shook his head. "Eva sneaked a look at Thurston's phone and told me what the texts said. Just what I said. 'Chedda . . . Beretta.' I offered to testify to that."

"Hearsay on hearsay," I said. "Not a chance at admissibility."

"That's what Strickstein said, but the way I see it, the whole downtown power elite was backing Thurston. The newspaper, the television stations, the Dolphins. Nobody wanted to see the big hero take a fall."

It wasn't true. The media had roughed Thurston up. But again, the family's perception is skewed. How could it not be? Garner could see the world only through the lens of a grieving father. He also was a man of the earth and soil. He had a natural distrust of the suits downtown, and when the murder trial careened off the tracks, he assumed the worst.

"The fix was in," he'd told me minutes earlier.

"Really, it wasn't."

"How would you know?"

"I've been doing this a long time. I would have sensed something. Strickstein fought hard."

"She supposedly subpoenaed the texts from AT&T, and they're gone. Down some black hole. Ain't that a little fishy?"

Now big, fluffy cumulus clouds, looking like scoops of vanilla ice cream, gathered to the west, but the sun still glared overhead. I tried to find the irrigation canal, figuring that might lead me back to the farm-house. That's when I heard the growl of an engine. I turned. Headed down the muddy row, directly at me, was a pint-size forklift. It was probably used for moving pallets of fertilizer or containers of mulch, but just now, lift raised, it seemed to be intent on spearing me.

I shielded my eyes, trying to make out the driver but couldn't. "Hey! Stop!" I yelled.

It kept coming, perhaps thirty yards away.

I turned and started running, shoes sinking into the mud.

Still the forklift came at me, gaining ground.

Jeez, I gotta be able to outrun a forklift.

No, I couldn't.

The lift was twenty yards behind me now, and I was going full speed through the stand of trees. As I ran, I swatted away the fat, veined leaves. The sea grapes, hard as marbles, pounded my face.

An image came to me then. Cary Grant in his gray suit, dash-ing through the cornfield, pursued by the crop-dusting plane. Other than the suit, I bore no resemblance to Grant. I'm just a heavy-legged, shaggy-haired, ex-linebacker with a bum knee, a crooked nose, and, at the moment, one shoe. I shot another look over my shoulder. The forklift was ten yards from spearing me like an olive on a toothpick.

A tree limb snapped across my face, wet leaves stinging my eyes. In front of me, I saw something—a flash of metal—but I couldn't make it out. The object grew larger, and now I saw it was a four-wheel ATV with a thick-necked man aboard.

I cut into an adjacent row, but my knee buckled, and I flopped face-first into the trunk of a sea grape tree. My forehead hit with a *thwomp*, and, for a moment, my vision faded to black.

Bleary-eyed and woozy, blood trickling from my forehead, I got to one knee. The forklift and the ATV were wedged into the mud on either side of me.

I heard a man say, "Grab the rake."

Another voice: "You take the tank."

I blinked twice, squinting into the sun. There seemed to be a contingent of men standing over me, all big and blocky.

"You're trespassing, mister," one of them said.

I tried to focus on the trunk of the tree that had bashed in my head. There seemed to be two trees. "I'm seeing double."

"We're twins, asshole," one said.

"No, I mean it. Unless you're quadruplets, I'm seeing double."

They hovered over me, a quartet of elephants, blocking out the sun. I couldn't make out their faces, but I knew who they were. "You're Brick and Slade, right?"

"We're your worst nightmare, asswipe."

"Worst nightmare. Jeez, you watch too many movies. Bad movies."

I felt something poking my ribs. Grabbed at it. A wooden handle. "What the hell?"

"Take it," one of the elephants said. Now there were only two. I shaded my eyes. Big and sunburned, blond crew cuts, bib overalls, and combat boots that might fit a Tyrannosaurus rex.

I grabbed the handle and got to my feet. I was holding a heavy rake with lots of ragged teeth. "What's this for?"

"Hit me with it," Brick said. Or maybe it was Slade.

"Why would I do that?"

"Because you're a trespasser and a troublemaker."

"And an asswipe," I reminded him. "But I'm not gonna hit you."

"Sure you are, and then I'm gonna be in reasonable fear of great bodily harm. Ain't that right, Slade."

"Or even worse, fear of imminent death," Slade said.

Oh, so that's where this was going. The Stand Your Ground law.

"That's what you told the jury. Thurston could kill our sister because the big pussy was in reasonable fear of imminent death or great bodily harm."

I said, "So, when I hit you with the rake . . ."

53

Slade grabbed a hose attached to the tank attached to the ATV, turned the nozzle, and sprayed me with a liquid pungent with ammonia. I coughed and sputtered and squeezed my eyes shut.

"Brick's gonna defend himself with deadly force," Slade said.

I wiped my face with the sleeve of my suit jacket and grabbed the rake handle with both hands. Damn thing was heavy. I calculated the odds of taking out both of them before getting my ribs fractured once they started stomping me with those size-sixteen combat boots.

"You won't get away with it," I said.

"Maybe not. We don't have the juice downtown Thurston has."

That again. They were their father's sons. Only younger, bigger, stronger. And meaner.

"Look, the case wasn't fixed. Strickstein did her job, and I did mine. If it makes any difference to you, I just told your father I want to help. I'm going to look into those missing texts."

"What about the phone calls?" Slade said.

"What calls?"

"Whenever Eva and that asshole would fight, she'd come down to the farm to get away from him. I'd check her out to make sure there were no bruises."

"'Cause if there were," Brick interjected, "me and Slade would have kicked the living piss out of him; I don't care how much weight he can bench press."

"Did he abuse Eva?" I asked.

"She said no, and we can't prove different. But one night she's over here on the phone with Thurston, and they're yelling back and forth, and she puts him on speaker. He's drunk and slurring his words and cussing her out. 'Ho' this and 'bitch' that. And then he says—"

"I bring pain, bloodstains on what remains," Slade said.

"And a bunch more rhyming, rapping shit," Brick said. "We told the prosecutor about that, but she goes, 'Oh, that's too vague. Plus it's hearsay. I can't get it in.'"

"It's not hearsay," I said. "The defendant said it, so it's a party admission, but I'm not sure what it's worth. Thurston's quoting a song. Notorious B.I.G.'s 'Warning.' Apparently he's very fond of it."

"We know that, asswipe. We Googled it. The prosecutor says we can't testify to anything because, as family, we're not credible. Then she says Thurston's threats don't fit with her theory of the case, that—"

"That it was a spontaneous argument, not a planned killing," Slade said, finishing his brother's thought.

"Not what I would have done," I said, "but who's to say it's an unreasonable strategy?"

Just then a four-wheel ATV sloshed toward us in the adjacent row of trees. Clyde Garner pulled to a stop, got off, stretched out his back as if his lumbago was bothering him, and said, "What are you boys up to?"

Brick and Slade studied the tops of their muddy boots. They looked as if their father might put them over his knee and spank them.

"Hans and Franz here said they were gonna kill me," I said, "but I think they were just trying to scare me."

"Did they?"

"It's possible I peed my pants, but I put up a brave front."

"Okay, boys, back off. Mr. Lassiter ain't our enemy. He's a tool of the system, for sure. But I think he might just be ready to switch sides."

IN THE ELEVENTH JUDICIAL CIRCUIT IN AND FOR

MIAMI-DADE COUNTY, FLORIDA

In re: Investigation of Jacob Lassiter, Esq.

Pursuant to Florida State Section 918.12, to wit, Jury Tampering.

Investigation No. 2016-MDC-GJ-149

Partial Transcript of Grand Jury Proceedings

Q: [By ASA Strickstein] Ms. Wang, what is your occupation?
A: [By Daiyu Wang] Security technician for Miami–Dade County.

Q: Where do you work?
A: At the Richard E. Gerstein Justice Building in the civic center.

Q: Do your responsibilities include maintaining the video surveillance cameras inside and outside the Justice Building?
A: They do.

Q: Did my office ask you to produce all exterior tapes showing the front steps of the building, the fountain, and the sidewalk leading to the jurors' parking lot on Monday, August 8, between 4:30 and 5:30 p.m.?
A: Yes.

Q: What special instructions did I give you?
A: You showed me a photograph of a lawyer named Jacob Lassiter and asked if I could find him on any of the videos. The video produces long shots, so faces are not always easily made out.

Q: Do you have any special training in facial recognition?

A: I have taken several courses given by the FBI. One of my jobs is to look at the photos on outstanding arrest warrants and watch in real time as people enter and leave the Justice Building. You'd be surprised how many wanted people show up when their friends or family members have a court date.

Q: Did you find Mr. Lassiter on the tapes?

A: Yes, at 4:57 p.m., he exited the building on the south side. I copied a seventeen-second clip for your office.

Q: Ladies and gentlemen of the grand jury, please direct your attention to the monitor. Ms. Wang, please narrate. [Turns on player]

A: There's Mr. Lassiter, coming down the steps carrying a briefcase and walking across the patio.

Q: Walking faster than people around him?

A: It seems so.

Q: As if to catch up with someone?

A: I suppose.

Q: And there! I'll stop the video. Where are we?

A: The sidewalk that separates the jurors' parking lot from the general lot. Mr. Lassiter has caught up with a man I did not recognize but you told me was Manuel Gutierrez, a juror in the Thurston murder trial.

Q: I'll run a few more seconds. There! What do you see?

A: The men are walking and talking. Mr. Gutierrez gestures toward the jurors' lot.

Q: What is that at the left-hand edge of the screen?

A: The rear grill and partial license plate of a car I have identified as a 1971 Plymouth Barracuda belonging to Manuel Gutierrez.

Q: Let's roll the video until it ends. Ms. Wang, please continue.
A: Mr. Lassiter and Mr. Gutierrez walk toward the parking lot and disappear out of range of the camera.

Q: As if walking to Mr. Gutierrez's car?
A: In that direction, yes.

Q: Thus, ladies and gentlemen of the grand jury, Ms. Wang has corroborated the testimony of Manuel Gutierrez, who told you that Mr. Lassiter approached and spoke to him in the parking lot. We submit this adds credence to Mr. Gutierrez's further testimony about the cash bribe. Ms. Wang, you are excused.

Home Remedies

"Ouch, Granny! That stings."

"Crybaby. Always have been."

Granny Lassiter was dabbing a mixture of crushed garlic, cayenne pepper, and coconut oil into a cut on my forehead, just above my right eye. The wound had started as an abrasion from a series of Sugar Ray Pincher's jabs. Then the damn sea grape tree had jumped in front of me and opened a full-blown cut that stung like hell. The pain had one benefit. It made me forget about my headache.

We were on the back porch of my little coral rock pillbox of a home in Coconut Grove. The evening was still, the fronds on a scrubby palm tree hanging limp in the soggy air. Granny Lassiter, who was actually my great-aunt, best we could tell, was a woman of indeterminate age, and she sure as hell wasn't going to enlighten me. She'd raised me from a pup in her tin-roofed cottage on the gulf side of Key Largo. Now she helps me raise my nephew, Kip. Tonight Granny wore khaki cargo pants and a T-shirt with the slogan: "Good Girls Go to Heaven. Bad Girls Go to Florida."

"Why can't you use an antiseptic cream like everyone else?" I asked.

PAUL LEVINE

"Them chemicals will angry up your blood," Granny explained.

"Jeez, I want a doctor."

As if on cue, the screen door opened and Doc Charlie Riggs toddled out of the house, holding a mason jar filled with an amber liquid that looked suspiciously like bourbon.

"You rang?" Charlie said.

"I meant a real doctor."

Charlie harrumphed and gave me the once-over. "Looks you're about ready for the autopsy, so just tell me when to sharpen my scalpel."

Doc Riggs was a real doctor, of course, albeit a retired one. He'd been county coroner until he got fired for being fair, which is to say, not favoring the prosecution in autopsies of homicide victims. He was in his usual baggy shorts, flip-flops, and Miami Marlins jersey. Not the Major League Baseball team. The minor league Marlins from the International League in the 1950s. Charlie claimed that as a small boy he saw the immortal Satchel Paige pitch for the Marlins, and who am I to call him a liar?

Charlie had a scraggly gray beard and lopsided spectacles, and over the years he's helped me in numerous homicide trials and even more personal tribulations. Now he sipped from the mason jar and smacked his lips. "I miss your home brew, Granny, but Pappy Van Winkle is a decent second choice."

"At least you won't go blind," I said.

Charlie wrinkled his nose and sniffed the air. "What smells like swamp stew out here?"

"That would be me," I admitted, "but you can blame Granny."

Doc Riggs examined my face and scowled. "I don't like your pupil dilation."

"I don't like the situation in the Middle East, so we're even."

He put an index finger about six inches from the tip of my nose and slowly moved it back and forth. "Follow the finger."

60

I could feel my eyes moving left and right, an effort that intensified my headache. Charlie harrumphed again.

"When you called me on the cell today," he said, "you told me you were on the turnpike headed for home."

"Yeah?"

"You should have been here in forty-five minutes, an hour tops. But it took you two hours."

"Maybe I stopped at a liquor store to get your Pappy Van Winkle."

"Nope. That's been in your cupboard for a while."

"Okay, Charlie, I missed the turnpike exit, and when I finally got off, I turned west instead of east. But after twenty minutes, my quick wits told me the Everglades was not South Miami."

He said, "Uh-huh," but his tone was one of disbelief and disapproval.

"I was preoccupied. Thinking about everything the Garners told me. And Pincher, too. It's been a helluva day."

"Uh-huh." Seldom has such an innocuous sound seemed so damning.

"C'mon, Charlie. Pincher told me Stacy Strickstein was going after me for jury tampering. Can you believe that?"

"I believe it. Twice."

"What's that mean?"

"On the phone, you said Strickstein was going after you for jury tampering. So now you've told me twice. Have you forgotten the first conversation?"

"Of course not."

"Uh-huh."

"Stop with the uh-huhs! Okay, I forgot. It's been a stressful day."

"Tell me what happened at the tree farm."

I told Charlie about my encounter with the Garner clan as he was taking my pulse and testing my reflexes. I gabbed for several minutes while Charlie poked at me.

"What do you think, Charlie? All those loose ends, starting with the missing texts between Thurston and Jelly Bean Drexler?"

"Did Clyde Garner ever see the texts himself?"

I shook my head, an effort that caused bowling balls to ricochet inside my skull. "Eva saw them on Thurston's cell phone and told her father. Strickstein said the carrier couldn't come up with them."

"So you can't even prove the texts existed. And you know how families of victims get confused in their grief and anger. His memory of what his daughter told him might be sketchy. He could be exaggerating. Or lying. Or it's possible his daughter made it up."

"Why would she do that?"

"For sympathy. Family support. To justify a decision to leave her husband. Who knows?"

I certainly didn't.

"I keep thinking what you told me about the knife wound," I said.

"My opinion was meaningless, Jake. I couldn't state with certainty that the wound was self-inflicted."

"In my gut, I know you were right. I can feel it."

"Feelings aren't evidence."

"I've been doing this a long time. Thurston played me, and then he played the jury. He's damn good at it, Charlie."

Doc Riggs seemed to be studying me with concern. "What?" I asked.

"Let's drop Thurston and talk about you, Jake. Did you experience any dizziness today?"

"Maybe a little. It's hard to remember every sensation when you've taken two beatings."

"What about double vision?"

I considered evasion. It comes rather naturally. But instead I said, "Yeah, some blurriness, a little double vision. But it went away."

"Say after me, 'Peter picked a peck of pickled peppers.'"

"Easy. Piper packed a pot of speckled mackerel."

"Damn it, Jake. This is serious. How many concussions did you have playing football?"

"I don't know, and I don't care." The first half of that sentence was true. But the rest . . . well, I'm not stupid. Stubborn at times, sure, but I read the papers. At least the sports section, and that's where the scary news has been of late. Former NFL players with brain damage, seemingly a new name every week.

"Concussions," I said. "Are we counting the time in high school I ran into a goalpost headfirst at full speed?"

"Were you concussed?"

"I was unconscious for a few seconds or maybe longer. Who knows? It was practice, and we didn't have a doctor on the field. Coach didn't use the word *concussion*. Actually, I'm not sure he knew the word."

Charlie sighed. "But you think you suffered a concussion."

"Probably. My first of many."

"What else do you remember about the incident? Did you undergo any tests, have any treatment, do any therapy?"

"Best I recall, Coach made me run wind sprints for bending the goalpost. Plus I had to sweep out the wood shop for a month to earn money for a new one. Does that count as therapy?"

-12-

Shake and Bake, Jake

To pacify Charlie, I tried to remember all my head bangers, going back to Coral Shores High School in the Keys, through my days at Penn State and my minicareer with the Dolphins. At the same time, Granny was plastering my forehead with a bandage soaked in apple cider vinegar. As if the garlic, pepper, and coconut oil hadn't hurt enough.

"Ouch!"

"Hush up, you big baby," she said for about the third time. "Tomorrow I'll cut some aloe leaves in the yard and squeeze the juice on your wounds."

Charlie cleared his throat and looked at me sternly. "Jake, you still haven't answered my question about the number of concussions you've suffered."

I shrugged. "In high school we didn't keep track or even know we had them. I'd get my bell rung, and everything would go dark for a second or two. An assistant coach with the medical training of a gas station attendant, which he happened to be, would put his hand in my face and say, 'How many fingers?' I'd answer, 'What fingers?' But he always said the same thing, 'Shake and bake, Jake. Shake it off and get your ass back in there.'"

"That's so damn dangerous," the doc said, "considering what we know now. I'm reasonably certain you were concussed today. Based on your description of your sparring session with the State Attorney, I'd say that's when it happened, but you didn't do yourself any favors head-butting the tree. You need to rest for a few days, maybe longer. I'd like to suggest some tests to be run."

"No time, Charlie. I've got work to do. Plans to make. Big decisions."

Charlie fished into his shorts and found a meerschaum pipe that he jammed, cold, into his mouth. He chewed a moment on the lip and said, "Maybe put all that on hold."

I waited for Granny to head back through the screen door into the kitchen. I hadn't planned to say anything to Charlie, but I knew I could trust him with any secret. "Thunder Thurston," I said when Granny was back inside. "Something has to be done about him. He's a monster."

"Damn it, Jake. We're talking about you. Your health, your well-being."

"Okay, I promise. We'll talk about me, but please hear me out about Thurston."

Charlie let out an exasperated sigh. "All right. Thurston's a monster."

"It's true! I tracked down all the rumors. In high school an ex-girl-friend said he beat her up. At Florida State, a student said he date-raped her. When he was a rookie with the Dolphins, a South Beach model said he tossed her out of a moving car. He denied everything and was never charged. Don't you get it, Charlie? He hurts women and gets away with it because he's been a star athlete since he was sixteen years old. Every time there's a chance to stop him, the powers that be simply enable him. And me? I'm his latest enabler. I helped him get away with murder."

"Now, that isn't true. You just did your job."

"I've got a new job. I'm gonna stop Thunder Thurston. Permanently."

This time he didn't harrumph. More like a *hmmm.* He chewed the pipe some more and finally said, "I've known you since you were a rookie in the PD's office who couldn't find the courthouse door with a road map. I've watched you mature. I've seen you take on cops and judges and prosecutors, and once in a while, your own clients. But what you just implied, threatened really . . . Jake, that isn't you."

"What's that supposed to mean?"

"I say this as a dear friend, someone who admires you, loves you like the son I never had . . ."

"Yeah? Spit it out, Pop."

"You suffered a concussion today in your ill-advised bout with the State Attorney and perhaps aggravated it in your dustup on the tree farm. You're having post-concussion syndrome, and you're not making sense."

"If it makes any difference, I wanted to kill Thurston before Ray Pincher decked me."

"It doesn't. My fear is that you're ill. Whether it's psychological or physical or a combination of the two, I don't know. But I think there might be something seriously wrong."

"Such as?"

"Oh, come on, Jake. You know very well what I'm talking about. All the former NFL players with chronic traumatic encephalopathy."

"I don't want to think about that right now."

"That's understandable. It's an incurable disease. Ninety out of ninety-four former players who manifested symptoms of brain damage turned out to have it when they were autopsied."

"I know you love carving up brains, but could you hold off on mine for a while?"

"Living players are being diagnosed now. Your former teammate Mark Duper for one."

"Super Duper. I love that guy."

It was true. I admired the courage of the pint-size wide receiver. I'd heard about Duper's problems from other teammates, and I felt for the guy. He had memory loss and panic attacks, and had been involved in unexplained acts of violence. Only recently had degenerative brain disease been suspected. I chose to remember him the way he played, fearless while running suicidal routes over the middle.

"Duper would catch a frozen rope from Dan Marino and then get bounced around like a pinball," I said.

"Too much bouncing for his brain."

"I'm not gonna lie. I've thought about brain damage. I've talked with former teammates. But I'm as sharp—or as dull—as ever, Charlie. Besides, there's no treatment for CTE. What good would it do to know, except you and Granny would make a big fuss over me?"

"Stubborn jackass!" Charlie said. "Do it for me, okay?"

His tone shocked me. The doc rarely got angry. But sometimes yelling at me was the only way to get my attention. If Charlie cared that much about me, I should do the same.

"What do you want me to do, Charlie?"

"Just go see Dr. Helfman for a standard neurological workup. If anything is squirrely, she'll tell you about the next step, which is probably a PET scan of your brain. If everything is okay, we'll go drinking. If not, we'll still go drinking."

"Fair enough. I'll take whatever tests she recommends as long as they don't involve enemas."

"Fine, and while you're at it, forget about Thunder Thurston."

I shook my head. "Sorry, Charlie. Whether I'm checking out or sticking around, I'm still gonna do the same thing. Bring down Thunder Thurston and bring him down hard."

-13-

Son of Muck City

At 11:47 the next morning, I had my chance to kill Thunder Thurston. He was leaning over the balcony railing of his Fisher Island condo, firing his forty-five-caliber handgun at gulls and terns soaring over Government Cut, the passageway for cruise ships at the Port of Miami. One of his size-fifteen feet was off the marble tile, and the torso of his massive frame was just at the tipping point.

One push and whoosh, Fly, Thunder, fly!

Can I do it?

Do I have the cojones?

He weighed 235 pounds, but I could drop into a crouch, snag both ankles, and fire up hard. I could flip him over the railing and watch him flail through the air and splatter onto the pool deck far below.

I had my defense ready. He had threatened me—not the birds— with the forty-five. Even took a shot at me. Forensics would reveal gunpowder residue on his right hand. So I acted in self-defense.

One problem. There were four potential witnesses in the living room of his seventy-five-hundred-square-foot chrome-and-glass condo. At the moment, they were preoccupied playing volleyball. That's right, inside the penthouse. The apartment had been two stories, and Thurston spent a million bucks ripping out the second floor. Now the living room had a twenty-four-foot ceiling and a regulation sand volleyball court.

Four young women who resembled college cheerleaders were bouncing around, kicking up sand, and squealing with delight. The volleyball court was surrounded by a patch of artificial grass. The necks of several bottles of Cristal peeked out of the ice in a picnic cooler. A silver cocktail tray held champagne flutes and a pile of cocaine a foot high. Could they see onto the balcony through the floor-to-ceiling glass? Were they watching? Were they sober?

The two teams were organized by "tops and bottoms," two of the leaping ladies wearing only bikini tops and the other two only bottoms. Except for the uniforms, the teams could have been lifted from a Pepsi commercial with two Anglo women, one Hispanic, and one African-American. Thurston had always been an equal-opportunity corrupter.

I had perhaps three seconds to kill the murderer. I hesitated, thinking about possible flaws in my defense.

Motive? Why would Thunder turn a gun on me?

I would have to come up with something. Unless I changed my story.

Accident!

Thurston leaned over too far.

"One second he was here, Officer. And then he wasn't."

But I waited too long. Thurston turned and faced me, the forty-five still in his hand.

"Damn birds are too small to hit," he said.

"Have you tried a shotgun?" I suggested helpfully. "Because right now, the only thing you're liable to kill is a sunbather over at South Pointe." I gestured toward the park on the other side of the channel.

He studied me a moment. "You look like shit, man."

True, my encounters with Pincher and the Garner twins had left me bruised, abraded, and puffy. Or, as Granny said this morning, "Your face is all swole up."

Thurston, on the other hand, was as handsome as ever. He had a rock jaw, wide-set eyes, and a torso those Greek sculptors in antiquity might have mistaken for Hercules. He wore running shorts and a bright-white T-shirt. A gold chain thick enough to tie down a cruise ship hung around his neck. Dangling from the chain were two fist-size gold nuggets that formed the number twenty-two, in homage to his Dolphins jersey. To shield his eyes from the afternoon glare, he wore oversize aviator sunglasses, similar to the ones favored by R&B singer R. Kelly.

"It took you long enough to get here," he said.

"Sorry, Your Majesty," I said.

"You got a major case of bad attitude, lawyer."

He spoke with a crispness to his enunciation. He'd told the story many times, how he'd been embarrassed by his diction when he left Belle Glade for Florida State. Around the time of Thurston's birth, his hometown made national headlines with a double whammy of bad news: the nation's highest crime rate coupled with the highest AIDS-infection rate. The population was largely African-American with a sizable Haitian minority. As a boy Thurston's accent reflected both groups, but by his second year in the NFL, after voice and speech lessons, he was a highly paid spokesman for breweries and apparel companies.

A pair of Florida blue jays flew close enough to the balcony for me to notice they carried acorns in their beaks. Thurston whirled and fired a series of shots, hitting nothing but air. The blue jays banked like fighter jets and headed across the cut toward South Beach. Party time, maybe.

"Damn! You should have been here yesterday," Thurston said. "Some asshole was flying a drone right off my bedroom window. I took it out with one shot."

That might have been true, but then again with Thurston, you never knew.

"Drone had a camera. Might have been one of those asshole Internet gossip sites. Everybody is after the dirt on the son of Muck City."

"So why'd you call me?" I asked.

"You said you were gonna take care of Garner for me. Then I don't hear from you. Now, you show up like this. Did that old man kick your ass?"

"His boys had some fun with me, but the State Attorney did most of the damage."

"You're too old for that shit."

I hadn't planned on being here. I'd taken Charlie's advice and phoned Dr. Helfman first thing in the morning. She was going to skip lunch and see me at noon. But heading down Dixie Highway toward the University of Miami's medical facility, I pulled a U-turn when Thunder called my cell.

He needed to see me right away and wouldn't say why. I'd already told him that the NFL would rescind his suspension within seventy-two hours, and he could rejoin the Dolphins in camp. He was in no hurry. Like most veterans, he viewed preseason games as an excellent way to suffer heat exhaustion and unnecessary injuries.

I could have refused my client's invitation and just have gone on with my day. But after our angry words yesterday, that might have made him suspicious. I didn't yet have a plan to dispatch Thurston. Pushing him off the balcony would have been reckless. Who knows what witnesses might be sunning themselves or what drones with cameras might be flying by?

My headache had subsided to a series of jarring *thumpety-thumps*, and my mind was reasonably clear. Despite Charlie's urging, I really didn't want a medical checkup. Maybe I was afraid neurological tests would reveal oatmeal where my brain should be. I chased those thoughts as an ocean breeze rustled the canvas overhang on the balcony's seating area. The only decent weather in Miami in the summer is two hundred feet off the ground, within spitting distance of the Atlantic.

Thurston lowered his massive frame into a fancy chaise of Italian design, dozens of multicolored straps sagging under his butt. "So, what do you have for me? What you gonna do about Garner crapping all over my boat? Dockmaster says it'll cost twenty grand to clean that shit up."

"I've seen you drop more than that on champagne and caviar at Liv."

Thurston's eyes narrowed. "Whose side are you on, lawyer?"

"The side of world peace. I don't want Garner or his boys hurting you."

"That ain't happening."

"Or you hurting them."

"I'm making no promises."

I took a seat facing him. The fancy Italian chaise wasn't as comfortable as it looked. "I feel an ethical and moral obligation to defuse the situation."

"What the hell does that mean?"

"Which word are you having trouble with Thunder? *Moral* or *ethical?*"

He pointed the forty-five at me. "You're a lot bigger target than a damn bird."

Motive! I insulted Thunder, and he pointed the gun at me. Unfortunately, he's no longer dangling over the abyss.

I gave him a scoffing laugh. "You're a brave man when you have a gun in your hand and you're facing a hundred-pound woman or a fifty-year-old ex-jock with bad knees and a torn-up shoulder."

He glared at me, one of those boxer-at-the-weigh-in, gonna-whip-your-ass-and-rape-your-woman glowers. Then he lowered the gun and laughed so hard the trapezius muscles of his neck vibrated. "That's why I like you, Lassiter. Your crazy ass ain't scared of me."

"Then maybe you'll listen. I want you to call Clyde Garner and apologize."

"What?"

"Express your deep remorse for what happened to Eva. For what *you* did to Eva."

"Screw that. Bitch stabbed me."

"She could have sunk that knife into your heart, and you wouldn't have felt a thing."

He mulled that over a moment. "You throwing shade at me, dude?"

"Just saying maybe you should show some empathy for her family."

"Any other bright ideas, lawyer? I gotta work out."

"Charity. I want you to make a one-million-dollar donation to a charity of the Garners' choosing. Maybe it'll go to shelters for abused women, but that's up to them."

"No way! That'd be like I feel guilty, which I don't."

"And I want you to take an anger management course."

"Fuck you and the Porsche you didn't ride in on!"

"I've taken the course myself, Thunder, and it works."

"Next time take a course for stupid lawyers."

"You forgetting I just won your murder trial?"

"What I ain't forgetting is you wanted me to plead to manslaughter."

"Only after I concluded you lied to Coach Duncan and you lied to me."

"I would never deceive Johnnie. He's the best man I've ever known. As for you, Lassiter, you could have bailed if I offended your girlie-man sensibilities."

"No way the judge would have let me out so close to trial."

"So why'd you fight so hard for me in court?"

"Couldn't help myself. I don't know how to go half-speed. Plus I had no idea the jury would buy your bullshit story."

"At least you admit it. I won the case, not you."

"You're right. Next time you shoot somebody, call Roy Black."

"He got a better rep than you?"

"Immensely."

I heard movement inside the apartment. The sliding door opened, and a giant waddled out. Okay, not a real giant.

Jelly Bean Drexler.

-14-

Zero Chill Dude

Rashan "Jelly Bean" Drexler weighed about as much as your average refrigerator but wasn't quite as nimble or quick on his feet. Instead of the sculpted torso of his pal, Drexler was an amorphous blob of chest merging with stomach, a yard-wide butt, blubbery thighs, and feet the size of a sea lion's flippers. He wore a vintage Oakland Raiders jersey and nylon running shorts, though I doubted he'd done any running since his days as a truant, shoplifter, and versatile juvenile delinquent. On that sea mammal's feet were, fittingly, orange flip-flops, which should have sued him for abuse.

"Jell, I'm glad you're here," Thurston said.

Drexler didn't say a word, unless a crunching sound qualifies as speech. His chin was angled toward the sky as he sucked out the contents of a bag of potato chips the size of a duffel bag.

"Dawg, I been thinking about what you said the other day," Thurston continued.

Crunch. Crunch. Crunch.

Thurston turned to me. "Lassiter, Jell's got my back."

"And one of your Ferraris," I reminded him.

"Jell says he oughta negotiate my new contract."

"Great. He can use the haggling skills he learned selling drugs on street corners," I suggested helpfully.

Drexler tossed the empty chips bag over the balcony railing, where it soared higher in an updraft. "Lassiter, you a zero chill dude."

"If that means I'm not cool, guilty as charged. But Jelly Bean, you're just a hanger-on. A mooch. A leech."

"Screw you, benchwarmer! I'd be balling today if I hadn't blown out my knee."

"Blown out your stomach is more like it."

He worked his face into a scowl that tripled his double chins. "In high school, they called me The Hammer."

"Only thing you hammer these days is the buffet table at the Biltmore . . . on Thunder's tab."

"You don't get it, Lassiter," Thurston said. "Me and Jell are fam. We've known each other our whole lives. We shared a lot."

"Same probation officer," I agreed.

I wasn't upset. No way did I want to be Thurston's mouthpiece, in or out of court. At the same time, parasites like Jelly Bean Drexler pissed me off. A year ago I had advised Thurston to put his money into safe investments like tax-free municipal bonds. But Drexler overruled me, and Thurston opened a South Beach nightclub. He comped his five hundred closest friends, and they comped their friends. The bartenders stole, the valet parkers stole, booze disappeared, and "Thunder Dome" lasted two months while burning through $6 million. I took satisfaction knowing that Thurston's loss was good for the local economy.

"Without Jell, I would have dropped out of Florida State my first semester," Thurston reminisced. "My teammates made fun of the way I talked back then, and they were brothers! Brothers from Miami and Lauderdale, not Muck City."

"They looked down on us," Drexler said.

"Made me feel stupid," Thurston said.

"You were never stupid," I said.

"I know that now. Back then only Jell believed in me. He'd do anything for me, and I'd do anything for him. Without Jell, I'd be back in the muck cutting sugarcane."

"You're wrong! He didn't sweat through your two-a-days," I said. "He didn't carry the ball thirty-three times against the Gators when they were trying to twist your legs into wishbones. And he sure as hell didn't take your speech courses or your algebra exams. You did it, Thunder. You pulled yourself out of the cane fields, but you brought this parasite along with you."

Drexler moved closer to my chaise, his bulk blocking out the sun. "Whoever started rearranging your cracker face, I could finish the job."

"I didn't know the word *job* was in your vocabulary," I said.

"Chill, you two!" Thurston ordered.

While Drexler tried to frighten me by squinting, his chubby cheeks turning his eyes into narrow slits, a couple of things occurred to me. First, Victoria Lord's idea to get Drexler to flip on Thurston would never work. They were, as Thurston said, "fam." They grew up together in Muck City, and one would never turn on the other.

Second, maybe there was a bright side. The closeness of the two men only added credence to what Clyde Garner had told me. If Thurston had planned to kill his wife, who would he tell? The one man in the world he could trust, that's who.

According to Eva, Thurston had texted Drexler: *Bitch touch my chedda, feel my Beretta.* Maybe it was just a song to him. Maybe it was a lousy joke. Or maybe . . .

Rather than split his loot with Eva in a divorce, he'd planned to kill her.

Then there was the cell phone conversation Eva's brothers overheard. Even more threatening lyrics: "I bring pain, bloodstains on what remains."

Stacy Strickstein had claimed the prosecution couldn't recover the text messages, which had somehow been permanently deleted, if they had ever existed at all. The phone conversation, she said at first, was hearsay, which it wasn't. She then claimed that premeditation conflicted with her theory of the case and therefore she wouldn't use it, which was a dubious strategy.

So why had Strickstein been so lackadaisical preparing her case against Thurston? And now, after screwing the pooch in the murder trial, why was she going after me on some bullcrap bribery investigation? I had no idea.

"You got anything else to say, Lassiter?"

"Only this. You remind me of O. J. Simpson."

"He was shiftier. I'm stronger."

"Not talking about your running style. It's your split personality. The bullshit facade you present to the world. All sunny skies and charming smiles. Then the real you. Stormy weather and an evil heart."

Thurston was shaking his head. He looked more sad than angry. Finally he said, "Ever since the verdict came in, you've been different, Lassiter. Jell, he's the same. Always has been. He's my bro."

"So?"

"So you're fired."

IN THE ELEVENTH JUDICIAL CIRCUIT IN AND FOR

MIAMI-DADE COUNTY, FLORIDA

In re: Investigation of Jacob Lassiter, Esq.

Pursuant to Florida State Section 918.12, to wit, Jury Tampering.

Investigation No. 2016-MDC-GJ-149

Partial Transcript of Grand Jury Proceedings

[Continuation of Earlier Testimony of Manuel Gutierrez]

Q: [By ASA Strickstein] Mr. Gutierrez, you told us you opened the envelope Mr. Lassiter gave you and found ten one-hundred-dollar bills.
A: [By Manuel Gutierrez] *Sí.* One thousand dollars.

Q: And what else?
A: A note with a telephone number.

Q: What did you do?
A: Put the money in my pocket and that night I called the number. Mr. Lassiter answered.

Q: Tell the grand jurors about the conversation.
A: He tells me not to worry about nothing. He's using a burner, a disposable cell phone. There'll be no record we ever talked. He says he wants to come over to my house and asked me the address.

Q: And what did you say?

A: I give him directions, and he comes over real late, after midnight.

Q: What happened when Mr. Lassiter came to the house?

A: He takes his cell phone, the burner, and crushes it in his bare hands. *Él es muy fuerte.* He's very strong. And he says, "Shitbag, this is your head if you tell anybody about our deal."

Q: What deal was that?

A: He gives me another twenty-four thousand in hundreds, and I promise to work like hell in the jury room for him. And even if I couldn't convince the others, I'd vote not guilty until hell freezes over or both Castros die. I'd hang the jury for him, if that's what it took.

Q: What did happen in the jury room?

A: On the first vote, it was close, eight to four for guilty. I was relieved, because I had help. Three other people arguing for innocence. I don't know, maybe Mr. Lassiter paid them, too. Anyway, on the second day of deliberations, I did a lot of talking and by the third day, we came back not guilty.

Q: What did you do with the money, sir?

A: The day after the verdict, I bought a big-screen TV down at Sound Advice on Dixie Highway. The Sony eighty-inch model. When I get it home, Lourdes, that's my wife, she says, "Where do think we're gonna put that? It's bigger than the living room." And I said, maybe we can build an extension, and she wanted to know where the money was coming from, and I told her. That was my mistake.

Q: Then what happened?

A: She went to mass and came home and said *La Virgen Maria* told her I had to call you.

Q: And what did you do?

A: Sometimes I say no to my wife, and sometimes I say no to the Virgin Mary. But together they're too tough for me.

-15-

Deep-Carpet Lawyers

hope Thunder Thurston appreciates how great a lawyer you are," Marvin Fishbein said.

"I think our feelings about each other are mutual," I replied.

"Good! Grand! You won an impossible case, and the dividends are just starting to be reaped, my friend."

Actually, we were not friends. These days, I worked for Fishbein, the managing partner of Harman and Fox, an old-line, deep-carpet, stuffed-shirt law firm dating to the days William Jennings Bryan sold Coral Gables property from the back of a trolley car. Mr. Harman and Mr. Fox had long since ascended to that great courtroom in the sky . . . or perhaps the boiler room in the opposite direction.

Fishbein was a relatively decent guy for someone who made his bones as a lawyer by busting unions and cheating hourly workers out of overtime and sick leave. Unlike some of his partners, Fishbein had no pretensions. He was here to make a lot of dough by doing as little work as possible for filthy-rich corporations with scant social conscience.

This was my second tour of duty with the firm. Two decades ago, after proudly passing the bar exam on my fourth try, I'd landed a job in the public defender's office. The PD's clients are a dangerous lot, and I had my share of sociopaths and schizophrenics, not to mention the paranoids who see their own lawyers as part of the vast conspiracy against them. I've watched a defendant break a chair over his lawyer's head before the court officers could intervene. That's why the PD's office found it helpful to have an ex-linebacker at the defense table, his neck too thick for a proper knot in his discount-store polyester tie. Which explains how I got my first gig as a mouthpiece on the government payroll.

When Harman and Fox made Fishbein its hiring partner all those years ago, he discovered that virtually no one in the cushy suite of offices had actually tried a case in the past decade. They had litigators, paper shufflers who took depos, sent out boilerplate interrogatories, pestered the court with voluminous motions . . . and eventually settled everything. The firm needed a trial lawyer.

As an assistant public defender, I was in court every day. I tried cases with little time for preparation and virtually no money for investigation. Like all the PD's, I lost a lot, basically because virtually all my clients were guilty of something, though not necessarily of the crimes with which they'd been charged. I also lost because the presumption of innocence was a lofty ideal, pretty much ignored by judges and jurors.

Yeah, I know. The sign above the judge's bench reads **WE WHO LABOR HERE SEEK ONLY THE TRUTH**. And for years, I've said, "There ought to be a footnote. Subject to the truth being ignored by lying witnesses, concealed by sleazy lawyers, excluded by inept judges, and overlooked by lazy jurors."

Basically public defenders are wounded knights, wearing rusty armor, straddling spavined steeds, and hoisting splintered lances. They ride into battle, free of fear and impervious to pain.

That's why Marvin Fishbein hired me the first time. For a while I enjoyed the perks. From Harman and Fox's office on the fifty-second floor of a Biscayne Boulevard high-rise, I could see Bimini. I had an expense account, stone-crab lunches at the Bankers Club, a staff of paralegals and investigators, and an assistant to tote my files and pick up my dry cleaning.

But it didn't take long to figure out that *seeing* Bimini was not the same thing as *being* in Bimini. If anything, the gauzy view of the island across the Gulf Stream only emphasized the fact that I was not fishing, windsurfing, or just snoozing in a hammock. Then there were those damnable time sheets. Accounting for every quarter hour of the day, leasing out my life in fifteen-minute bites. I quickly realized I was not big-firm-partnership material.

I would have quit . . . had I not been fired. Punching out that date rapist and earning a public reprimand from the Florida Supreme Court speeded my departure. So I hung out my shingle and flew solo.

Now, all these years later, Fishbein called again with virtually the same problem. His young lawyers were Ivy League intellectuals without street smarts, particularly Flagler Street, where the county courthouse was located. As for my past, all was forgiven. Fishbein claimed he now respected my willingness to deck a belligerent client. Supposedly that tale has been told—and enhanced—over the years. In one account, I hung the client out the window by his ankles. In another, I marched him to the roof of the building, lashed him to the flagpole, and hoisted him to the sky.

"You're Lassiter the Legend," Fishbein had said when wooing me back.

After all the flattery, I chomped and swallowed the bait. Harman and Fox covered my overhead—my secretary, Cindy, my coffeemaker and copy machine—paid a handsome salary without my having to keep time records or wear a tie in the office. The firm gave me the honorary title "of counsel" to signify that I was neither a filthy-rich partner nor a workaholic young associate.

Now I was in Fishbein's corner suite, listening to Marvin gab, which he preferred to actually working. A black turkey vulture was perched on the ledge outside the window, giving us the evil eye. As all Miamians know, the dirty birds fly to Florida each winter and return to Ohio—or someplace else normal—each spring.

Fishbein spent a moment asking about my battered face, and I took a moment telling lies. He asked about Granny, my nephew, and my love life—fine, fine, and empty—and I kept wondering just what he wanted.

"Do you play golf, Jake?"

"Not so much. I can hit the ball a mile but not straight. I've got no short game. Also, I cheat."

"Good to know. But I'll tell you who plays. Cyrus Frick."

I shrugged, and outside the window, the vulture ruffled its feathers.

"General counsel of Biscayne Life Insurance Company," Fishbein said, admiration coating his voice like whipped cream in his Frappuccino. "Not assistant general counsel or deputy general counsel. But the big enchilada."

I grunted my appreciation that Fishbein hit the links with such an impressive fellow, thinking I knew what was coming, hoping I was wrong.

"You know the main job of an insurance company's general counsel, Jake?"

"Just guessing, Marv, but I'd say starving widows and orphans to death."

"Hiring outside counsel."

"My second guess was adjusting the thermostat in hell."

"Love your irreverence, Jake, though not all the partners do. Now, I've been letting Frick win at golf for the last fifteen years, and he's finally brought us a case."

"You're the rainmaker," I admitted.

"We eat what we kill," Fishbein said, proudly.

On the window ledge, the vulture cocked its head, as if eavesdropping.

"But you get credit, too, Jake," Fishbein continued. "Cye read about the Thurston verdict and thought you're the man for Biscayne Life Insurance."

"Does he want me to sell double indemnity policies like Fred MacMurray in that old movie?"

"You're a great kidder, Jake. Cye wants you to defend his biggest case, a life insurance claim that's a bit of a sticky wicket. It can't be settled. It's gotta be tried, and it needs a lawyer with brass balls to do it."

"I hate insurance companies," I said.

"You don't have to love your clients."

"True. But I've long believed it's best to have a client I like, a cause that's just, and a check that doesn't bounce."

"Sorry, Jake, but you've only got one out of three here. Insurance companies pay the rent and a helluva lot more."

"Can't someone else do it?"

"Jake, you're my Clydesdale. My workhorse. You don't piss your pants when a witness sandbags you or curl up and die when a judge rules against you."

"If I did, I'd be very wet and very dead. You've got an insurance trial team in the office. Why not give them the case?"

"Trial team!" He spat out the words. "Sure, they alphabetize their files. They outline their opening statements and prepare storyboards of their cases. They plan! But you know what Mike Tyson said about plans?"

"Everyone has a plan," I said, "until they get punched in the mouth."

"Precisely, my friend. You're my counterpuncher. You get hit; you hit back harder. I need you, Jake. The great firm of Harman and Fox needs you. And to get to the point, I'm not asking. You're gonna defend Biscayne Life Insurance."

I was stuck. Fishbein was ordering me to handle the case. It's the first time that had happened since I'd reenlisted at the firm. Face it—I was a buck private in Fishbein's army.

What the hell have I done?

I've given up my independence for security, that's what. For a juicy paycheck, a bay-front view, and cocktails at lunch.

What had I been thinking?

I had told Fishbein the truth. I really hate insurance companies. Carrying their flag into battle was akin to being the devil's handmaiden. But what could I do? I was trapped in a personal hell of my own making. I felt feeble and weak and angry, too. And what about everything else going on in my so-called life? How was I going to deal with Thunder Thurston, not to mention the grand jury probe, if I was wrapped up in this crummy civil case?

With utterly no choice, I said, "Tell me about the case, Marv," I said. "Where do I start?"

-16-

Obituary, Second Draft

Marvin Fishbein smiled broadly and pointed to a cardboard box in the corner of the suite. The case file, no doubt. Not that Marv would have opened it. It had been decades since he'd read a pleading, much less written one.

Still he was able to summarize what general counsel Cyrus Frick had told him. The company wrote a half-million-dollar life insurance policy on a female cage fighter named Carla Caruana. The name rang a distant bell, probably because my nephew, Kip, watched mixed martial arts on television, and it's impossible not to be drawn in when two men—or women—are savagely beating each other in high definition.

Carla the cage fighter was the single mother of two children, Joshua, eight years old, and Elizabeth, six. A little more than two years ago, when Carla was thirty-one, she was a top competitor in the Ultimate Fighting Championship. But she suffered several injuries and worried about her future in the sport. She tried to buy disability insurance, but no company would write a policy for someone whose occupation made wingsuit flying seem tame. She did, however, pass the physical exam for the purchase of a $500,000 term life insurance policy from Cyrus

Frick's company. So she bought the policy and named her children as beneficiaries.

Not long thereafter, Carla Caruana's career started going downhill. She was sidelined with injuries. Her income fell. She started drinking. She might have become addicted to painkillers.

"Now, here's where it gets sticky," Fishbein said. "The policy had a one-year exclusion for death by suicide. She attempted suicide before midnight on the three hundred sixty-fifth day after the policy was issued."

"Attempted?"

"To wit, she took a lethal combination of pain pills with three different sleeping medications and about a fifth of vodka, at about ten thirty p.m., roughly ninety minutes before the policy would have vested and suicide would be covered."

Yeah, he really said "to wit."

"When did she die?" I asked.

"Excellent question, Jake. Not until four forty-two the next morning, at which time death by suicide clearly would have been an insurable risk."

"Your golfing buddy denied the claim, and here we are," I said.

"Exactly. A delicious legal question, don't you think?"

"I'm not sure anything about a young mother's suicide is delicious," I said. "What's the case law say?"

"All over the waterfront. Maybe it's the time of the attempt that controls. Maybe it's the moment of death. Maybe it's even more complicated. What if she was brain-dead at five minutes before midnight, even though her heart kept beating several more hours?"

On such minutiae does our legal system turn, I thought. *Pettifoggery as high art.*

"Why not just pay the half mil to the kids?" I suggested.

"Ah, were it only so easy. Before the lawsuit was filed, the estate's lawyers made a demand for the policy limits, and Frick replied with a rather strongly worded letter."

"How strongly worded? Denials of claims are pretty much boilerplate."

"Did I mention that Frick has a drinking problem? No? Well, apparently, he'd gotten sauced before writing the denial."

Fishbein picked up a single sheet of paper from the corner of his desk. He read aloud: "Dear learned counsel. Alas, your plea on behalf of the two alleged orphans falls on deaf ears. An insurance company is not a charity. An insurance policy is not a love letter. Your client's suicide renders the contract null and void, and if I may say so, did more harm to her precious children than this denial of benefits ever will. On the other hand, perhaps the little dears are better off without their pill-popping, muscle-brained, tattoo-parlored, cage-fighting holy terror of a mother. In that vein, our counteroffer is zero, zilch, nada, plus all the lint you can lick out of my navel."

"Unbelievable," I said. "Callous. Mean. Crude. Inhumane."

"There's one more line. You know the standard template at the end of lawyers' letters?"

"Sure. 'Please be governed accordingly.'"

"Cye changed it a bit."

"I'm listening."

Again, Fishbein read aloud. "In closing, learned counsel, go shit in your hat."

I was already picturing the trial. The tearful children would be sitting in the front row. Frick's letter would be projected on a screen, his outrageous insults highlighted in bright yellow for the jury.

"Once Cye sobered up," Fishbein said, "he researched the law and saw the case was a toss-up."

"Maybe on the law, but if it gets past summary judgment and goes to the jury, the insurance company is toast. Burned toast."

"Cye recognized that. So he finally offered policy limits, the five hundred grand, plus interest. Rejected."

I mulled it over a moment. Smart plaintiff's lawyering. Once Frick wrote the nasty letter, the insurance company was in the precarious position of a bad-faith denial of benefits. As long as the suicide didn't exclude coverage as a matter of law, the policy limit—$500,000—disappeared. The jury could award virtually any amount it wanted to punish the company.

"About as bad as bad faith can be," I said.

"Afraid so."

"The plaintiff's lawyer will ask the jury for four or five million."

"If the jury returns anything north of a million, the company will fire Cye and we can kiss any more business good-bye."

My dormant headache was kicking up again. I got to my feet and walked to the window. The turkey vulture spotted me, flapped its wings, and headed north along Biscayne Boulevard toward the American Airlines Arena. I stretched my back, leaned over, and picked up the box of files.

Estate of Carla Caruana vs. Biscayne Life Insurance Company.

How much whiskey would it take to get through the paperwork? Tonight I would be paying the price for selling out. This was shaping up to be even worse than I imagined, and I had pictured the fires of hell with me shoveling coal into the boiler. I took a moment to kick myself when I was down.

Jake, old buddy, how the hell can you work for Marvelous Marv and Frick the Prick? They're everything you hate. How low can you go? Just how much of your soul will you sell for a paycheck?

"Marv, may I ask you a personal question?"

"Sure. As long as it's not about that receptionist with the enhanced boobs."

"Are you ever plagued by existential angst?"

"You mean, what are we doing here? How should we live our lives? What's it all about?"

"Yeah."

"Never gave it a thought. And I suggest you don't, either. Too much thinking, you'll end up on the shrink's couch. Just do, Jake. Don't think."

It occurred to me that Marvin Fishbein was either an idiot or a genius. Or a genius in his idiocy. He certainly didn't lose sleep at night over ethics and morals and personal responsibility. And me? At the moment, I had no choice but to stow all that in a box in my backyard storage shed.

"I'll have Cindy file my notice of appearance," I said.

"Excellent! Jake, if anyone can win this, you can. You've got hard bark. You can stiffen the spine of judge and jury. You won't let sympathy or emotion play into the ruling. You're cold-blooded, like me."

Vultures, they say, can projectile vomit ten feet or more. Where was my black-feathered friend? Right now I could beat him in a hurling contest.

"Thanks, Marv. Maybe that can be in my obituary."

He gave me a puzzled look as I imagined an addition to my obit: *Jake Lassiter, a cold-blooded Miami lawyer who got murderers off the hook and starved orphans on behalf of insurance companies, died yesterday of equal doses of bourbon and regret . . ."*

I started for the door, lugging the box of files, heavy as a coffin. "Who's the knight on the white horse?" I asked, over my shoulder.

"How's that, Jake?"

"Who's the plaintiff's lawyer?"

"Take a guess."

"A heavyweight. Maybe Stuart Grossman in the Gables."

"Nope. Try again."

"Some out-of-town bigshot. One of those Texas guys with a name like Racehorse or Six Gun."

"Closer to home, my friend. Steve Solomon and Victoria Lord. You know them, right?"

-17-

Hundred-Dollar Bills

I told Marvin Fishbein that Solomon and Lord were friends, but he already knew that. He implied that maybe they owed me a favor from the time I represented Solomon in what turned out to be a bum rap. I told Marv they didn't operate that way, and, if anything, they would work even harder to win with me on the other side.

That's the way it works. You want to show your mentor how good you are. Student spanks the teacher, that sort of thing. Marv expressed confidence that I had a bigger bag of tricks and sent me on my way.

A minute after leaving Fishbein's office, I was standing in the corridor, waiting for the elevator, the cardboard box containing the Caruana file balanced on one knee.

"Hold up, Jake!"

It was not-so-marvelous Marv, huffing and puffing his way toward me. "Forgot one thing. Just a little housekeeping matter."

I pivoted toward him, sending pain through an arthritic knee that had been hyperextended countless times and scraped by a surgeon half a dozen times. "Yeah, Marv?"

"Forgot to tell you. The firm got served with a grand jury subpoena. They asked for records of bank transactions involving Thunder Thurston."

I put on my puzzled look. "I don't know anything about it." That was true, as far as it went. I didn't know anything about the subpoena. But surely the subpoena was related to the grand jury investigating me for bribing a juror. No way would I share that info with Fishbein. The grand jury operated in secret, which was good in one respect. The partners at Harman and Fox would be clueless about the investigation. But there was a downside, too. Without knowing the identity of the witnesses or the nature of the evidence, it was nearly impossible to blow the investigation out of the water before any damage was done. Damage being an indictment styled *State of Florida vs. Jacob Lassiter*.

Pincher, my old pal, was no help. With Stacy Strickstein a likely opponent in the upcoming election, he was afraid to even look over her shoulder, much less fondle the evidence. Even worse, based on what he'd said before coldcocking me, Sugar Ray thought I might be guilty.

All these thoughts distracted me from the puzzling question of the moment. Why did Strickstein want the firm's bank records?

"What do you think the grand jury is after, Marv?" I asked, in my tone of absolute innocence.

"I was hoping you knew. I reviewed the documents before we produced them. Thurston's deposits to the operating account were in order. All legal fees."

"What about his corporate account, Thurston Pro Bowl Enterprises?"

"Subpoena didn't ask for it, so we're not producing it."

"Trust account?" I said. "Thurston paid a fifty-thousand-dollar cost deposit during pretrial discovery."

"It balances to the penny. Everything kosher."

There was something in his tone. "Marv?"

"Well, maybe nothing. But just before the trial, you authorized a check on the trust account for twenty-six thousand and change."

"We only spent about half the cost deposit. I returned the excess."

"But the check was made payable to cash, Jake, and your signature appeared on the back."

"Thunder asked for the balance in cash, so I cashed the check and gave it to him in hundred-dollar bills."

"Personally?"

I shook my head. "I had a courier deliver it."

Fishbein raised his eyebrows, just a bit. "There was no record of a signed receipt in the file."

"I'm sure Thurston got the cash or he would have yelled about it, maybe with a gun in his hand."

"Even so, Jake. Sloppy. Not like you."

"Sorry, Marv, but when you're prepping for trial, little things like receipts and courier confirmations slip through the cracks."

That was true, of course. That's why high-rise firms like Harman and Fox have assistants, paralegals, and clerks on call 24-7. It's not my job to handle minutiae. But just now I was wondering and worrying what had happened to that cash.

"Okay, no biggie," Fishbein said. "I wonder why the grand jury cares about any of this."

Cash. Cash and bribery of a juror.

His wondering seemed to require an answer, so I told two lies in one sentence. "I have no idea, Marv, but from now on, I'll be more careful with the paperwork."

IN THE ELEVENTH JUDICIAL CIRCUIT IN AND FOR

MIAMI-DADE COUNTY, FLORIDA

In re: Investigation of Jacob Lassiter, Esq.

Pursuant to Florida State Section 918.12, to
wit, Jury Tampering.

Investigation No. 2016-MDC-GJ-149

Partial Transcript of Grand Jury Proceedings

Q: [By ASA Strickstein]: Ladies and gentlemen of the grand jury,
you are going to hear from Mr. Alberto Sacata. If we were in trial,
I would take several minutes to qualify him as an expert witness.
In this proceeding, I will simply proffer to you that Mr. Sacata is
chief latent fingerprint examiner for the Miami office of the Florida
Department of Law Enforcement. He has testified more than eight
hundred times and has been qualified as an expert witness in seven-
teen of the twenty judicial circuits of Florida. Mr. Sacata, is that a
fair summary?

A: [Alberto Sacata] Yes, ma'am. I'm also the past president of the
International Association of Identification, the premier organization of
fingerprint, firearms, and crime scene examiners.

Q: Let me show you exhibit seven, Mr. Sacata. Have you seen it before?
A: Yes, it's one stack of hundred-dollar bills, twenty-four in number.

Q: Did you test these bills for latent fingerprints?
A: Yes.

Q: Do you have an opinion whether there were latent prints of value on any of that currency?

A: Yes, there were. Seven latents of value matched the exemplars of a Mr. Manuel Gutierrez.

Q: And the others?

A: There were left thumbprints of value on twenty-one of the twenty-four bills along with partial right thumbprints sixteen of the twenty-four bills.

Q: Anything remarkable about the location of the thumbprints?

A: The left full prints were all on the left-hand side of the bills, below Benjamin Franklin's face. The partial right prints were slightly above and to the right.

Q: Telling you what, Mr. Sacata?

A: The bills had been stacked, all facing the same way. A right-handed person was holding the currency in the left hand and sliding each bill off the stack with the right thumb.

Q: Were you able to form an opinion as to the identity of the person who made these prints?

A: Yes.

Q: Please explain.

A: Three days ago your office provided me with the booking file of Mr. Jacob Lassiter, a Miami lawyer, who had been briefly jailed for contempt of court a few years back. More than once, actually. He was fingerprinted, and I used those prints as the exemplar for the comparison.

Q: And?

A: I can state to a reasonable degree of scientific certainty that Mr. Lassiter's thumbprints are on the currency, and that he likely left those latents while counting out the stack of bills.

-18-

Dirt on Plaintiff

Granny made chicken-fried steak for dinner. And that wasn't all. Cream gravy and mashed potatoes drowning in butter. Deep-fried ears of corn, fried okra, fried green tomatoes, and biscuits dripping in honey. Best I could tell, the biscuits were not fried. Neither was the sweet potato pie for dessert.

Burp.

It was 8:00 p.m., and I had not yet gone into cardiac arrest, so I decided to do a little work. I retired to my study, a fancy name for a room too small to be a bedroom. An old, half-inflated football sat forlornly on my messy desk. The score of a long-ago Penn State victory over Pitt was scrawled in blue, the ink as faded as my memory of the game.

I unpacked the *Caruana vs. Biscayne Life Insurance* box and opened a bottle of Jack Daniel's. Judging from the heft of the file, it would be a four-Jack night. I sank into an ancient recliner of cracked brown leather and started reading and sipping.

There were no surprises in the pleadings binder. Until I filed my appearance today, Cyrus Frick had been handling the case with an in-house team of lawyers. They had moved for summary judgment on the legal ground that the act of suicide constituted "one transaction" that occurred when Carla Caruana swallowed the pills and drank the booze prior to midnight. It was irrelevant, they argued, when death occurred. Even if she had lingered for a year in a coma, the "transaction" of the suicide occurred within the one-year exclusion period, and the insurance policy was void.

It was not a frivolous argument, and I could make it without blushing. But I needed an analogy. Lawyers love analogies. It helps simplify things for the dunderheads, by which I mean the judges, not the jurors.

It came to me rather quickly, perhaps nurtured by the sour mash whiskey and my college education, even though I amassed mostly C's and a few B's at Penn State. I had majored in theater, because that's where the girls were, but I had also taken a physics course, because I got confused at registration and thought I was signing up for phys ed.

I learned a bit about the Big Bang and every once in a while I stumble across a brainy show on PBS with nifty animation about the cosmos and creation. It's the stuff we discussed late into the night back in college when I had some intellectual curiosity fueled by beer, pizza, and marijuana. So here's what I was thinking.

About 13.8 billion years ago—give or take—the universe was formed. At first, preuniverse, there was just this speck of matter that had zero volume but infinite density. Yeah, I know, try wrapping your non-Einstein mind around that. Then, boom, the Big Bang, a flash of unimaginable brightness, and that speck became a seething, roiling mass of plasma billions of light-years across. Pretty much from here to eternity.

But there wasn't any matter, not as we know it. Just clouds of protons, neutrons, and electrons heated beyond any measurement. It took about four hundred thousand years for the clouds to cool and hydrogen atoms to form, and everything went dark again. Those dark ages lasted one hundred million years, and only then did the first stars emerge.

So . . . when was the universe created? At the Big Bang, when there really wasn't anything except those invisible subatomic particles? Or when the hydrogen formed? Or one hundred million years later when stars formed?

The "transaction," it seems to me, occurred in that first split second, that flash of light, even though definable matter did not yet exist. First there was nothing, then there was something, no matter how invisible, infinitesimal, and unknowable. The process had begun. Creation.

Similarly, Carla's suicide was transacted when she consumed the pills and booze and the metabolic process began deep inside her, a process that would end her life a few hours—not one hundred million years—later. At least that was my theory concocted under the influence of Mr. Jack Daniel's.

Next I turned to the plaintiff's paperwork. Victoria Lord had written the opposition brief. Much like its author, the legal argument was cool, dispassionate, and very smart. No wailing, no crying about orphans, as lesser lawyers might be inclined to do. Singing emotional arias wouldn't sway the court on a motion in which the law—not passion—prevails. In Victoria's view, there was a two-part transaction. What transpired prior to midnight was part one, an "attempted" suicide. Part two, Ms. Caruana's death at 4:42 a.m. the next day, completed the suicide. Therefore, the policy was in full force and effect when the suicide exclusion expired at midnight.

There was no Florida precedent directly on point, and cases in other jurisdictions were split. So the defense motion for summary judgment would be a crapshoot. I would argue that there was no liability as a matter of law. If I won, a jury would never get to hear the case, and Joshua and Elizabeth Caruana wouldn't get a dime. If I lost, the case would go to a full jury trial, and Solomon and Lord could warm up the calculator, one with a lot of digits.

I was only on my second tumbler of Mr. Daniel's when I opened a file marked CARLA CARUANA, INVESTIGATIVE. There were half a dozen photos of Carla, posing in a red-white-and-blue, star-spangled, two-piece fighting outfit. She was a brunette with a thick neck and solid core. Muscular thighs, prominent deltoids, and long arms corded with veins. Some photos included her children, who looked to be around six and four, meaning the pictures had been taken about two years ago. The boy posed in a boxer's stance. The freckle-faced girl hugged her mother's waist.

Next came a subfile marked INVESTIGATIVE NOTES. WORK PRODUCT AND PRIVILEGED. On the outside binder, someone had handwritten:

Dirt on plaintiff!

I wondered if I should wash my hands now or later. Oh, those damn insurance companies and their private eyes. Whatever it was, Cyrus Frick would be expecting me to use it. Some days I just hate my life.

I opened the file, which was divided into subsections:
SUSPENSIONS FROM COMPETITION
CRIMINAL CONDUCT AND ARRESTS
PRESCRIPTION AND ILLICIT DRUGS
AUTOPSY REPORT
The first page had an unsigned, handwritten note:

Unwed mother! Unfit mother! Evidence of bad reputation. How do we get all the dirt into evidence?

Washing my hands would not be enough. I needed a cold shower in lye and bleach. How could I defend the insurance company using its below-the-belt tactics? Short answer, I couldn't. Next question, how do I keep from being fired? No answer.

My headache was in high gear. Maybe it was stress related. I would try to keep track of what was happening in my life every time it felt like someone smacked my skull with a sledgehammer.

I thumbed through the rest of the "Dirt on Plaintiff" file and came across a DVD. On the label someone had scrawled in blue marker:

Caruana Clips: The Life and Crimes

A smart-ass insurance lawyer or PI playing off "The Life and Times," I imagined. That's what passed for humor in Cyrus Frick's office.

I sipped at my whiskey, preparing to roll up my sleeves and dig into the dirt. Just then I heard my nephew, Kip, yelling. "Uncle Jake! C'mere! Quick!"

-19-

All-Time Blooper Reel

At the sound of Kip's voice, I unfolded myself from the recliner and stood, my right knee clicking where bone rubbed against bone. The dirt file—and my further descent into the suburbs of Hades—would have to wait.

"Hurry, Uncle Jake!"

I've been raising Kip since his mother, my half sister, Janet, took off for places unknown, although jail or a crack house were two likely destinations.

Kip was in the eleventh grade at Biscayne-Tuttle, a private school comfortably located on the shore of Biscayne Bay. The tuition was hefty, another reason I needed the gig at Harman and Fox. I wanted my nephew to be around smart kids, to get a good education, to have advantages I lacked, growing up poor in the Upper Keys. Kip was a third-string wide receiver on the school's football team. Unlike his block-of-granite uncle, he didn't have the frame for the sport, and I pretty much hoped he would quit and join the chess club.

I found the towheaded kid sitting cross-legged in front of the television in the Florida room. A three-ring binder, his high school football team's playbook, was open on the cocktail table. I would have preferred an algebra text.

At the moment Kip was watching football. It took only a second for me to recognize the jerseys: New York Jets and Miami Dolphins.

Oh no, not that.

"Uncle Jake, you made the all-time NFL blooper reel. So cool!"

"Jeez, where are they showing this crap?"

"ESPN Classic. You're like immortal!"

"Story of my life. A blooper reel."

On the screen, the old clip looked as if it had been shot in black-and-white, thanks to the swirling snow and misty fog in the Meadowlands on that crummy December day. I was on the suicide squad—the kickoff team—and made a helluva head-on tackle at the Jets' thirty-five-yard line. These days a helmet-to-helmet hit would draw a fifteen-yard penalty for targeting, but in the dark ages it was just another teeth-rattling smackdown.

The kick returner flew one direction and the ball the other, spinning on the frozen turf, and somehow ended up in my hands. I slipped on the icy field, and one of the Jets' blockers got a hand on me, but I tore away.

"Kip, did you see that? My knee hit the ground."

"Yeah?"

"By contact! The play should have been blown dead."

If it had, none of the rest would have happened.

On the screen there I was, number fifty-eight, whirling around, ball clutched against my belly, and churning at full speed.

The wrong way. Toward the Dolphins end zone!

I'd suffered a concussion on the tackle, the team doc would later tell me. The wooziness and skull-crushing headaches would come that evening. But in those next few seconds, I felt glorious, rumbling downfield, holding the ball aloft as I crossed the goal line. A contingent of New York Jets piled on top of me. Laughing their guts out.

Safety! Two points for the enemy.

My only NFL score, and it was for the wrong team. Not only that, we lost the game by a single point.

"And that's how the name Wrong Way Lassiter was coined," the announcer said cheerily.

"Kip, you saw it, didn't you? Down by contact."

"I guess."

"And the official was right there. Why the hell didn't he blow the whistle?"

"I dunno, Uncle Jake."

"It's the story of civilization, Kip. Officials failing to blow the whistle."

My nephew chewed on his lower lip a moment. "Are you an anarchist?"

"Hell, no. Why do you say that?"

"Just something we read about in civics class."

"Glad you're learning something. Don't be one of those Americans who can name more housewives of Beverly Hills than justices of the Supreme Court."

"I'm thinking about becoming a lawyer."

"Don't you dare!"

"Why not?"

"The so-called justice system is polluted."

"So? I'll clean it up."

"Try, kid. Lousy judges, lazy lawyers, sleeping jurors. Officials don't blow the whistle, and injustice prevails."

"You *are* an anarchist, Uncle Jake."

The bloopers show thankfully moved on to someone else's humiliation. There was the butt fumble, where Jets quarterback Mark Sanchez spastically slid face-first into the rump of his own lineman, dropping the ball, which was returned for a touchdown. At least I had company.

"If you really want to be a lawyer," I said, "I'm gonna make you an offer you can't refuse."

"Yeah, what?"

"You know a lot about mixed martial arts, right?"

"I can name every men's UFC champ from flyweight to heavyweight."

"What about the women?"

"I can even spell Joanna Jedrzejczyk. She's women's strawweight champ."

"Great. I'll pay you five bucks an hour."

"That violates minimum-wage laws, Uncle Jake."

"Plus room and board."

He gave me an eleventh grader's dismissive look and said, "What do I gotta do?"

"You made me watch the damn blooper reel. Now I've got something for you. You ever hear of Carla Caruana?"

"Duh. Crazy Carla was like the number two bantamweight till Ronda Rousey cleaned her clock. Then Carla got suspended for some crap in another match and arrested for busting up a bar. Then you know what happened?"

"She committed suicide," I said.

"Yup. First she cracked, then she croaked."

Croaked.

Teenage boys are so lacking in empathy. Maybe they can't help it. All those raging hormones with no place to go. Okay, one place to go.

"Don't be disrespectful, kiddo. Carla Caruana was a mother raising two little kids by herself."

"Yeah, and she checked out on them. So who do I feel sorry for? Her or them?"

"All I'm saying—"

"She's even worse than my mom, who ran away from home. Ran away from me, really. But at least Mom's not dead. Not that we'd know. Or care."

Ouch.

Sometimes I forget just how much Kip has been wounded. I seldom see his pain because he hides it under the shell he has built to protect himself.

"Your mom's addiction is an illness, Kip."

Covering for my worthless half sister, a check forger, drug abuser, and worst mother in the history of Florida with the possible exception of Casey Anthony. I let myself entertain those uncharitable thoughts but didn't want Kip to follow my lead. "Whatever," Kip said.

Sometimes, I try to teach life lessons. "Try not to be judgmental about someone else's problems."

"I know. I know."

"Whether it's your mom or Carla Caruana or a kid at school. Be kind. Have empathy."

"Okay."

"Remember *To Kill a Mockingbird*?"

"How could I forget? You keep talking about it."

"Do you remember what Atticus Finch told Scout about judging other people?"

"You made me memorize it when I started calling Billy Maranski 'Billy Moronski.'"

"Say it now."

"Ah, jeez. Not again."

"Say it. With feeling. Like you mean it."

Kip sighed and recited: "You never really understand a person until you consider things from his point of view, until you climb inside his skin and walk around in it."

"What's old Atticus talking about?"

"Empathy, Uncle Jake."

"Exactly. Now, in that spirit, let's work on Carla Caruana's case."

He had a puzzled look.

"What, Kip?"

"Granny said you're working against Carla's kids."

"That's true."

"So, who's your empathy for? An insurance company?"

A ringing phone saved me.

"Hold that thought, Kip. We'll get to work in a minute."

I answered the phone. Doc Charlie Riggs. I love the old coot, but I knew he was going to bust my chops.

IN THE ELEVENTH JUDICIAL CIRCUIT IN AND FOR

MIAMI-DADE COUNTY, FLORIDA

In re: Investigation of Jacob Lassiter, Esq.

Pursuant to Florida State Section 918.12, to
wit, Jury Tampering.

Investigation No. 2016-MDC-GJ-149

Partial Transcript of Grand Jury Proceedings

[ASA Strickstein]: Ladies and gentlemen of the grand jury, I will now summarize the evidence so that you may vote on whether to return a true bill, an indictment, or a no-bill, in which case the suspect, Mr. Lassiter, will not be indicted. Now, to summarize—

[Foreperson J. Berkowitz] Ms. Strickstein, we haven't heard from the defense.

[ASA Strickstein] In the grand jury proceeding, you hear only from the state's witnesses. Should you indict Mr. Lassiter, the defense will have ample opportunity to present its case at trial.

[Foreperson] Have you asked Mr. Lassiter whether he wishes to talk to us, give his side?

[ASA Strickstein] That's rarely done, Mr. Berkowitz. It would require Mr. Lassiter waiving his Miranda rights and appearing before you without counsel. Neither he nor his lawyer would agree to that.

[Foreperson] You're sure, Ms. Strickstein?

[ASA Strickstein]. Perfectly. Admissions Mr. Lassiter makes could be used against him at trial. If he gives one story to you, he is stuck with it at time of trial. Any deviation would destroy his credibility and possibly subject him to perjury.

[Foreperson] But you haven't asked him to appear?

[ASA Strickstein] Nor do I intend to, Mr. Berkowitz. Now, before I summarize the testimony, please note that you are only to determine if there is probable cause that Mr. Lassiter committed a crime. And unlike a trial, that standard of proof is not "beyond a reasonable doubt." It is much lower than that.

[Foreperson] It's a little bit confusing, Ms. Strickstein.

[ASA Strickstein]. Then let me quote the law. To indict Mr. Lassiter, you need only "a reasonable ground of suspicion supported by circumstances strong enough in themselves to warrant a cautious person to believe he committed a crime."

[Foreperson] Still, it would have been nice to hear from the defense.

[ASA Strickstein] Your concern is noted. To reiterate, it takes twelve votes from your panel of twenty-one members to indict. Now, I will begin by summarizing the testimony of Manuel Gutierrez. As you recall . . .

END PARTIAL TRANSCRIPT

-20-

Henry the Eighth and Me

When I answered the phone, Doc Riggs asked how my doctor's appointment had gone, and I told the truth. I had canceled the exam when Thunder Thurston called, telling me to come to his condo.

Charlie hammered me awhile, calling me a "chucklehead," a word you hear these days about as often as *nincompoop* and *birdbrain*. Carrying the phone, I walked from the Florida room back to my study, ready to dig into the dirt file on Carla Caruana.

"Damn it, Jake! Stay away from Thurston," the doctor ordered.

"That should be easy. He fired me."

"Good." He paused a second, and I could almost hear him thinking. Worrying thoughts. "You didn't do anything untoward, did you?"

"Like try to kill him? No, but I thought about it."

"I beseech you, Jake. Let it go."

"I had a chance. I almost made the move, almost tossed him off his own balcony."

"Are you saying that just to give me a heart attack?"

"If that's what I wanted, I'd have invited you over for Granny's chicken-fried steak."

"You're behaving irrationally. You know that, right?"

"Give me credit. I didn't kill him."

"Thank God."

"I wasn't ready. But that could change."

"Damn it! Forget Thurston. Start thinking about yourself. When are you going to get those neurological tests?"

"Stop worrying. I'm not drain bamaged."

"Very funny. Did you know that Henry the Eighth had CTE?"

"If that was in the play, it must have been in the second act after I fell asleep."

"I'm serious, Jake. The real Henry the Eighth suffered numerous head injuries while jousting, including the time a lance penetrated his helmet visor."

"Ouch! Reminds me of a Bills lineman who used to stick his fingers through my face mask and try to gouge my eyes out, so I'm feeling for old Hank."

"Once a horse fell on Henry, and it was lights out for an hour. After that, he began behaving crazily. He had Anne Boleyn beheaded, if you recall."

"As if it were yesterday. But I only ride horses on the merry-go-round. So no worries, Charlie."

"I'm not letting up on you, Jake. This is too important."

Kip joined me in the study. He had made a pit stop in the kitchen and was now slurping a root beer through a straw.

"I'll try to work in a doctor's visit when I'm not busy helping filthy-rich insurance companies steal oatmeal from the mouths of orphans," I told Charlie.

"I'm not pussyfooting around anymore! Get yourself checked out!"

The old coot was exhausting me. There was no use arguing any longer, so I said, "I'll see Dr. Helfman. I'll do the tests. I promise. And if it's bad news, you've got first dibs on the autopsy."

I hung up, and Kip gave me a look.

"Are you sick, Uncle Jake?"

Damn. Me and my big mouth.

"Not at all. That's just Charlie being Doc Riggs. Did you know he never had a patient who lived?"

"That's because he was the coroner."

"Just an excuse. But I feel great. A tiny headache now and then."

He looked somber, not the usual Kippers. "You'd tell me if you were sick, right?"

"Kip, what are you worried about?"

"Nothing."

But his face said something else. I thought about our conversation. We had been talking about his mother, who had abandoned him. His natural father? Nobody knew exactly who that might be. Granny was getting along in years. That left me. I was pretty sure I knew what he was thinking.

"Do you know how much I love you, kiddo?" I said.

He shrugged his shoulders. "You never say."

"That's because I grew up at a time when guys didn't go around blubbering about their feelings. But I have feelings."

"I guess."

"Remember when we used to jump into the water at Venetian pool?"

"Yeah, it was a game to see who could jump the farthest. You'd let me win."

"That's how I said I loved you. And reading you to sleep at night, when I played all the characters in the stories. That's another way. But now I just want to say it flat out. I love you, Kip, and I always will. I won't abandon you, and I won't let you down."

For me, that was a hell of a lot of emotional sharing. In my younger days, I wouldn't have been able to do it. But a man changes as he senses his own mortality. And this boy, well, at the risk of dishing out soapy clichés, he touches my soul. Sometimes when I look at him, I get a little teary-eyed and a flock of doves beat their wings inside my chest. Or maybe it's just heartburn. But I love him. That's for sure.

After a moment of thinking it over, Kip said, "I love you, too, Uncle Jake."

"Great. Now that we've resolved the touchy-feely issues, let's rumble. Teach me all you know about cage fighting."

-21-

Ground and Pound, Lay and Pray

Once we were back in my study, I poured my third Jack Daniel's—or was it my fourth?—opened the dirt file, and slipped the "Life and Crimes" DVD into my desktop computer.

Kip, on his second root beer, had agreed to work for slave wages and was talking up a storm. "Crazy Carla was equally good at sprawl and brawl and ground and pound."

"In English, Kippers."

"A sprawler and brawler stays on her feet. She's a boxer or kickboxer or karate fighter. But a grounder and pounder is like a wrestler. She takes her opponents to the mat and then beats the stuffing out of them or forces them into submission with a painful hold. Crazy Carla did both. Punched and kicked standing up, then a takedown, and kapow! She used her fists and elbows and then maybe an arm bar. She'd ground and pound, and her opponent would lay and pray."

It seemed barbaric to me, not a sport at all. And I've played a game where a tight end belly-laughed after crushing my Adam's apple with a well-timed forearm. The video started playing. First up an ESPN feature called *Cage Fighters: La Femmes Fatales*. The insurance company investigators had edited out the other women, so we watched twelve minutes about Carla Caruana, or as Chris Berman, the announcer, said, "The triumphant yet ultimately tragic story of Carla Caruana."

Carla was born and raised in Apopka, north of Orlando, and took up soccer in elementary school. She was the star of her high school team, and the video showed her scoring with several acrobatic scissor jump-kicks, where she basically somersaulted backward and booted the ball into the goal upside down. She also scored with uncanny headers that seemed to rocket into the net at precise angles just out of the goalie's reach.

By the time Carla got to the University of Florida on a soccer scholarship, she had taken up kickboxing and karate. Home video showed impressive power in her sidekicks and round kicks, in which she occasionally went airborne.

"That's a karate kick called the flying butterfly," Kip told me.

In the summer after her sophomore year in college, Carla was working part time at Disney World, walking the park as Snow White, posing for pictures with families. In her costume, she didn't look particularly muscular or athletic. She encountered three fraternity boys from nearby Rollins College who teased her, making lewd remarks and pulling at her wig.

Which was when she unleashed a series of kicks and punches to one guy's head, the other's nose, and the third guy's groin. She left them bruised, bloody, and gasping for air. She got fired, of course, but also started a new career path.

Cage fighting. Mixed martial arts in the octagon.

"They told me I was too pretty to get hit in the face," she said on the video. "But I thought of myself as an athlete, not a girlie girl."

During that time she became romantically involved with a cage fighter from Australia. They were together long enough for Carla to get pregnant—twice—and for her lover to scurry back Down Under after the second child was born.

I watched a series of Carla's bouts in Las Vegas over a several-year period. She often punched and kicked her way to technical knockouts.

The DVD kept playing. More interviews, more matches. And for me, more Jack Daniel's.

"Watch this!" Kip said. He'd apparently seen several of the matches live, which explained the pay-per-view charges on my cable bill. "That's the Honduran Hurricane she's fighting."

Carla used a head kick followed by a left-right combination, and the Honduran Hurricane fell backward, unconscious. A KO in forty-seven seconds.

A few more matches and, as Kip had promised, there was some grounding and pounding. A couple of wins by submission with an arm bar, one of which dislocated her opponent's elbow.

Carla took some punishment, too. Kicks and punches to the head jarred her, and she lost consecutive TKOs to Cat Zingano and then Ronda Rousey in a championship bout. Diagnosed with the first of several concussions, she took a forty-five-day noncontact suspension. And then three more over the next two years.

Okay, Carla. I feel for you. I've been there, done that, suffered Lord knows what consequences.

"Uh-oh," Kip said. "This is the match from Anaheim against Lady Tiger."

On the monitor, Carla decked her opponent with what I would call a flying-roundhouse-spinning-holy-shit kick to the temple. Lady Tiger went down as if felled by a sniper, and Carla leapt on her, using one elbow to pin her head to the mat and smashing her face with the other fist. Five, six, seven punches, and blood spurted from Lady Tiger's nose. Lady Tiger tapped the mat in submission, but Carla didn't stop punching. The referee tried to pull her off Lady Tiger, but Carla tossed an elbow into his ribs and kept pounding away.

"Six-month suspension," Kip said. "Like I told you, Uncle Jake, she cracked."

On the monitor, a furious Carla was speaking—or rather yelling—at a press conference. "You know what I think about the UFC and its rules? This!" She shot the bird at the camera.

"Suddenly, Crazy Carla went from the number one challenger to a pariah," ESPN's Chris Berman intoned. "She lost her lucrative endorsements, and her personal life spiraled downward."

The next scene showed Carla in her kitchen, making breakfast for her children. As she poured cereal, Carla spoke quickly, in a hyped-up stream of consciousness that wasn't easy to follow. The gist seemed to be that she didn't care if she was a cage fighter or cleaned birdcages at the zoo.

She began missing appointments, including photo shoots for commercials and hearings for UFC reinstatement. She would forget to pick up her children from school. In an interview on an Orlando television station, she slurred her words and her eyes were glassy. The caption asked: "Local Hero: Substance Abuse Problem?"

Clearly Carla's life was out of control.

While the video played, I sipped more whiskey and thumbed through the rest of the file. During the suspension, Carla was arrested three times. The first was for DUI when she drove onto the Florida Turnpike by way of an exit ramp. Interestingly, both the Breathalyzer and the blood test showed no alcohol and only minute traces of painkillers. The second arrest was for disturbing the peace. Neighbors complained when Carla began throwing clothing and bedding out the second-story window of her townhouse. Pillows, towels, skirts, blouses. She was trying to jam a mattress through the window when police arrived. Then there was assault and battery in a bar. A man offered to buy her a drink, and she decked him with one punch. Bystanders say he asked if she was Ronda Rousey.

The DUI and disturbing the peace were dismissed, and the A&B was still pending when Carla took her own life. On the video somber music played, and Chris Berman lowered his voice to reflect the mood.

A police car and the coroner's wagon were parked outside Carla's town-house. The screen cut to a close-up of the suicide note:

I can't take it anymore. It's gotten all jumbled up in my head. Last night the demons floated over my bed again. Liz and Joshua, I'm so sorry. I love you more than you can ever know.
Mom

When the funeral scene came on, I found the autopsy records. While skimming the pages, I said, "Kip, stay away from drugs."

"Jeez, I know. What was Crazy Carla on?"

I scanned the toxicology report. "A smorgasbord of prescription drugs, starting with oxycodone, the main ingredient in OxyContin. Plus hydrocodone, the biggie in Vicodin."

"Painkillers," Kip said.

"How do you know that?"

"Everybody knows that. Anything else?"

"Antianxiety medications were her main course. Diazepam. That's Valium. Seasoned with alprazolam, known to its many fans as Xanax. Plus a hint of temazepam, which is Restoril. Then there was a healthy dose—or maybe an unhealthy dose—of alcohol in her bloodstream."

"There was a vodka bottle next to the note," Kip said. I'd seen it. The video—taken by crime scene techs—had lingered ghoulishly on a still shot of a bottle of Belvedere.

I needed more time to process the information. A thought was scratching at me. A loose strand or two. This is what I do. Find loose strands. Tie a few together. Maybe they become a handsome sweater, maybe just a hairy ball of yarn.

I found Cyrus Frick's timeline of the last year of Carla's life. Nothing was apparent that would change the outcome of the case. But all the events after the suspension from fighting seemed to be threads that tied together. The bizarre conduct. One day a loving, caring, responsible mom. The next an addict and barroom brawler. Then the unthinkable. A single parent willfully checking out, leaving her kids alone and terrified. Who would do that? What had happened to Carla Caruana?

"It's gotten all jumbled up in my head."

Carla, what did you mean by that?

I wanted to get inside her mind, so I approached her death from a different angle. Everyone was so focused on the *time* of the suicide that they had ignored its *cause*.

Just why did a single mother, thirty-one years old, end her own life? What were those "demons" she saw over her bed? I rewatched the interview from Orlando, the last one of her life. The slurred words, the glassy eyes. Naturally, everyone assumed drugs or alcohol.

But what if? I thought I might have it.

Solomon and Lord had missed the clues. Otherwise my pals would have amended their complaint and come up with a scenario that would have eviscerated the insurance company's defense.

If I'm right, I'm the only one who knows what really happened to Carla Caruana.

"What's going on, Uncle Jake? You've gotten real quiet."

"I've figured it out."

Kip sucked at the straw, slurping at air. "You figured out the secret to winning the case?"

"I'm afraid so."

He chuckled. "What's that mean?"

The boy deserved an answer. I wished I had a better one. "Because, Kippers, I can't decide whether I want to win or lose."

-22-

Stick with Socrates

I tried to shoo Kip out of my study, but he wouldn't budge. I told him I wouldn't pay him the five bucks an hour I'd promised, and he still didn't move. Where oh where did he get that stubbornness?

"I don't understand, Uncle Jake. Do you want to lose the case?"

"Part of me wants to lose, but another part won't let me take a dive."

Just like the Thurston murder trial. I wanted to toss pillow-soft jabs and lazy hooks. Then the bell rang, and I flew out of my corner, swinging anvils and sledgehammers.

My nephew looked confused. Who could blame him? I always taught him to set his goals high and work harder than anyone else to achieve them. When he got a summer job stocking shelves at a supermarket, I told him to arrive early, work faster than the guy next to him, and never complain. When he went out for football, I told him to train hard and treat every practice as if it were a game. When he first asked a girl to go to the movies, I told him make sure his fly was zipped.

The subtext of all of this was to win.

Win. Win. Win.

I drilled it into him.

And now just look at me.

"So you saw something in the video, Uncle Jake?"

"And in the files. But not just one thing. It's a tapestry."

"What does that mean?"

I poured more Jack Daniel's into the tumbler. I likely had reached my limit, but losing count, how was I to know? "A tapestry is woven from thousands of threads, and when it's finished you don't see the threads anymore. You see a picture that wasn't there when you started. In Carla's case, Solomon and Lord see the threads but not the final picture."

"So what's in the picture?"

"Don't want to say just yet."

"Are you going to sandbag your best buddies? Drop a bomb on them at trial?"

"Let me ask you a question, because your answer might help me decide. Who's your best friend at school?"

"Manny Dominguez. You know that."

"Let's say you and Manny are competing in debate and you each reach the finals of the championship round."

"Manny's on the sailing team, not debate."

"Go with me on this, Kip. It's a hypothetical. You really want to win because the champ gets a thousand-dollar prize and a trophy five feet high."

"Cool." Kip had suddenly become interested. "What's the second-place finisher get?"

"He cleans the toilets in the boys' locker room for a month."

Kip reached for my tumbler of whiskey, and I made no move to stop him. "That's not fair," he said.

"Neither is life, kiddo. Now, you and Manny are in the library, preparing for the finals. You happen to look at his notes, and you see he's made a terrible mistake."

Kip took a sip of the whiskey, scrunched his face, and quickly put down the tumbler. "Like what mistake?"

"I don't know. He confuses Madagascar with Manitoba. It doesn't matter. It's a huge goof that will cost him the debate. So the question is, do you tell him?"

Kip shrugged his bony shoulders. "Why would I?"

"Fairness. You go into the debate on a level playing field."

"Why should it be level? Manny made the mistake, not me. And I want the thousand bucks." He looked toward the monitor, which showed a freeze-frame of Carla Caruana's coffin. "What would you do, Uncle Jake?"

"At your age, same as you. When I was a young lawyer, same deal."

"And now?"

"Winning isn't everything."

"It's the only thing! You told me Vince Lombardi said that."

"Old school."

"*You're* old school!"

"But still learning. I don't care about the money or the trophies anymore. I care about a just and fair result."

"Thrasymachus said there was no such thing as justice."

"Trashy who?"

"Old Greek guy we read about in philosophy. Socrates said justice was cool, but Thrasymachus said it was just a word invented by the victors to rule the losers. Like, we won the war; now we make the laws."

"Might makes right?"

"Yeah, I guess."

That was such a depressing thought, I took another gulp of the whiskey. "You don't believe that, do you, Kip?"

"I believe it happens, but it's not right," Kip said.

"Good. Stick with Socrates."

"Is that what you're doing in Carla Caruana's case?"

"I'm not sure. Did Socrates believe the ends justify the means?"

"That sounds more like Machiavelli. He said if you're good all the time, you'll be ruined. But you can choose when to be good and when to be bad to reach your end result."

"A choice. That's appealing."

"So, what's it gonna be, Uncle Jake?"

"I think I'm going to follow Socrates. But with just a pinch of Machiavelli."

-23-

In the Coroner's Cooler

At just before midnight, I called Solomon and Lord on their land-line. Steve Solomon answered on the third ring.

"Am I calling too late?" I asked.

"We're in bed."

"Ooh, sorry."

"No problem. Victoria's researching on her laptop, and I'm reading the *Sports Illustrated* swimsuit issue."

"Reading?"

"The pictures have captions. Did you see Ronda Rousey on the cover?"

"Funny you mention that. We need to talk about cage fighting."

"Why?"

I told Solomon he'd be getting my notice of appearance in the *Caruana* case, and he made a loud hooting sound, then put me on speaker.

"Jake Lassiter, insurance lawyer! My pal, my best man, has turned Grinch! Vic, do you believe this?"

"Frankly, I'm surprised," she said evenly. Victoria was always the levelheaded one of the team.

"Not my choice," I said.

"I warned you, Jake." Solomon chortled. "This is what happens when you sell out. You work for the Man. You owe your soul to the company store. Oh, we're gonna have fun kicking your big butt."

"Before you do a victory dance, can we talk?" I asked.

"Don't bother offering policy limits. We already rejected it. This is a *mucho grande* bad-faith case."

"If you get past summary judgment," I said.

"Victoria's doing the research right now. At the hearing she'll dance rings around you, you big slab of meat."

"Sometimes I wonder why we're friends, Solomon."

"Because you like hanging around Victoria, but I'm cool with that."

I took a deep breath and wondered where to start. I had decided to tell them my theory of what had really happened to Carla Caruana. To do it, I had to resist the urge to make this a duel between Solomon and me.

"So why are you calling?" Victoria asked.

My bedroom window was cracked open, and I heard the whistle of a Metrorail train coming from the other side of South Dixie Highway. One last moment to reconsider. But, no, I would do what I thought was right, even if it violated statutes of the legislature, rules of the court, and customs of the practice of law. The ends would have to justify the means. My means.

"I read the file tonight and found a rather bizarre change of behavior in your client the last year of her life," I said. "Suspensions, violence, arrests, a pattern of irrational conduct she'd never manifested previously."

"Forget it, Jake!" Solomon said. "That stuff's prejudicial and not probative. We're doing a motion in limine to keep you from putting all that crap in."

"Can you keep quiet for one minute, Solomon? I'm not going to put it into evidence. *You* are."

"Why the hell would we do that?"

"You're going to highlight it, hang a lantern on it, and use it against me."

"I don't see how or why."

I paused. The breeze was slapping palm fronds against the window pane, and the faint scent of jasmine filled the room. I was hoping they would figure it out so that I didn't have to tell them. That might preserve a shred of my lawyerly ethics and dignity.

"Victoria, you're the brains of that operation," I said. "Do you see where I'm going?"

"Not yet, Jake. Maybe I can't see the forest for the trees."

"Jake, you're a brother to me," Solomon said. "But let's face it. You're a ham and egger. No chance you caught something Vic missed."

I ignored the insult and kept going. "If the issue is *when* the suicide occurred, I have a good shot at winning summary judgment, and everybody goes home. But if the issue is *whether* a suicide occurred, you're going to survive the motion and get to the jury on liability and bad faith. You'll win millions."

"Whether she committed suicide?" Solomon asked. "She left a note. It wasn't an accident. No way we can win if we go that route."

"You'll put the note in evidence, too."

"How much you been drinking tonight, Jake?"

"Not enough. Carla's note said, 'Last night the demons floated over my bed again.' She was hallucinating. Probably from dementia. Are you with me?"

"Dementia," Victoria said. "Keep going. I think I know where you're headed."

"Where?" Solomon demanded.

"If you're right, Jake, I can't believe we missed it," Victoria said.

"I probably would have, too, if Charlie Riggs hadn't been haranguing me about how my brain is filled with rusty bolts."

"Concussions," Victoria said. "You're talking about Carla's multiple concussions."

"From the time she was in middle school playing soccer. Then kickboxing and karate, and when she started cage fighting, the doctors lost count. Her behavior reflected severe forms of post-concussion syndrome. The question is whether she was suffering—"

"From chronic traumatic encephalopathy," Victoria said, up to speed now.

"Bingo. I assume the brain was preserved in the autopsy."

"In the coroner's cooler," Victoria said.

"You need to get it to a neuropathologist right away. If I'm right, and Carla suffered from CTE, you've got a different case."

"I'm not following," Solomon said. "Whether or not she had CTE, she still committed suicide."

"Victoria, there's still time to break off your engagement," I said. "There are lots of eligible bachelors out there, a few with law degrees, and one living a few blocks away."

"Volition, Steve," she said. "Intent. The conscious desire to end her own life. If the brain tissue reveals CTE, we can claim that Carla lacked the mental capacity to form the necessary intent required of suicide."

"Bingo again," I said. "You'll defeat my summary judgment motion because I no longer have a purely legal question. Cause of death will be a question of fact for the jury. And who will they rule for, your innocent orphans or my filthy-rich insurance company, as personified by Cyrus Frick, general counsel and chief prick?"

"Ring up the cash register," Solomon said. "Jeez, Jake, forget all that crap I just said about you. And it's okay when you flirt with Victoria, but don't make it a habit."

"Jake, why are you doing this?" Victoria asked.

"Because Jake's our best friend," Solomon guessed.

"Nope," I said. "Not doing it for you."

"Then for the kids," Victoria said. "Carla's children."

"I'll be happy for them if this works out. But, no, not for them, either."

"What then?" Solomon asked.

"Me. I'm doing it for me."

-24-

What about Lassiter?

The phone rang, waking me up.

The LCD display said 2:44 a.m.

In my experience, a middle-of-the-night call is not from my banker with the happy news that an accounting error has been discovered and I'm far richer than I thought. The call is not from that terrific woman who dumped me fifteen years ago because I was too immature to commit, and she wants to give me a second chance. More likely it's a helpful neighbor screaming that my house is ablaze, and I should get the hell out.

"Mr. Lassiter, this is George Gonzalez over at Fisher Island Security."

"If Thunder Thurston is firing a gun off his balcony again, call someone else," I said. "He's not my client anymore."

"It's not him, sir. Not exactly."

"What then?"

"I've got a fellow in the guardhouse here who's a lurker, and he says you'll vouch for him."

"Lurker?"

"Trespasser. Vandal. He came over on the three p.m. ferry in a tree farm truck, had some palms in the back—"

"Palms!" thundered a voice on the other end of the line. "They're screw pine trees, not palms, you jerk!"

"Mr. Gonzalez, is that Clyde Garner in your guardhouse?"

"The man doesn't know a pine tree from his pubic hair!" Garner's voice echoed in the background.

"It's him, sir, and he's very belligerent," the security guard said. "He came over here with some trees, as if he had a landscaping job, so none of my staff gave him a second look. And, in fact, he planted a tree outside Palazzo del Mare. I believe you know who lives in one of the penthouses."

"Thunder Thurston. On top of the world."

"Yes, sir. And what's embarrassing for my staff, Mr. Thurston's vice president specifically put Clyde Garner on the no-ferry list."

"Hold on. Did you say vice president?"

"Rashan Drexler, vice president of Thurston All-Pro Enterprises."

I laughed. Apparently Thurston had found a way to make Jelly Bean's mooching tax deductible.

Gonzalez continued. "After he planted the tree, Mr. Garner put a bronze plaque in the ground. It said—"

"I'll tell him!" Garner yelled in the background. "Give me the phone."

A moment of fumbling around, and then Garner's voice: "I had a plaque made, Lassiter. It said, 'In memory of Eva Garner, slaughtered by the coward Marcus Thurston.' These bastards just dug it up."

"Calm down, Clyde, and hand the phone back to the guard."

A moment later Gonzalez said, "About an hour ago, we noticed Mr. Garner sitting in his truck outside Palazzo del Mare. He must have been there for nearly ten hours. Just lurking. Obviously he poses a security threat. We're aware of the vandalism of Mr. Thurston's boat."

"Clyde Garner is in mourning. Maybe cut him a break."

PAUL LEVINE

"That's why we're calling you instead of Miami Beach Police. If we put him on the next ferry, will you take responsibility, Mr. Lassiter?"

"I'll give you my address. Tell Garner to come right over. I've got a bottle of bourbon with his name on it."

* * *

It was 3:37 a.m. when Garner pulled into my driveway and knocked on my door.

"Your chinaberry tree needs trimming," he told me as we walked to the back porch. "Some damn fine live oaks on your street, though. The one at the corner of Avocado and Douglas, that's got to be three hundred years old."

"Really? I'll give you my address. Tell Garner to come right over. I've got a bottle of bourbon with his name on it."

"Really? I'll have to ask Granny if she remembers it as a kid."

We sat in wooden Adirondack chairs, and I poured some Pappy Van Winkle into two tumblers. The air was warm and moist, and the lavender bougainvillea carried the faint scent of honeysuckle.

"You ever figure out why that half-assed prosecutor screwed up the case?" Garner asked.

"No, sorry. I've been . . . distracted."

He sipped at the bourbon, so I joined along, closing my eyes, savoring the golden warmth. A night of Jack Daniel's and an early morning of Pappy Van Winkle, and the world seemed to have rounded off its hard edges, leaving everything in soft focus.

"You forgot all about Eva, didn't you?" Garner said in a challenging tone. "You forgot everything I told you."

"Not at all. Strickstein didn't try to introduce evidence of prior assaults that, if they fit a pattern, might have been admissible."

"Which you said was probably her strategy not to create an issue for appeal."

"Nobody wants to try a case twice."

"What else do you remember?"

132

"She also told you that the cell phone carrier couldn't find the texts from Thurston to Drexler. And she wouldn't let your boys testify to what they heard Thurston say on the phone. Both the texts and the conversations involved song lyrics that may or may not have been threats."

"So you haven't forgotten." He took a long, slow, sad pull on the Pappy. "You just haven't done anything about it."

"I've got my own problems with Stacy Strickstein."

"Want to tell me what?"

I shook my head. "I haven't even told my granny."

"So what about Eva? Have you just given up so you can get on with your life?"

"I tried to get State Attorney Pincher involved. A plan to sting Thurston in a drug deal. Pincher won't touch it."

Garner grunted his disapproval. I noticed that he had drained his glass when I wasn't looking, so I poured him another. "I'm sorry, Clyde. Really."

He stared into the darkness of the night and said, "I knew there would be unending grief. I just had no idea there would be such pain. Physical pain. Barrel staves strapping my chest, each day a little tighter. One day, they'll squeeze the last breath out of me."

"How can I help you?"

His laugh was more of a scoff. "Well, add one more item to your list of things not to do."

"What's that?"

"Like that idiot told you, I sat in my truck outside Thurston's building all day and into the night. I watched people come and people go."

"Anyone in particular?"

"Bunch of young women in bikinis. Giggling and carrying on like the fools they are. Then there was that big fat sack of shit who opens doors for Thurston and probably reminds him to wash his hands after crapping."

"Jelly Bean Drexler."

A police siren wailed in the distance, and a neighborhood peacock screeched its reply.

"Just before six o'clock, a white Ford Taurus with Florida plates pulls up to the condo. The valet takes the car, and a woman goes into the lobby and heads to the elevator."

He waited, daring me to ask a question.

"Are you telling me it was Stacy Strickstein?"

"Dark-haired woman in a business suit. Looked like her, but from where I was parked, I couldn't be sure."

"What floor did she go to?"

He shrugged. "No way for me to tell."

I threw up my hands and nearly spilled my drink. "So you've got nothing."

He appraised me, a slight smirk on his face.

"What aren't you telling me, Garner? You look like you've got a meal to serve, but so far it's barely an appetizer."

"What do you think, Lassiter? What do you think I did?"

"Well, I know you stuck around at least until the mystery woman came down the elevator. I'm assuming you put yourself in a position for a closer look. But even if you tell me it was Strickstein, you can't place her with Thurston unless—"

"The bastard walked her out of the elevator, through the lobby, and waited with her till the valet brought her car."

"Holy crap!"

"Did I mention she wasn't carrying anything when she went in, and when she came out, she had a small duffel bag, like you downtown suits take to the gym?"

"Oh, man. It's getting better. Where were you when they came out of the building?"

"I'd gotten out of the truck and unloaded a wheelbarrow while she was inside. When they came out, there I was, just an old farmer in a straw hat and coveralls, spreading mulch around a little tree. An invisible man. I wasn't ten feet away from them. One shotgun blast, I could have killed them both."

"Thankfully you didn't. Could you hear anything they said?"

"Twenty years ago, I would have heard everything. But I been around too much farm equipment for too many years. She was speaking way too quiet. Whispering really. Thurston was louder, but I could only make out three words."

"I assume it wasn't 'praise the Lord.'"

"Thurston said, 'What about Lassiter?' And she said something back. But damned if I could hear it."

-25-

The Steeplechaser

I couldn't go back to sleep.

The Pappy Van Winkle didn't help.

A slice of Granny's Key lime pie didn't help.

I wanted to talk to the State Attorney. Ray Pincher had been avoiding my calls. The last time I saw him, he called me corrupt and flattened me in the ring. But the rot was coming from inside his own office. That's what I wanted to tell him. Stacy Strickstein aka Strychnine was after me to cover her own tracks. She was dirty. Not me!

Pincher had a rigid schedule. He awakened at 5:30 a.m. seven days a week. Today I would call him at 5:31. Roughly an hour to go.

I flipped through the several hundred television channels the satellite brings us. No, I didn't want to buy genuine imitation pearls from one of the home shopping networks. Sports Center was running baseball highlights, which seemed to be evenly divided between thunderous home runs and batters striking out. Life isn't like a highlights show. Life is a two-hop grounder to the shortstop, a pop fly with the bases loaded, and an occasional base hit that squeaks into the outfield. At least that's my life.

I clicked through the movie channels and happened onto one of my favorites. Paul Newman in *The Verdict*. A down-and-out lawyer, battling the bottle and overwhelming odds. A malpractice case tainted with false medical records, lying doctors, conniving lawyers, and a corrupt judge. Just another day in the justice system.

I tuned in just as Newman was finishing his closing argument, which seemed a lot more highfalutin than any of mine. "Today you are the law," he told the jurors. "Not some book, not the lawyers, not a marble statue, or the trappings of the court. Those are just symbols of our desire to be just. They are a prayer, a fervent and a frightened prayer. In my religion, they say, 'Act as if ye had faith . . . and faith will be given to you.' If we are to have faith in justice, we need only to believe in ourselves. And act with justice. See, I believe there is justice in our hearts."

Move over Atticus Finch.

I wanted to apply the movie's philosophy to my own life. But I had no faith in justice. Plus, I didn't believe in myself. And I wasn't sure I had justice in my heart. How, then, could I act with justice? My life was not as tidy as a movie script.

I took a personal inventory starting with the *Thunder Thurston* case. When the jury retired to its claustrophobic little room, I was sure we had lost. I remembered replaying my closing argument in my head.

Violent wife . . . bloody knife . . . reasonable fear. Stand Your Ground. Bullshit, bullshit, bullshit. And bullshit.

I'd piled it high, never expecting to win. How had I?

Strychnine claimed I bribed a juror!

But she's the one cozying up to my homicidal client and leaving his condo with a mysterious duffel bag.

What am I saying? Mysterious, hell!

A bag filled with money. What else could it be? Thurston's dirty jockstrap?

Just what crap is she calling cornbread and feeding to the grand jury?

My inventory was not yet complete. Let's not forget *Caruana vs. Biscayne Life Insurance Company*. If the Thurston murder trial was the criminal case I most wanted to lose, it now had a civil case for company. Is this what it has come to? *Am I of so little faith, all I want is to lose?*

How did I get here? In the past, I always tried to win, hoping for a result that was compatible with my notions of fairness, or at least one that didn't make me vomit in the lawyer's lounge. To win, I leapt over every ethical hurdle, as a steeplechaser does a barrier. If I cleared the top, I landed in a ditch, muddied and waterlogged, but I kept chugging along. I don't know exactly when I discovered that the water hazards were endless, the mud was quicksand, and my legs heavy as logs. At some point, I must have known that I would flop facedown, and the other runners would trample me into the muck as they sprinted effortlessly toward the finish line.

* * *

At 5:31 a.m., I called Pincher on his cell.

"Ain't gonna talk to you, Jake."

"Ray, you're gonna want to know what's happening right under your nose."

"Ain't listening."

"Ray, Strychnine is dirty!"

Click.

I was undeterred. On Mondays, Wednesdays, and Fridays, Pincher works out in the gym where he so recently knocked me ass over elbows. On Tuesdays and Thursdays, he rides a bike from his Cutler Bay home to Matheson Hammock, a county park on the shore of Biscayne Bay. There, with the sun rising over the Atlantic, he does his tai chi or some other ridiculously healthy endeavor. It was a Thursday. This morning he would have company.

I pulled on a pair of Penn State running shorts that were both too snug and too short and a T-shirt with the logo, "Lawyers Do It in Their Briefs." My running shoes smelled as if they'd been left outside in the rain, but they still fit.

I made a pot of coffee, filled it with ice cubes, and poured the liquid into an insulated pitcher I placed into a backpack.

I checked on Kip. Still sleeping.

And then Granny. Still snoring.

I left by the front door. The moon peeked out of a purple sky. The sun was still sleeping, but the air was already warm. My thirty-year-old Caddy convertible was in the driveway. I patted a fender and checked the body for peacock poop. All clear. The personalized license plate still asked, "JUSTICE?"

Yeah, I think it's a good question.

I left the old beauty sitting alone and forlorn and started jogging west on Poinciana toward Le Jeune Road, my pace slow, my footfalls heavy. About four blocks north, my pals Solomon and Lord would be asleep in their little bungalow on Kumquat. Solomon's torch-red Corvette would be out front, its license plate bragging, "I-OBJECT."

Yeah, guess where he got that idea?

I turned left on Le Jeune and headed toward the Gables Waterway. Loosening up, starting to sweat, the morning sticky-humid and heating up. I wondered what Pincher would say when I told him his chief homicide prosecutor was dirty. Maybe apologize for sucker punching me, for even entertaining the thought I'd bribed a juror.

By the time I got to the bridge, I was feeling stronger. In the waterway, two kids in a Boston Whaler headed toward the bay for a morning of fishing. I circled the roundabout and headed down Old Cutler Road under a canopy of banyan trees. Once while jogging the very same path, an iguana fell out of a tree and smacked me on the head. My reaction? About the same as the day I was windsurfing and an Atlantic ray—startled by my board—leapt from the water and sailed past my face.

Yeah, bellowed like a bull under the branding iron.

I passed the ritzy gated community of Gables Estates, every house on the water, and finally turned onto the shaded path that led through Matheson Hammock down to the open bay. The path cuts through a swatch of black mangrove trees, their roots climbing out of the marsh like skeletal legs. The tide must have been high because the path was covered with a foot of water. Or maybe global warming already was close to drowning us on this low-lying peninsula.

Inhaling the salty broth of the marsh, I splashed through the water and emerged into the bright sunlight. Only one bicycle was locked to the rack at the edge of the parking lot. Ray Pincher's Cannondale Quick 5. I could see the State Attorney on the seawall a hundred yards away, skipping rope, bare-chested.

When he saw me approach, he seemed to pick up speed, showing off, his torso glistening with sweat.

"Ah, the Jakester," he greeted me. "Pretty early in the morn and yet too late in the day to foul the air with your clouds of pettifoggery."

"Is that some kind of riddle?"

"Surely you know what I'm talking about."

"Nope."

He stopped skipping. Leveled me with a gaze. "I assume the reason you've been calling me, the reason you're here . . . is that somehow you found out."

"Gotta plead ignorance because I don't have a clue."

He cocked his head, appraised me. He must have known I was telling the truth, because there was a touch of sadness in his eyes. "Jake, my old friend, I'm afraid I've got bad news."

IN THE ELEVENTH JUDICIAL CIRCUIT IN AND FOR

MIAMI-DADE COUNTY, FLORIDA

INDICTMENT

STATE OF FLORIDA

vs.

JACOB LASSITER

IN THE NAME AND BY THE AUTHORITY OF THE STATE OF FLORIDA:

The Grand Jurors of the state of Florida, duly called, impaneled, and sworn to inquire and true presentment make and for the body of the County of Miami-Dade, upon their oaths present that on or about the eighth day of August 2016, within the County of Miami-Dade, State of Florida, JACOB LASSITER did unlawfully and feloniously tamper with a petit juror, to wit, one Manuel Gutierrez, by illegally delivering unto him United States currency in the amount of Twenty-Five Thousand Dollars with the intent to obstruct the administration of justice in violation of Florida Statute Section 918.22, to the evil example of all others in like cases, offending against the peace and dignity of the State of Florida.

J. Berkowitz

Foreperson of the Grand Jury

-26-

Bum Luck

"What's the bad news, Ray?" I asked.

"You've been indicted. Bribing a juror."

"This is crap!"

"On the brighter side, you're only looking at five years max."

"Strychnine's framing me."

"Plus automatic disbarment, of course."

"Thurston's in on it, though I don't know how or why."

I felt sweat pouring from me, not from the run, not from the heat, but from the reality that my life was spiraling down the drain.

"I never bribed anyone!" I yelled at Pincher. "You know me better than that! C'mon, Ray! Bribery? What the hell!"

Pincher let me rage for a while until I ran out of breath. Then he hung the jump rope around his neck and said, "You got coffee and almond croissants in that backpack?"

"Iced coffee. No croissants."

"It'll have to do."

I poured the coffee into plastic cups and Pincher said, "C'mon, Jake. Walk with me."

We took the paved path that runs a semicircle around a saltwater pond at the bay's edge. The morning had warmed, and the incoming tide washed seaweed onto the rocks. After a moment, Pincher said, "I've seen Strickstein's evidence. Tell me your side of the story."

"You wearing a wire?"

"Not unless it's up my ass. And if I'd said yes, would it change your story?"

I shook my head. "You first, Ray. What's the state got?"

"Oh, nothing much. Just your coconspirator, the bribee, testifying about a hand-to-hand transaction with you. Two transactions really, twenty-five grand in all. He said you told him to either bring back an acquittal of Thunder Thurston or at least hang the jury."

"That's it? One witness? One-on-one, defense wins."

"Did I say I was done? Your fingerprints are on the money, and a surveillance camera caught you within whispering distance of the juror outside the Justice Building."

"What juror? Who the hell says I did this?"

"Surely you remember number three, a guy named Manuel Gutierrez."

Oh, him.

I was going to stop right there and say I wanted to speak to my lawyer. But I didn't stop. It's funny, but the advice we give our clients is very hard to follow ourselves.

I took a pull on the iced coffee and said, "The guy with the restored Barracuda."

"That's him. Did you talk to him outside of court?"

Damn.

We all do stupid things. Little things we don't expect will lead to tragedy. One day I tried opening a coconut with a sledgehammer. I missed and cracked a paver in the driveway. But it didn't create a giant sinkhole that swallowed my house. Talking to the juror? Could that be the beat of the butterfly's wings that caused a hurricane?

"I saw Gutierrez next to his 'Cuda, and I complimented him on the car. I'd known from the juror questionnaire that his hobby was restoring old jalopies, so if you want to know the truth, I was currying a little favor. No big deal."

"Unethical."

"So slap my wrist. I didn't give him money."

We paused on the path at the farthest point from the beach. Two kite surfers were dragging their gear into the water, the kites bright orange and red. It didn't appear to me that the wind had yet come up. No whitecaps on the water.

Pincher said, "Gutierrez swore under oath that you sat in his car and put a thousand bucks in his glove compartment."

"That's a lie! No way that can be on surveillance tape."

"It's not. When you caught up with Gutierrez, you both were out of camera range."

"So the state's theory is I'm just wandering around the juror parking lot with a thousand bucks in my pocket looking for someone to bribe? This is nuts."

"Let me finish, Jake. You sat in his car. You gave him a cell number to call, which he did later that day. That's how you tested his willingness to play ball. You ascertained he was a willing conspirator, so you asked his address and came to his house after midnight. You gave him another twenty-four thousand in hundred-dollar bills, and he agreed to get your acquittal or hang the jury. You showed him your cell phone. A burner. You crushed it in one hand and said that would be his head if he ratted. And like I said, your prints were found on the bills."

My tinnitus had flared up. I should have been hearing the gentle slap of waves against shore, but instead there was the insistent buzz of radio static. I half expected Orson Welles to interrupt the static with a news bulletin about an invasion from Mars.

"Where do you want me to begin, Ray?"

"I've always found a good place to start is the truth."

I took a deep breath of soggy air and exhaled. And then another one, trying to relax. I'd been wrong about the wind. The kiteboarders had gotten up and were hopping a light chop that had formed in the bay where the wind was stronger. They were headed in the general direction of Stiltsville, off the tip of Key Biscayne. A young man and a young woman, probably in their twenties. Cutting across turquoise water under a cloudless sky. In my imagination, their minds were as clear as the sky. *Did they know how lucky they were? Of course not. The young cannot help their inexperience and occasional stupidity. But what was my excuse?*

I said, "First, I wouldn't have asked Gutierrez for his address. I had the juror questionnaire with all of that. Second, I've got arthritis in my fingers from fending off too many pulling guards. No way I could crush a cell phone with one hand. Third, the only stack of hundred-dollar bills with my prints would have been the cost deposit I returned to Thunder Thurston. I counted the money when the bank cashier handed it to me."

"Indeed you did. There's bank video showing it. Problem is, Thurston says he never got the cash, and there's no signed receipt."

"If the money ended up with the juror, Thurston has to be lying."

"The machine believes him."

I gave Pincher my blank look.

"Thurston volunteered to take a polygraph. Denied getting the cash from you and denied bribing Gutierrez. Said he didn't know if you bribed the juror, but with these allegations, he'd have to fire you, which I assume he's done."

Damn.

I was exhausted. It felt as if I'd just gone several rounds in the ring with Pincher, and he was using my gut as the heavy bag.

Now I envisioned a revised obituary:

"Jake Lassiter, a disbarred Miami lawyer who got murderers off the hook and starved orphans on behalf of insurance companies before being

145

convicted of bribing a juror, died yesterday in his cell at Gadsen Correctional Facility . . ."

I drained my coffee and said, "I came over here to tell you that Strychnine is dirty. She's got something going with Thurston. In the murder trial, she didn't use her most damning evidence—"

"I know all about it. Strategy decisions. You'll get nowhere with that."

"Yesterday she sneaked into Thurston's condo. I've got an eyewitness."

"Sneaked in, did she?"

"Not under cover of darkness, but why the hell was she there? Why did she go in empty-handed and come out carrying a duffel? And why did Thurston say to her, 'What about Lassiter?'"

"Why do you think?"

"Because Thurston is paying her off and they're conspiring against me."

"I'm just guessing, but I'd bet Strickstein was preparing Thurston to testify against you at trial. Not a major witness, more like chain of custody on the currency. Thurston will say you never gave him the cash. That keeps it in your possession until you gave it to the juror. As for the duffel, maybe he gave her an autographed football."

"That's ridiculous."

"Sure it is. But unless you can prove it was cash, that's their likely story."

"That son of a bitch Thurston. I should have thrown him off his balcony when I had the chance."

"I'm going to forget I heard that."

"I swear, Ray. I could kill the guy."

He made a tut-tutting sound. "You may think revenge is sweet. But trust me, Jake—it's a bitter dish. Like I told you at the gym, redemption is sweeter than wine."

"You're a helluva gasbag, Ray. You know that?"

"Training at seminary, no doubt."

I looked toward the horizon. The kiteboarders had gotten airborne, far into the bay. I envied them even more.

"Why is Strychnine doing this?" I said. "Why the hell go after me?"

Pincher laughed, but there was no joy in it. "Jake, don't you get it? It ain't you Strychnine's after."

"That's the first time you called her Strychnine."

"But not the last."

"If she's not after me, why indict me?"

"It's just your bum luck that you're my friend. You're the shaky bridge that leads to me. You're collateral damage."

"Strychnine wants to indict you?"

"She's raising money to run against me. She's never held office, and outside the legal community, she's unknown. Her only chance to beat me is to knock me out of the election. So, sure, she wants me perp-walking in front of the cameras, preferably just a few days after you do."

"What the hell did you do?"

"A bit like you, Jake. You talked to a juror. Didn't seem like a big deal, as long as no one found out. And I have my little secrets, too."

Eight Days to Oblivion

An osprey with talons as sharp as steak knives flew circles just offshore, looking for breakfast in the shallow water. Little bumper fish, dumb as dirt and without benefit of counsel, wriggled their last few strokes.

Ray Pincher watched the osprey and spoke in soft, measured tones. I waited for him to tell me just how I fit into Strychnine's plans to become state attorney and what she had on him.

"There's a tsunami rising up from the sea," Pincher said, "and in Miami, there's no high ground."

I knew he was speaking metaphorically, but I still shot a glance at the horizon, where the ocean met the sky.

"Do you know why the indictment against you is sealed?" he asked.

I shook my head. "Maybe Strychnine thinks I'll flee to Argentina if word leaked. I expect there'll be a knock on my door any day, and I'll be arrested."

"Not for eight days."

"Eight?"

"The first day anyone can file to run for state attorney. The day I *always* file."

"So my arrest is supposed to embarrass you? That's all she's got?"

"Hardly. But it's a first step. The *Herald* headline will be something like: 'Pincher Ally Indicted in Corruption Probe.'"

"What corruption probe?"

"Why do you think Marvin Fishbein called you about a job after all these years?"

"He needed a trial lawyer."

"And of the thousand or so he could have hired, he picked you, a guy his firm fired years ago."

A couple of burned-out synapses sparked and I said, "*You* told Marvelous Marv to hire me!"

The osprey dive-bombed the water, talons aimed like sabers. A splash and the bird came up with a juicy little jumper.

"Do you remember we had lunch about six months ago?" Pincher asked. "You were complaining about how slow business was. Hungry young lawyers were cutting fees to get clients. White-collar cases had dried up. Drug arrests were way down. So I called Fishbein, and, yeah, he was looking for someone. But frankly, Jake, you were a tough sell."

"So why'd you do it? Just to help me out?"

"Who was the first guy to call you with congratulations?"

"You. About nine-oh-one a.m. on my first day. I hadn't even hung my merit badges on the wall."

"I didn't just call to say attaboy."

The memory came back quickly. "You asked me to bundle campaign contributions from the partners at Harman and Fox as soon as I was settled in."

"Which you did, and I thanked you for it."

"It wasn't that much, Ray. Most gave the legal limit, a thousand bucks, but in the overall scheme of things, that's not a lot."

He waved his hand, a dismissive gesture. "Those are the reported amounts. Not the cash."

It took me a moment to catch on. "Oh, shit Ray! You can't take cash."

"Right. And *you* can't talk to a juror. But you did and I did."

He was quiet a contemplative moment before continuing. "I thought I had no choice. Do you know how much television time costs in the Miami market? You can't run a countywide campaign these days without taking cash. Everybody does it."

I let the news sink in. The sun was higher in the sky now, an overhead broiler. The osprey had flown off, either satisfied with breakfast or scouting new territory for lunch.

"Do you remember my stopping by Harman and Fox for a meet and greet?" Pincher asked.

"Sure. I set it up. Coffee and *pastelitos*."

"After my five-minute canned speech in the conference room, Fishbein invited me into his office. Handed me twenty-eight checks from the partners for a thousand bucks each."

"All kosher so far."

"Then Fishbein smiled and said he had a present for me. An attaché case made of the finest-quality alligator skin."

"Shark would have been more appropriate. What was inside?"

"Exactly two-hundred fifty thousand dollars. A breathtaking sight."

"What was in it for Harman and Fox? Why violate the law to help you?"

"The new courthouse complex. A three-hundred-million-dollar bond issue. Ordinarily the county commission hires one of those fancy New York law firms for the paperwork. Harman and Fox wanted a piece of that pie."

"Two million in attorneys' fees," I said.

"Roughly. So why not spend a fraction of that to get the business?"

"You can deliver the bond issue?"

"Fishbein and his partners are sophisticated enough to know there's a bond committee appointed by the county commission and I'm just one member."

"But—"

"But enough members of the commission owe me favors so that, yeah, I can probably deliver it. That's what I told Fishbein. I used the word *probably*."

I must have given a look that reflected my feelings. Disappointment. Disillusionment. Disapproval. Dis-a-lot-of-things.

"What's your problem, Jake? Somebody has to get the bond work. And like I say, I never promised. But that's a nuance that would be missed by any grand jury run by Strychnine."

"How'd she find out?"

"Marv Fishbein got arrested for DUI and started blabbing about being my best friend and how he was bankrolling my campaign with cash. When he sobered up he recanted, but word had gotten to Strychnine, and she's about to bring him into the grand jury. Meanwhile, she's subpoenaed all my finance committee records. We're delaying as long as we can, but when she puts it all together, she'll see we're paying out more than our disclosure documents say we're bringing in."

"A prima facie case of campaign finance fraud. And a possible bribery indictment, as well."

"She'll shoot for both."

"As far as the election goes," I said, "either one will sink you and end your career. Just as a jury-tampering charge will do to me."

"That's about it, Jake. So if you think Strychnine is dirty, you have eight days to prove it, or we're both going down."

-28-

Road Trip

Just who the hell is pushing my eyes back into my skull?

That's the way my headache felt as I walked rather than ran home from Matheson Hammock. A pair of strong thumbs, jamming my eyeballs.

Legs heavy, body sweaty, ears banging with a *ker-thumpety-thump* of kettledrums. By the time I got home, both knees were sore.

Showered. Shaved. Put on a navy-blue suit, white shirt, burgundy tie. Outfitted for work. Or a funeral.

Driving north on Dixie Highway, I listened to a local idiot on sports talk radio—"Canes football team needs more thugs"—before flipping to the classic country station. As if I wasn't already in the dumps, here was Hank Williams warbling, "I'm so lonesome I could cry." Somehow he put a little tremolo in his voice between the syllables in *lonesome*. I admire artistry wherever I find it, particularly if I lack similar skills. Since I can't carry a tune or paint a picture or build a bridge, I have a lot of admiring to do.

I called Cindy, my trusty secretary. Not "assistant" or "paralegal." She's been with me nearly twenty years and insists she doesn't want a promotion.

"*Jefe*, you finally coming into work?" she jabbed me. "Phone's been ringing off the hook with PBNs."

Potential New Clients.

"Tell me."

"They're not all blue chips, to tell you the truth. Got a mom who wants to sue the parents in her kid's kindergarten class for not showing up at his birthday party. Cost of the cake plus mental distress."

"Next, Cindy."

"The case of the rained-out vacation."

"Meaning what?"

"Guy wants to sue the Dominican Republic because it rained every day at his resort."

"Anything else?"

"Oh yeah. A guy from Broward just got five years for aggravated assault. Stomped another guy pretty bad."

"A straight appeal. That's better."

She didn't react.

"Cindy, what aren't you telling me?"

"He stomped the guy while wearing Air Jordans. Now he wants to sue Nike for failing to warn him the sneakers were dangerous weapons."

My cell beeped with an incoming call. I checked the display just as I guided the old Caddy onto I-95. Steve Solomon.

"Later, Cindy."

I helloed Solomon and he yelled back at me, "Road trip!"

"What are you talking about?"

"Jakie, Jakie, Jakie! I take back every shitty thing I ever said about you, and I apologize for every shitty thing I'm gonna say later."

"Meaning?"

153

"I just got off the phone with Dr. Melissa Gold, neuropathologist and big deal in neuroscience at UCLA. I'll e-mail her CV to you."

"Yeah?"

"Your hunch was right, pal. The autopsy proved it. Dr. Gold sliced and diced Carla Caruana's brain tissue. Brown-and-red splotches. Tau protein."

"I have no idea what that is."

"She'll explain it. The diagnosis is CTE. And what did that cause, my pal? Dementia! Just like you said, Carla couldn't form the legal intent to commit suicide."

"The doctor said that based on brain tissue? She connected the dots between dementia and legal intent?"

"Not exactly. But she'll give us enough scientific mumbo jumbo to beat your summary judgment motion and get to a jury."

"Congratulations, Solomon. But I'm a little distracted right now."

"Get undistracted. We're flying to LA in the morning for Dr. Gold's depo. She's in Santa Barbara for a doctors' convention, and we'll depose her after her morning speech. You gotta be there to represent the forces of darkness, also known as Biscayne Life Insurance."

"No can do. I have things to take care of here. Important things."

"You're not being rational. What's more important than two orphans?"

I wanted to tell Solomon I had eight days to get evidence that Stacy Strickstein was dirty and that I was clean, or at least not filthy. Once the indictment was unsealed, I would be arrested. And even if I was later acquitted, my career would be in tatters. How would I get new clients? The only pitch I could come up with was: "Hey, I beat a bum rap, and I can do the same for you."

It didn't play. No one wants a jailbird for a lawyer.

I told Solomon none of this. If he knew the jam I was in, he would come up with crazy ideas and distract me even more. So, it would be quick trip to California, and then when I got back, I could . . .

Could what?

Where would I even start?

I didn't know, and Solomon was yammering at me.

"We gotta get Dr. Gold's depo taken, transcribed, and filed before the summary judgment hearing next week," he said.

"By 'we,' you mean you and Victoria. Please try to remember I'm on the opposite side."

"Okay, that's rational. Jake."

Rational *seems to be the Solomonic word of the day.*

"But whatever personal problems you have, put them on hold, okay?" he continued.

"Do I have a choice?"

"That's my pal. C'mon, we'll have fun. You, Vic, and me. Like the old days. You ever eat abalone?"

"Sure. Whenever we played in Oakland or San Francisco. I like it in garlic and butter."

"That's the spirit. Abalone and some fine California wine. See you in the morning. American flight 1403. First class on a triple seven. I've taken the liberty of booking you a seat."

"You take a lot of liberties, Solomon."

"Flight's at six fifty-nine a.m. Don't be late. I'm gonna snooze the whole way, so I'm putting you next to Victoria. You can flirt with her for six hours. Tell her she'd be better off with you."

"She already knows that, Solomon. But it doesn't make any difference to her."

"True. But why is that?"

"For whatever reason, she loves you, Solomon. And love isn't rational."

-29-

Meet Me in Havana

At 6:15 the next morning, I was blearily walking along Concourse D at Miami International Airport. I'd had a double shot of Cuban coffee at the La Carreta stand, a little sister of the Calle Ocho restaurant. The caffeine should have jolted me awake but didn't, although it kick-started my pulse rate. It also hatched a new headache. Within moments, a percussive rhythm in my skull seemed to be keeping time to my elevated heartbeat.

I never rescheduled my appointment with Dr. Helfman, and in case I'd forgotten—which I hadn't—Charlie Riggs reminded me again last night. So did Granny, with Kip joining in. They were ganging up on me. I told them I didn't have time.

"Make time!" Charlie had ordered. "The sand is running out of the glass, my friend."

Now, rolling my carry-on past brightly lit stores, I fought off the urge to buy a T-shirt with a drawing of what purported to be the state bird. A giant mosquito. I was only yards from my departure gate when my cell rang. Caller ID was blocked.

"Who's awake at this hour?" I answered.

"Mr. Lassiter. Why are you at the airport?"

Woman's voice. A shade of mockery in her tone.

"Who is this?"

"There's a flight to Havana departing Gate D-37. Is that where you're going, one step ahead of the law?"

Oh, crap.

"Strychnine. Is that you?"

"Assistant State Attorney *Strickstein*," she corrected me.

"You have me under surveillance? For a lousy third-degree felony, you have someone following me?"

"This case is bigger than you can imagine. Perhaps you should talk to your friend Raymond Pincher about that."

"I doubt Sugar Ray would want to talk to a hardened criminal like me."

"Really? I have some excellent long-lens shots from yesterday. You and the State Attorney conspiring on the beach."

"*Perspiring* on the beach is more like it."

"I'm the one you should be talking to, not him."

"I didn't realize *Let's Make a Deal* was still on the air."

"It can be, depending on what you have to trade."

A high-pitched squeal came over the concourse speaker, announcing that first-class passengers and parents with unruly children could board flight 1403 to Los Angeles.

"I gotta go, Strychnine."

"Assistant State Attorney *Strickstein*," she repeated.

"And you're busting your ass to drop the *Assistant*, aren't you?"

I caught sight of Steve Solomon and Victoria Lord hurrying toward the gate. Solomon waved me to join them. I gestured with the cell phone and held up a finger. *One minute.*

"I have a witness who nails you on a hand-to-hand bribe," Strickstein said. "Automatic disbarment and five years in prison. What do you have for me?"

"How about a mojito at the Nacional in Havana? As long as there's still no extradition treaty, I'm buying."

"All I need from you is your sworn statement that Ray Pincher asked you to bundle campaign contributions for him."

"Not a problem. He did, and I'll say so."

"And that he insisted the contributions be in cash."

"No way. Didn't happen. Ray said to do everything by the book, and I did."

"Were you present when the State Attorney discussed the court-house bond issue with Marvin Fishbein?"

"I don't know they ever discussed it, so I'm certain I wasn't there."

"When your memory improves, call me. You can consider it a race."

"Who am I racing?"

"Marvin Fishbein, of course. Whoever flips first stays out of jail. Whoever doesn't will be indicted for campaign finance fraud and bribery of a public official. In your case, that would be tacked onto your jury-tampering charge. Three convictions, Lassiter. We'll go for habitual-offender status. How does thirty years sound?"

"Like you're desperate. *Adiós*, Strychnine. See you in Havana."

A new announcement told us that people in steerage and latecomers might want to put some giddyup in their step and hustle onto the plane. I got into the line and punched in a number on my cell.

"Fishbein," Marvin answered.

"Don't say anything, Marv. Assume your phone is tapped for this and every other call."

"Jeez, Jake. I've been subpoenaed. What the hell?"

I could hear the fear in his voice. "Stay calm, Marv. The state has no case unless one of us talks."

"You're sure?"

"The prosecutor virtually admitted it. So I need you to hang tough. You can do that, right?"

"I don't know, Jake."

"Not acceptable. I'll see you in a couple of days. Hang in there for me, Marv."

"For you? I don't give a good crap about you. What about me? My good name? My family?"

He was babbling. I could almost see his hand shaking. "Okay, not for me, Marv. For truth. For justice. For redemption."

"What the hell are you talking about?"

"It's complicated. I'll explain when I have more information, but it's Strickstein who's in jeopardy, not us."

If Fishbein's line was bugged, so much the better. Let Strychnine wonder what I had on her. Of course, the answer was *nada*. But today's mantra was confusion to the enemy.

"Jake, I can't go to prison. I'm not like you. I'm not tough enough."

"You're not going to prison, Marv."

"My rectum's sacrosanct, Jake. Only thing goes up there is the colonoscopy tube."

"Pull yourself together. I'm getting on a plane—"

"You're fleeing! Where, Jake? Buenos Aires?"

"Los Angeles. I'll be back in two days. We're gonna bring Strickstein down. It's all going to work out."

"How? You have the goods on her?"

"You wouldn't believe what I've got," I said with calm certainty. Like big-time poker players, trial lawyers are skilled at bluffing. Even though I held a garbage hand, I put enough joy in my voice to make it sound like four aces. "If anyone's going to prison, it's her! Not you, Marv. And not me. We'll be drinking champagne and eating caviar when they haul Stacy Strickstein off to jail."

PART THREE

"Repetitive head trauma chokes the brain and turns man
into something else."

—Dr. Bennet Omalu, portrayed by Will Smith in
the film *Concussion*

"The NFL is now conceding something already known.
The sheer number of deceased players with a postmortem
diagnosis of CTE supports the unavoidable conclusion
that there is a relationship, if not a causal connection,
between a life in football and CTE."

—In regard to National Football League Players
Concussion Injury Litigation, Opinion of the
United States. Court of Appeals, Third Circuit,
approving class action settlement of former players'
claims, April 18, 2016

-30-
The Night That Never Was

Steve Solomon was already reclining in 1A, the bulkhead seat by the window. There was no 1B or 1C, as airline cabins are designed either by pranksters or engineers with little knowledge of the alphabet. Next to Solomon was a wide first-class aisle and then seats 1D and 1G. Victoria was settling into 1G, farthest from Solomon, so I took 1D, closer to him across the aisle.

As Solomon had promised, we were on an American Airlines Boeing 777 with swiveling leather recliners. Hit a switch and the recliner becomes a flat bed that sinks into the privacy of a wraparound cocoon, like a shaded chaise on a beach at a fancy resort.

"Who were you talking to so intently on the phone?" Victoria asked.

"Kip," I lied. "He wanted to wish me a safe trip."

Had I been speaking to Kip, he would have asked if I'd left him money for pizza but never would have wished me Godspeed. He is, after all, a teenage boy.

"Such a nice young man," Victoria said. "How's he doing in school?"

"Okay, I guess. But he's playing football, and his coach is a hard-ass."

"Aren't they all?"

"I'm worried that Kip's trying to be like me."

"That would have its drawbacks. Have you talked to him about it?"

"A little but I don't want to stifle him, either."

The steward came by with warm cashews and cold mimosas. Across the aisle Solomon asked for two Bloody Marys. Then he removed his shoes and stepped into a pair of slippers from the airline goodie bag. He put on an eye mask and sank back into his comfy bed, out of view. I yelled at him across the spacious aisle. "Aren't you going to work on your questions for Dr. Gold?"

"Nope," came the muffled reply from inside the cocoon. "I'm better when I'm spontaneous."

"I can't help you if you put her under oath and she sandbags you."

"Chill out, Jake."

"You're reckless. Did I ever tell you that?"

He grumbled an unintelligible response.

I said, "Give me a copy of Dr. Gold's report, so I can prep my defense."

A voice from inside the flat bed echoed, "Got nothing in writing. Wasn't time."

That was probably true. But historically it's been the strategy of plaintiffs' lawyers to instruct their experts not to prepare written reports. That way, nosy defense lawyers can't prepare for depositions and hearings.

"So you're ready, right?" I pestered him.

"I was born ready."

"You realize the importance of the depo, right, Cowboy?"

Solomon's head emerged from inside his cocoon and then the rest of him. He raised his eye mask and turned toward me. "Hey, Mom. I've done my homework. Okay?" He picked up his first Bloody Mary from the tray and drained it in one gulp.

"Once the depo starts, we're no longer pals," I told him. "I have to defend my client, whether I like it or not."

"Ooh, I'm scared now. Vic, are you scared?"

Next to me, Victoria said, "Would you boys please stop?"

"I'm going to sleep," Solomon said, "so you two do whatever you do when I'm not around."

"Basically, I tell Victoria she's making a huge mistake," I said.

Solomon grunted and disappeared again into the flat bed.

* * *

Somewhere over Texas I washed down four Tylenol with a mimosa. I figured the vitamin C would ward off scurvy, and the champagne expressed my thanks to the French people for the Statue of Liberty and Edith Piaf.

"Headache?" Victoria asked.

"Little one," I lied.

Trying to man up the way all my coaches taught me. Once during two-a-days in the August heat, I'd collapsed and puked within splashing distance of Coach Shula's spikes. "Lassiter, get off my field!" he yelled. "Go die somewhere else."

I considered it an affectionate moment between mentor and student.

"You took a couple of pills right after we took off when you thought I wasn't looking," Victoria said.

"Busted," I admitted.

"Any dizziness or double vision?"

"Nope." That was true, but my ears were still ringing. More annoying than painful. A little like listening to Herb Albert and the Tijuana Brass play "Spanish Flea" a hundred times in a row.

"Charlie Riggs called me yesterday," Victoria said.

"You consulting with the old sawbones on the *Caruana* case?" I asked, though I was pretty sure that wasn't it.

"Actually, he called about you, Jake."

"Violating doctor-patient privilege. I'm gonna sue him."

"You were supposed get neurological tests."

"Life intervened."

"But you'll see a doctor, right?"

"I told Charlie I would, so yeah, I will."

She lowered her voice to a whisper, even though no one was listening. "You've stopped talking about vigilante justice. May I assume you've realized how crazy and dangerous that would be?"

"Thunder Thurston is on hold until I clear up some other things."

"On hold?"

"For now."

She sighed. "Want to tell me about the other things you need to clear up?"

I considered doing just that. The whole Strychnine disaster. My getting indicted. Harman and Fox's illegal campaign contributions. Victoria would have a measured reaction and probably good advice. But something kept my mouth wired shut. Maybe I was embarrassed to be caught in such a web. Maybe I was afraid Victoria would think I really had bribed a juror and was a conspirator along with Fishbein and Pincher in campaign finance fraud. Whatever the reason, I said, "Maybe later. I'm just not ready to spill my guts."

She appraised me a moment, then tossed me a question that wasn't so much from left field as from the last row of the bleachers. "You remember that night I came on to you?"

I let a moment pass, the only sound the drone of the huge engines. I cleared my throat to buy even more time, then said, "Nope. Can't say I remember anything like that."

"For a lawyer, you're a lousy liar."

"I'll work on it."

"Steve was in jail. I was angry with him because he lied to me about how he came to be holding the gun that shot Nicolai Gorev. For the record, Steve's a better liar than you are."

"I'll stipulate to that."

"I came over to your house very late. You were in the hammock out back. I'd been drinking. Ring a bell?"

"Never happened."

"I was wearing white short-shorts, and you took a long look."

"I would remember that. But nope."

"And platform sandals with long straps that circled my calves all the way to my knees."

"The night that never was."

"You really checked out my legs."

I kept quiet. Of course I remembered all that. And the stretchy pink tank top that showed her well-formed delts and small, perky breasts. The image was burned into my brain, no matter how many concussions I've suffered.

"It wasn't just that Steve lied to me about the shooting," she went on. "I thought he was having an affair with that Russian Bar girl."

"What Bar girl?"

"That night, you told me he wasn't seeing her, though it was in your interest to say he was."

"Sorry, no recollection of any of this."

"I tried to get you out of your hammock and into bed. Do you remember what you said?"

I shrugged and gave her my blank look. She sighed and gave me her exasperated look. "You turned me down. And you said, 'There was a time . . .'"

I zoned her out. I didn't need Victoria to tell me what I'd said because I remembered every word: *There was a time when I wouldn't have been man enough to say no. But those days are gone, and I'm not taking part in get-even sex. We're not going to wake up tomorrow hating ourselves and each other."*

Victoria was still pulling up the memory. "Then I said, 'I already hate you for turning me down.' And you got this real serious look and said, 'Tomorrow . . .'"

"Tomorrow, you'll thank me. Look, I need you. Steve really needs you. And when this is over, you and I will have a drink—preferably coffee—and laugh about tonight."

"Anyway, I want to thank you now," she said. "You could have taken advantage of me, to use a rather outdated expression."

"In my experience booze plus anger plus revenge sex equals regret in the morning."

"So you do remember!"

"I was speaking hypothetically. After a night of thrusting and parrying, oohing and aahing, after the moist heat cooled, and the morning sun sneaked through the blinds, we would be sitting at the breakfast table with coffee, toast, and a big pitcher of embarrassment. You would have gone back to Solomon, and our friendship would have been shattered."

"Hypothetically speaking?"

"Of course."

"For the record, we both love you."

"You kids are okay, too."

"So, if I make suggestions about your personal life," she said, "that's where it's coming from. A place of love and respect and friendship."

Oh, brother. What now?

Just what plans did Victoria have to improve my life?

-31-

Love, Jake. Love.

The giant jet engines droned on. Victoria let another moment pass. I would bet she was working on some idea that would involve feelings. Mine, not hers. She wanted me to be more open. We've had that conversation before. Okay, I admit it. I'm a bit of a throwback. But then I'm a guy. I don't hoist my emotions like a swallowtail flag on a sailboat. I keep things to myself and try to solve my own problems without pestering friends and family.

Then she surprised me. "Steve says the reason you're not seeing anyone is that you're hung up on me."

"Untrue. I'm just particular."

"Really?"

"I have my standards. I try not to date fleeing felons, bail jumpers, and women who've killed their lovers. Otherwise, I'm open to meeting most anyone."

"Seriously, when was your last relationship?"

"Not that long ago. What's her name? That stewardess with dry skin."

"They're called flight attendants, Jake."

"Not when we were dating. Come to think of it, she worked for Eastern. Or was it TWA?"

"You need to get back in the game before it passes you by."

"It?"

"Love, Jake. Love."

"I wouldn't know where to start. These days more than ever, I feel like a brew and burger guy in a pâté and chardonnay world."

Victoria let out a *hmmm* sound, picked up an airline magazine, and glanced at the cover, though I figured she wasn't really interested in traveling to Antarctica. She was doubtless still working on that feminine urge to improve my life, despite my best efforts to resist change.

The silence got to me, and I said, "Okay, you think I need a doctor and a girlfriend. Is that about it?"

"I also want you to trust me. And Steve, too. If you're having problems, don't shut us out."

"When I have something to report, you'll be the first to know."

"Okay, then, I'll share something with you. Steve and I have been subpoenaed before the grand jury."

"What!"

"They want canceled checks of all campaign contributions to Ray Pincher and all our bank records for the past six months."

"That damn Strychnine," I said.

"Stacy Strickstein. Yes, I called her. Asked what it was all about. She said to ask you."

I felt my neck heating up. I've known prosecutors who indict wives and parents of suspects just to coerce guilty pleas. This was a page from the same book.

"I was bundling contributions for Pincher," I said. "You and Steve gave me checks of two hundred fifty bucks each, and I passed them to the campaign finance chairman. Some people I solicited wrote their checks and then, unbeknownst to me, slipped cash under the table."

"Not Steve and me."

"I know that. Strychnine knows it, too. She's just harassing you because we're pals."

Victoria thought about that a moment. "That explains the last thing she said to me."

"Yeah?"

"She said, 'When I'm done with Lassiter, he won't have a friend in this town.'"

"Not to worry, Victoria. I don't need a lot of friends, as long as I have the two of you."

-32-

Depo, California Style

At LAX we picked up our rental, an oversize black Chevy Suburban with heavily tinted windows that would do nicely for the Secret Service or a gangster rapper. Steve Solomon's choice, naturally.

Solomon offered to drive, and I offered to lie down in the backseat. After the six-hour flight, my back was seizing up, and the headache from hell would not go away. Victoria plugged the address of the Four Seasons Biltmore into her phone, and we headed toward Santa Barbara.

It was one of those seventy-two-degree, endless-blue-sky Southern California days . . . with horrendous traffic. We were inching north along the 405 when Solomon began regaling us with stories of his days as a shortstop with quick feet but a feeble bat on the University of Miami baseball team.

"We had a nine-game road trip out here my senior year," he reminisced. "UCLA, Pepperdine, and UCSB. Finished in Santa Barbara with a three-game series, where I stole five bases."

"And haven't yet returned them," I suggested.

"Four hits, all singles, two on bunts, and three walks in the three games."

"I bet you don't remember which team won the series," I said.

"What crap are you giving me now, Jake?"

"The three games. Miami versus UCSB. Who won the series?"

"Who can remember? It was a long time ago."

"But you remember all your at bats. All your stolen bases. Probably how many times you scratched your crotch."

"So?"

"You weren't a team player. It was all about you all the time. Steve. Steve. Steve."

"Jeez, the third-stringer is giving me shit."

"Boys, please play nice on this trip," Victoria pleaded.

But I wasn't letting up. "Your egocentricity is a character flaw, Solomon."

"Victoria, can you believe this? The guy who wants to kill his client is lecturing me on character."

"Former client," I said.

"Oh, that makes a difference. Tell it to the judge!"

"Steve! Jake! This is going to be a really long day without you two swinging your dicks in my face."

That shut us both up.

It seemed like hours, but twenty minutes later Solomon took the exit onto the 101 and headed north by northwest through the San Fernando Valley and toward Santa Barbara.

* * *

The Four Seasons Biltmore has a colonial Spanish-style main building with an orange-barrel-tile roof and lushly landscaped, discreetly cozy little bungalows. The front of the hotel sits just yards above Butterfly Beach on the Pacific Ocean. The back looks out on the Santa Ynez Mountains. Mediterranean-style homes are visible in winding clusters along the mountain roads. Local civic boosters call the town the

American Riviera. Maybe that's a stretch, but still, it's a pretty plush spot.

As Floridians, we're not impressed by oceans and beaches. But mountains that come down nearly to the shore? Well, that kicks sand in our faces.

In the conference area of the hotel, placards announced sessions for several hundred neurologists who'd gathered here, not for the ocean and sunshine, but education and schmoozing. Some of the lectures sounded particularly thrilling. There was "Cerebellar Cognitive Affective Syndrome: Implications for Neurology and Psychiatry." And "Rational Therapeutics for Prion Infection and Its Relevance to Alzheimer's Disease." A final placard announced a talk given by Dr. Melissa Gold: "Traumatic Brain Injury and Dementia."

Okay, we're getting warmer.

On the placard was small print summarizing Dr. Gold's findings, but it contained phrases like *amyloid precursor protein*, and my eyes were blurry from the long day of travel. Thanks to picking up three hours on the coast-to-coast flight, it was only midafternoon, but I was ready for a nap.

"Where's our conference room?" I asked Solomon.

"We're in Cali, baby," he said.

"Meaning what?"

"Would you rather stare at walnut paneling or babes in bikinis?"

Victoria said, "Are you asking me, Steve?"

"Metaphorically speaking," Solomon answered, trying to recover. "I mean wouldn't we rather be on the beach? The pounding surf. The salt air. The seabirds. The whole megillah."

"We're not taking the depo on a beach," I said.

"Technically above the beach. Follow me."

We exited the front of the hotel, walked past a groomed patch of birds-of-paradise, and crossed to the ocean side of the street. We entered the Coral Casino, a private beach club with a fifty-meter pool and two stories of cabanas built just above the sand.

"It costs a hundred fifty thousand to join the club," Mr. Know-It-All Solomon said. "When Vic and I win the case, maybe we'll sign up."

"Long trip to swim a few a laps," I said.

"You're too practical, Jake. You gotta let yourself dream."

A neatly groomed young man in a starched white shirt with epaulets led us to the second floor, where we entered an open walkway overlooking the pool, which ended where the sand began. We took the walkway to an alcove directly over the beach. There was a canvas awning overhead, but otherwise the alcove was open on all four sides. Just as Solomon had promised, there was salt air. And seabirds. I didn't see any women in bikinis on the mostly deserted beach. Just a few walkers and a golden retriever bouncing in the shore break, chasing a rubber ball.

"What do you think, Jake?" Solomon said.

"Sometimes you surprise me, Solomon. This is nice."

A round table with five chairs was set up inside the alcove. A young woman was already there, setting up her stenograph machine. She introduced herself as Mary Ortega, our court reporter. She was about thirty, wearing orange jeans and a white blouse. Santa Barbara casual, I supposed. She collected our business cards to enter our appearances on the transcript of record, cracked her knuckles to loosen up, and waited.

A moment later, Dr. Melissa Gold hurried along the walkway, carrying a leather valise and wearing a blue sundress festooned with white lilies. Strappy sandals with those big cork heels showed off her toenails, which were painted turquoise. "I hope you don't mind the way I'm dressed," she said. "After my talk this morning, I changed and walked on the beach to the wharf. It was invigorating!"

The woman had such natural cheer, we all smiled. Or at least I did. My eyes were on Melissa Gold, and I couldn't quite be sure of Solomon's and Lord's expressions.

"Dr. Gold, you look smashing," I said.

"Smashing?" Solomon rolled his eyes. "What are you, an English duke?"

"Steve!" Victoria warned.

"Sorry. Dr. Gold, I'm Steve Solomon. We talked on the phone."

The doctor was a tall, slender woman with reddish-brown hair that came to her shoulders and a sprinkling of freckles across her nose. Her eyes were a pale green flecked with gold. If she was wearing makeup, I couldn't detect it. Her cheeks were rosy, perhaps from her brisk walk along the beach. Solomon had given me a copy of her curriculum vitae, and working back from the year she graduated from college, I figured her to be forty-four years old. My incredible powers of investigation also determined—by looking at the naked ring finger of her left hand—that the lady was not married. And, yeah, she looked smashing.

"This is my partner, Victoria Lord," Solomon continued. "And that big slab of meat is Jake Lassiter, lawyer for the insurance company. You may regard him as the Prince of Darkness."

I managed to smile and nod and say hello all at the same time. She smiled back and said, "Mr. Lassiter, I hope you won't be too rough on me."

It sounded flirtatious, or maybe that was just her way of disarming me.

"He's a blistering cross-examiner," Solomon said before I could reply. "Brings the strongest witnesses to tears."

"Really?" The ocean breeze was whipping Dr. Gold's hair across her face. She gathered a handful and slipped on a band, creating a ponytail. Still looking at me, she said, "But Mr. Lassiter looks like such a pleasant man."

"That's the genius of his wickedness," Solomon said. "Lulls witnesses with his hypnotic charm, then tricks them into confessing horrendous deeds."

"Mr. Solomon exaggerates both my charm and my iniquity," I said.

Still smiling, Dr. Gold said, "In either event, I relish the challenge."

-33-

Two Stags Pawing the Dirt

In our little alcove, the court reporter administered the oath, and Dr. Melissa Gold promised to tell the truth. I believed her, but then I am a sucker for women who are smart, confident, and did I mention smashing? Yes, I did.

Below us on the beach, a dog barked happily. Three long-necked gray herons waddled along in formation, then took off, one after the other, like planes on a bombing mission.

Solomon began the easy task of qualifying Dr. Gold as an expert witness. Columbia University undergrad. MS in neuroscience and a PhD in molecular science from Yale. MD from Duke, board certified in neurology and neuropathology. A bunch of fellowships and papers and honors and currently director of the Center for Neuroscience at UCLA. In short, brainy about brains.

We paused a moment while a server delivered several three-tiered platters of cold seafood—oysters, clams, lobster tails—and two bottles of Perrier-Jouët in silver buckets. Different than the usual coffee and a Danish at my depos in the Harman and Fox conference room.

I glanced at Solomon, who grinned back at me. "If you're looking for your abalone, I sent them to the fish market in the harbor to get the freshest in town," he said.

Most of the time Solomon drove me nuts. But there were times when he just startled me with his graciousness. Which made me wonder if Victoria had the same reaction.

Solomon slurped down an oyster and returned his attention to Dr. Gold. He kept lobbing questions, and she kept hitting winners. She had studied athletes with neurodegenerative diseases and military veterans with battlefield brain injuries. She was the lead neuropathologist in the autopsies of twenty-four former NFL players, twenty of whose brains revealed chronic traumatic encephalopathy. She credited Dr. Bennet Omalu of Pittsburgh for discovering and naming CTE and Dr. Ann McKee at Boston University for helping identify the four stages of the disease.

Under Solomon's prodding, Dr. Gold modestly agreed that she was a "pioneer" in neuroimaging of cognitive dysfunction in former NFL players, using a modified PET scan, something that allowed living persons to be diagnosed, though not with 100 percent accuracy.

"Unfortunately, autopsies are a better diagnostic tool," she said ruefully.

Dr. Gold was part of the team that battled the NFL, which for years shamefully argued that there was no connection between multiple concussions and traumatic brain injury. Yeah, pretty much like the tobacco companies and lung cancer.

Dr. Gold mentioned how NFL Commissioner Roger Goodell had, until recently, steadfastly denied the link between the beloved game and death. "There's risks in life," Goodell famously said. "There's risks to sitting on the couch."

I would like to clothesline Goodell, smash the bastard with a forearm to the throat, then set his damn couch on fire. He could buy a new one with the $44 million the team owners paid him last year. What excuse could there be for the NFL falsifying its head-injury report-ing, omitting hundreds of concussions, and paying off physicians who found no link between concussions and dementia? Then, after staking out its indefensible position, the NFL hired tobacco company lawyers and lobbyists to press its case. Basically, the sport that replaced baseball as the national pastime had become a multibillion-dollar racketeering enterprise.

Solomon asked Dr. Gold to name some of the former players who had died from CTE. Her answer sounded like an all-time All-Pro team.

"Frank Gifford. Junior Seau. Earl Morrall. Mike Webster. Ken Stabler. Ollie Matson. Andre Waters. Cookie Gilchrist. Dave Duerson. Terry Long. John Mackey."

Dr. Gold paused after each name, as if conducting a memorial service for the victims of a mass disaster. She explained the medicine. Essentially traumatic brain injury leads to a disruption of the scaffolding structures in the neurons. And, yes, she'd written several peer-reviewed articles concerning CTE in former NFL players, both dead and alive. Then there was the really scary finding from a study she had just com-pleted. Repeated subconcussive blows to the head suffered by high school and college football players could cause brain damage later.

I sipped my champagne and said, "Why don't I just spare every-one undue time and the court reporter undue effort and stipulate that Dr. Gold is an expert in traumatic brain injury generally and CTE specifically?"

"So stipulated," Solomon said. "Thank you, Mr. Lassiter. Your col-legiality is appreciated. Dr. Gold, I'm now turning you over to my partner, Victoria Lord."

"What's with the handoff?" I asked, terminating my collegiality. "Solomon, I thought you were carrying the ball today."

"Vic knows more medicine than I do," he said.

"My bartender knows more medicine than you do. What's that got to do with it?"

"You want the truth, Jake? I don't want you objecting and cluttering up the record."

"So don't ask objectionable questions."

"If Victoria handles the depo, you won't object. Maybe it's because of chivalry. Maybe it's something deeper."

"Maybe it's because she's a better lawyer," I said.

Dr. Gold cleared her throat and looked at Victoria. "Are they always like this?"

"Always," Victoria replied.

"Men," the doctor said, with just a hint of a smile.

"I know," Victoria said, nodding. "They're like a couple of stags who paw the earth, lock horns, and push each other around. Then they just stop and look for something to eat. Who can figure them out?"

Both women laughed. They seemed to be sharing a moment that excluded Solomon and me. Then I realized it had doubtless been Victoria's idea to handle the substantive questioning herself. Woman to woman. So much easier to establish common ground. I admired the strategy.

"I nearly became a psychiatrist," Dr. Gold said. "Sometimes I wish I had. It would surely help in understanding men."

"The male animal," Victoria said. "Eternal puzzlement."

And they both laughed again.

-34-

Better Law Partner or Better Mate?

The sun was lower in the sky and the wind had picked up by the time Victoria began her questioning. I could see little goose bumps on Dr. Melissa Gold's bare upper arms.

Just sizing her up as a witness, I swear. Not checking her out.

Victoria asked the questions with her usual crisp precision and no excess verbiage. "Doctor, what is chronic traumatic encephalopathy?"

"It's a progressive neurodegenerative disease that particularly afflicts athletes who have suffered multiple concussions."

"What sort of athletes?"

"Boxers and football players mostly. But a recent University of Toronto study found that about one-third of all mixed martial arts events end with a head trauma event. Because of the nature of the sport, cage fighters are at an even greater risk of CTE than football players."

"How does CTE present itself?"

"By fibrous tangles of a protein called tau, which is visible in brain tissue under a microscope."

"Now, did you have the opportunity to examine brain tissue of the decedent, Carla Caruana?"

"I did."

"What did you find?"

"To the naked eye, the tissue appeared to be normal gray matter. No softness or apparent contusions as you would find in *dementia pugilistica*. That's the form of traumatic brain injury long associated with boxers."

"What we might call punch-drunk?" Victoria asked.

"A very extreme form. Similarly, Ms. Caruana's brain tissue showed no shrinkage that we associate with Alzheimer's."

"What tests did you perform on the brain tissue?"

"CT and MRI scans. Neither revealed any abnormalities."

"What then did you do?"

"The usual protocol. I used a staining technique developed by Dr. Bennet Omalu on several tissue samples and examined the slides under a microscope."

"And what did you see?" Victoria asked.

"Brown-and-red splotches. Angry splotches."

"Which turned out to be what, Dr. Gold?"

"A deadly buildup of tau proteins. A sticky sludge that kills brain cells. It is the direct cause of chronic traumatic encephalopathy."

Solid questions. Perfect answers. I liked watching people good at their work. Carpenters, bricklayers, even lawyers. Victoria spent a few minutes having Dr. Gold identify photographs of Carla Caruana's magnified brain tissue. Arrows pointed at the areas of tangled tau protein. The court reporter pasted exhibit numbers on the photos and would later attach them to the written transcript.

"Can you state to a reasonable degree of medical certainty that Ms. Caruana suffered from CTE?" Victoria asked.

Using the magical legal lingo to establish causation.

"Yes, I can," Dr. Gold said. "CTE is consistent with Ms. Caruana's history, as documented in the medical records. She suffered numerous concussions and often was not held out of competition in order to allow her brain to recover, likely increasing the damage. Under the microscope, her brain resembled that of an eighty-five-year-old with Alzheimer's. Her brain tissue was, in many respects, in far worse condition than many of the deceased NFL players who also suffered from CTE."

"Dr. Gold, based on your diagnosis, what symptoms and conditions would Carla Caruana likely have manifested in the last year of her life?"

"So many horrible things. Depression. Paranoia. Delusions. Confusion. Irritability. Memory loss. Bouts of explosive anger and violence. A virtual destruction of her life as she knew it."

"So that CTE would explain her seemingly irrational actions prior to death?"

"Yes. There is no other medical reason I could ascertain."

I knew Victoria was now about to embark on a string of leading questions. But with an expert, it's pretty much customary. Besides, I had no intention of objecting to anything. Not the refreshing, low-humidity weather. Not the sea, the sand, or the mountains. And not the delightful Dr. Melissa Gold.

"Would CTE have caused impairment of her decision making?" Victoria asked in her succinct style.

"Yes."

"Would she have been self-destructive?"

"Yes, that is highly consistent with CTE."

"And not be cognizant of actions she took?"

"That also is consistent with this form of traumatic brain injury. We often see victims of CTE taking self-destructive actions without being aware of what they are doing."

If Victoria were down on the beach collecting seashells, her bucket would be nearly full. But she wasn't done. "Even suicidal actions?" she asked.

"Particularly so. Many former boxers and football players suffering from traumatic brain injury have taken their own lives as their brains virtually disintegrate and irreparably damage their cognitive abilities."

Bingo! Please collect your prize.

I thought that should wrap it up. A plaintiff doesn't have to prove her entire case in the expert's deposition. Victoria had everything she needed to defeat the insurance company's summary judgment motion. Whether Carla Caruana had the requisite mental ability to volitionally commit suicide was now a jury question. And at trial the lovely Dr. Gold would spin her scientific tale, show her slides, and testify at greater length and in greater detail.

Victoria must have thought so, too. She paused and flipped through a legal pad, making little check marks as she went. Finally she said, "Your witness, Mr. Lassiter."

I stood and walked to the corner of the alcove directly over the beach. Just wanted to stretch my aching back muscles. A stocky middle-aged man in cargo shorts was surf-fishing, using a heavy pole to cast into the shore break.

"Dr. Gold," I began, still on my feet.

"Hold on, Jake," Solomon said. "I've got a question."

"Why?"

"I don't have to explain why. It's my deposition."

"Our deposition," Victoria corrected him.

"Good point," Solomon agreed. "Now, Dr. Gold—"

"Solomon, I have an idea," I broke in.

"Don't interrupt me, Jake."

"Hear me out."

"No!"

"Solomon, why don't you let me cross-examine, and if there's anything you want to clear up, do it on redirect. I won't object, even if you go far beyond the scope of my cross."

"Don't tell me how to take a depo!"

Mary Ortega, the court reporter, said, "You two are speaking too quickly for me."

I threw up my hands in surrender and stared silently out to sea. There were several oil derricks in the channel, and my headache now mimicked what I imagined to be the *chug-chug-chug* of the drill assembly biting into the rocky seabed.

"Now, Dr. Gold—" Solomon began again.

"Steve, is this necessary?" Victoria interrupted.

"Just one question, Vic," he promised, then turned back to the witness. "Dr. Gold, can you state to a reasonable degree of medical certainty that Carla Caruana's CTE caused her to commit suicide?"

There was an uncomfortable pause. Then Dr. Gold said, "Well, that is a question, as phrased, that combines medical issues with legal and behavioral ones."

In other words, no.

But she didn't say no. So Solomon could just shut his trap. Or withdraw the question and we could all go for a walk on the beach. But the cowboy couldn't resist taking another shot.

"I understand, Dr. Gold. But you already stated that the disease causes all those severe physical and mental problems, often resulting in self-destructive actions, so isn't it true that CTE directly caused the suicide?"

It was as if Captain Edward J. Smith ordered the helmsman of the Titanic *to steer directly into the iceberg.*

I walked back to the table and waited, with everyone else, for the answer.

"Actually, Mr. Solomon, I can't say that," Dr. Gold said.

I banged the table with my fist, and everyone jumped in their seats. "You're an asshole, Solomon! You went a bridge too far. Why would you ask a determinative question if you don't know the answer?"

"Is that an objection? Because you don't get to make speeches," he said.

"I object to your recklessness. I object to your laziness. I object to your very existence."

"Objections overruled," Solomon announced, quite judicially.

"I don't understand," Dr. Gold said. "Mr. Lassiter, aren't you the defense lawyer?"

"It's complicated." I turned back to Solomon. "You asked the ultimate jury question. Why? You don't need the expert to answer it, and only an idiot would ask it without prepping her. You have enough to get to trial, or at least you did before you muddied the water."

"Just give me a moment," Solomon said. "I'll clarify the question."

"How? You're a loose cannon, and you're firing at your own troops!"

"I guess Wrong Way Lassiter would know."

"Jerk off!"

"Jake, settle down," Victoria ordered. "You're overreacting."

I banged the table again, harder, and a lobster tail fell from the tiered tray. "Carla Caruana deserves better than you, Solomon. And so does Victoria."

"Better law partner or better mate?" Solomon fired back.

"Both!"

"Ha! There we have it! The truth comes out."

"Please slow down," the court reporter pleaded. "I can't keep up."

"Go off the record," I ordered her.

She lifted her hands from the keyboard with a dainty motion of a classical pianist finishing a concerto.

"And delete everything in the record from the moment Mr. Solomon said, 'Now, Dr. Gold.'"

"I can't do that, Mr. Lassiter," Mary Ortega replied, eyes widening. Obviously, litigation on the American Riviera hadn't prepared her for Miami lawyers.

"I'm ordering you to," I said.

"It's against our rules."

I stomped around the table. Grabbed the paper from the steno-graph tray and unfolded several pages filled with the magic shorthand indecipherable to the untrained eye. "There," I said. "Is that where Mr. Solomon started his brilliant line of inquiry?"

"No." Her hands shaking, Mary Ortega leafed back a few more pages. "There," she said.

I ripped off the pages and crumpled them. "I should make you eat these, Solomon."

He got to his feet. "You want to try? I'm a jock, too!"

"Anytime, Solomon. It won't be like stealing bases in college."

"You're demented, Lassiter. It's your brain Dr. Gold should be dissecting."

Melissa Gold looked at me and said, "Mr. Lassiter, I don't understand. Why are you so upset? Just what is your goal here?"

"Truth! Justice! Redemption! It would take too long to explain."

I jammed the crumpled pages into my suit pocket. I could light them on fire later. "Let's go back on the record and wrap this up."

The court reporter's fingers flew back to the keyboard.

"I have nothing further at this time," Solomon said.

Victoria said, "Your witness, Mr. Lassiter."

I realized I was still standing, towering above the others. I lowered myself into my chair and looked at my legal pad. There were a dozen pages of notes, a few doodles, and a reminder to buy air conditioner filters when I got home.

My eyes shifted to Melissa Gold, and she held my gaze. I didn't say a word. Neither did she. I could hear people splashing in the pool below us. I broke eye contact and watched a pair of seabirds land on the patio, hoping for crumbs from someone's club sandwich. I looked back at Dr. Gold, who cocked her head and raised her eyebrows, waiting. I knew what I wanted to ask but wasn't sure if I should. Maybe she would sandbag me. If she did, it could be worse than what Solomon just went through.

Oh, what the hell.

At long last, I said, "Only one question."

"Fire when ready, Mr. Lassiter," she said.

"Dr. Gold, will you have dinner with me tonight?"

-35-

Truth, Justice, Redemption

T he dynamics of the three of you are fascinating," Dr. Gold said.

"How do you mean?" I asked.

"You're on the opposite side of the case, but you seem to be helping Solomon and Lord. At the same time, you and Mr. Solomon appear to hate each other."

"No way, Dr. Gold—"

"Melissa."

"Melissa, I love the guy."

"You're being sarcastic."

"Not at all. He's the kid brother I never had. The smart aleck who goes out of his way to irritate me. When I try to teach him things, he's so damn stubborn, he fights every suggestion."

"What you call suggestions probably sound like orders to him."

"You *have* taken some psychiatry courses, haven't you?"

We were sitting outdoors at the Lark, a restaurant in Santa Barbara's Funk Zone, a gentrifying neighborhood of trendy bars, wine-tasting rooms, and art galleries in what had been an industrial area. We had walked about a mile from the Biltmore on a path along the ocean, enjoying the breeze and watching the shadows of the palm trees lengthen in the setting sun. A slice of the moon glistened, white as silk in the darkening sky. The early evening had turned cool, but a fire pit near our table gave off a warming glow.

I knew why I had asked Dr. Gold to dinner, but I had no clue why she'd accepted. There were two reasons on my part. First, I wanted to get away from Solomon and Lord. I've always been the third wheel in that party, and after my yelling match with Solomon, I needed time and space. Second, Melissa Gold was an intelligent and attractive woman. I am, after all, a guy. A battered and bruised gladiator, loser of several winner-take-all romantic contests . . . but still, until the day I die, a guy.

I wrapped my right paw around a heavyweight old-fashioned glass, which conveniently held an old-fashioned, a perfect combo of rye, soda, and bitters. Melissa was drinking a hummingbird. With pink grapefruit juice and foamy egg whites on top, it looked like a girlie-girl drink, but a jigger of gin made it the real deal.

"Before we walked over here," Melissa said, "I had a little chat with Victoria Lord in the restroom."

Oh, brother. Women chatting in restrooms. Men never have a clue what they say but always fear the conversations are about them, generally highlighting their many shortcomings.

"She's worried about you," Melissa said.

"No reason to be," I said.

She sipped her drink through a straw that drilled a hole in the egg whites. That bought a moment for her to decide what to say. "Victoria told me you're having severe headaches and blurred vision. Perhaps some disorientation. She also says your outburst at the deposition was very uncharacteristic."

I thought about covering it up, hiding under bravado. But for once I answered honestly. "I can be loud, but ordinarily I'm under control. Today I was on the verge of losing it. I was about a second away from tossing Solomon over the wall and onto the beach."

"Is that the first time you've entertained thoughts of that kind?"

Once I started telling the truth, it was difficult to stop. I took a deep breath and rolled the dice. "Actually, the other day I considered throwing an ex-client off his balcony, and it's a high-rise building. Seems my crazy self has a fixation regarding bodies and heights."

She measured her words as carefully as if weighing diamonds. "I find that somewhat frightening."

"Scares me a bit, too."

"What's beneficial is that you recognize you're having difficulty with impulse control."

"But each time I've resisted the impulse."

"So far, Jake. So far. May I ask what prompted these thoughts?"

Her tone was calm, cool, and clinical. I thought it best if I followed her lead.

"The ex-client is a murderer who went free because of me. I'm not gonna kill myself, so that left him. I guess my subconscious saw it as my only path to—"

"Truth, justice, redemption."

"Exactly."

"But logically you must know that an act of vigilante justice cannot be redemptive."

"Of course. But I don't always do what's logical."

Melissa made a *hmmm* sound. I'd just confessed to a crime I hadn't yet committed, and she was concerned. Who wouldn't be? Before she could cross-examine me any further about my homicidal tendencies, I said, "What else did Victoria tell you?"

"You were supposed to undergo neurological testing back in Miami, but you didn't."

"A few days ago, I got my bell rung sparring with the State Attorney. The same day I ran headfirst into a sea grape tree. One or the other probably gave me a concussion, but it's no big deal. I've been concussed a lot of times over a lot of years."

"Beginning when?"

"High school. In those days, the trainer would break a smelling salts capsule under my nose, and I'd run back into the huddle rather than inhale the ammonia."

"Have you had post-concussion syndrome before?"

"Lots of times. And the symptoms always go away. I've just got to give it a few days."

Our server, a friendly and well-groomed young man named Patrick, brought crispy brussels sprouts and a beet-and-butternut-squash salad that was a riot of colors: bright orange, mellow yellow, and dark red. Patrick told us the provenance of every ingredient, right down to the name of the farmer who grew the beets organically just a few miles away, should we want to pay him a visit. Brussels sprouts, he told us, are cruciferous veggies, related to cabbage. This particular batch, mixed with dates for sweetness and lime for tang, was descended from a royal family of crucifers just down the road in Camarillo.

If foodie heaven were a condo, we just bought the penthouse.

Melissa speared a beet and asked, "What would you say was the most troubling symptom after your most recent concussion?"

"I got a little lost driving home a few days ago. Missed my turnpike exit. Then when I finally got off, I turned west instead of east."

"Disoriented?"

"I guess."

"How do you feel at this moment?"

"Happy to be here. With you."

"Be real now, Jake. Later you can tell me you like my eyes, or whatever."

She smiled at me. I smiled at her. And I did like her eyes.

"No headache. Vision clear. Some tinnitus."

"Can you describe the sound?"

"Are you familiar with the *1812 Overture*?"

"The cannon fire?"

"Plus the clanging chimes and the stirring brass flourish."

Melissa daintily patted her lips with a napkin. "I could perform some very simple neurological tests in the morning. Noninvasive and nonthreatening."

I drained my old-fashioned and signaled the world's most knowledgeable server for another. The rye, he had already informed me, was High West from Park City, Utah, and had fragrant notes of cinnamon and clove accented with vanilla and caramel. It sounded like an ice-cream sundae, but it tasted like damn good whiskey.

"Nonthreatening?" I said. "What do you think I'm afraid of?"

"You tell me."

I wanted to hang tough. I wanted to say, "Nothing scares me! So bring it on. Gimme some of that traumatic brain injury, I'll kick its ass."

But the real me answered. "Truth is, Melissa, I'm worried what a doctor might find. Every week, there's news about another former NFL player descending into dementia or committing suicide. And now I'm immersed in autopsies and diseased brain tissue in this case. Who wouldn't at least ponder what it all means?"

She held her head at an angle and studied me, a delicious warmth in those sun-flecked green eyes. "That was hard for you, wasn't it?"

"Nah. Didn't hurt a bit."

She raised her eyebrows, and I folded like a Boy Scout tent in a gale. "Okay, it was a little hard. But easier than talking to Solomon and Lord about it. Or Doc Riggs, my pal back in Miami."

"Why's that, do you suppose?"

"I don't want to burden my friends. I'd rather help with their problems. But why I'm opening up to you, I have no idea."

"Maybe because you know that we'll never see each other again."

That took me aback. "I hope that's not true."

"We'll see, won't we?"

It could have been an awkward moment, but just then we were saved by the smoked pork bellies. Patrick served the platter with a two-minute description of the smoking process, the roasted blackberries and almond brittle that formed the sauce, and the garnish of pickled peppers that Patrick didn't pick. The dish had nearly gone cold by the time he finished his recitation.

Melissa tested the pork belly with her fork and said, "Victoria didn't go into detail, but she implied you were upset about a recent murder trial. I assume that's the one that prompted your homicidal urges."

"That's the one."

"So you rue winning that trial, and you hope to lose this one?"

"Correct again."

"You have cognitive dissonance. You're plagued by the clash between the duties of your profession and adherence to your ideals."

"A little fancier than I'd put it, but the notion is right."

"With perhaps a dash of middle-aged angst."

"I'm only middle-aged if I live to be one hundred, but, yeah, that's right, too."

She held my gaze and said, barely above a whisper, "You are a very intriguing man, Jake Lassiter."

"And you're a great listener, Melissa. But you haven't told me anything about yourself."

Just then, Patrick delivered my garlic-glazed lamb shank and Melissa's gnocchi with Dungeness crab and chorizo. As we ate, Melissa filled me in. Grew up on the East Coast, fell in love with the West Coast when she took summer session classes at Stanford. Married during her residency to another physician. Divorced. No children. Loves her work. Worries day and night about athletes who suffer multiple concussions. Lately studies are showing potential brain damage in high school football players, increasing her alarm even more. Divides her time between research and teaching classes at UCLA med school. Has a condo near the beach in Santa Monica, and, yes, she's visited Miami. Wouldn't mind being shown around by a native. I allowed as how I was just the man to do it.

"What's living in Miami like?" she asked.

"It's not just beaches and nightclubs. University of Miami has a fine medical school. Wonderful faculty." I gave her my best crooked grin.

She smiled but didn't say she'd be packing her bags anytime soon.

"But truth be told," I said, "most of the year Miami is hot, wet, and buggy."

"You mean muggy?"

"That, too. But buggy. Gnats we call no-see-ums. Cockroaches we call palmetto bugs. And mosquitoes we call damn bloodsuckers."

"Sounds delightful."

I polished off another old-fashioned and was feeling a bit warm. My tinnitus was also picking up. The noise in my ears was in high reverb mode, something like the wall of sound of the Crystals' "Da Doo Ron Ron." The bass drum in my brain seemed to be competing with several tambourines. I squeezed my eyes shut, but that didn't help. Slowly a wave of heat at the base of my neck crept up my skull. "I think I'm going to step outside for a breath of air," I said, getting to my feet.

"Jake, we are outside."

I looked around. She was right, clever woman. Decorative lights were fastened to an overhead trellis of wood beams.

"Why is it so warm?" I asked.

"The air temperature is about fifty-eight degrees. Are we too close to the fire pit?"

I looked. The flames were turning from orange to blue and back to orange again. Above my head on the trellis, the lights seemed to be moving closer and ever brighter, like high beams on the freeway.

No, wait. The lights aren't moving. It's me.

I was tottering back and forth.

"Jake! Jake, are you all right?"

"Junior Seau . . . Frank Gifford . . . Earl Morrall."

"What? Jake, please sit down." .

"Mike Webster . . . Ken Stabler . . . Ollie Matson."

"Jake, can you hear me?"

"Andre Waters . . . Cookie Gilchrist . . ."

"Jake!"

"Jake Lassiter . . ."

I was aware of Melissa reaching out for me. But the lights were spinning as the names of the dead echoed in my brain. I tried to latch on to the edge of the table, but it spun in a circle like a merry-go-round. Get too close to the edge, and you are flung into space.

I toppled sideways, just as I did when Ray Pincher had decked me.

I heard Melissa call my name one last time, but her voice trailed off like a train whistle in the distance, and I lost consciousness just before I hit the deck.

-36-

Cottage Hospital

I dreamed of a football game played by dead men.

Not zombies. Nothing so weird.

The men were very much alive in the game. Young and strong and fast. In their prime, but even my somnolent brain knew they were dead now.

A fine mist covered the field, so it was difficult to make out the stadium, but it seemed to be the Orange Bowl, as long gone as the players. Earl Morrall, with his crew cut and square jaw, wearing a vintage Dolphins jersey, lofted a perfect pass to Frank Gifford, the golden boy, in a Giants uniform. Gifford juked past Dave Duerson, in Bears blue and orange, and sailed into the end zone, untouched. My sleeping mind mashed it all up, not caring about team rosters or eras. An all-star dream team all linked by brain damage caused by CTE.

The game went on for a while until a blast of sunlight hit me. I blinked, saw it wasn't the sun. A miniature flashlight aimed a beam into my left eye.

"Where am I?" I said.

"Cottage Hospital," Melissa Gold said.

"Quaint name. You sure it's not a bed-and-breakfast?"

"It's good to hear you make a joke."

"Not joking. I'm hungry."

"That's a good sign."

"How long was I out?"

"Really out, seven minutes. In the ER you opened your eyes, but you were not fully conscious. You were speaking, mostly incoherently, though some curse words were pretty clear. You became agitated and your heart began racing, so the chief resident sedated you. That was roughly fourteen hours ago."

"So it's Saturday morning." Thinking I had six days before the indictment was unsealed, I was arrested, and my life was sucked down the storm drain and straight into the sewer.

"About nine thirty a.m.," she said.

"And you? Last night?"

She gestured toward a chair by the window. Blanket. Pillow.

"You stayed here? Ah, jeez. I'm sorry."

"Don't be."

I straightened up in bed, and she fluffed the pillow behind my neck, like the attentive caregiver she was. "Aren't you missing the conference today?" I asked.

"It's fine, really."

"No, it's not. I haven't been this embarrassed since I was sixteen and took my date to the movies. I reached in my wallet for a ten-dollar bill and out flew a condom."

"For the record, I've been on the pill for twenty-five years."

"Good to know."

"How do you feel?"

I tried to straighten my left arm. *Ouch.*

"Sore shoulder," I said.

"It took the brunt of your fall. Better than your head. What else?"

"Headache's diminished. Maybe a two on a one-to-ten scale. No tinnitus, but that usually kicks up in the evening like most symphony orchestras."

She held her right index finger six inches from my nose.

"Follow my finger."

"I'd follow it anywhere."

She wiggled her finger right and left and said, "Eyes moving in tandem, smooth and coordinated."

She shined her little flashlight in my right eye, then took it away, shined it again in the same eye, while looking at the left eye. "Consensual response normal."

"Isn't there a better grade than normal? For a consensual response, I mean?"

"Open your mouth and say, 'Aaah.'"

"I've been doing that for doctors ever since I was seven. No idea why."

"Open!"

I complied and gave her my best "Aaah."

"Uvula rises straight and in the midline."

"I thought only women had uvulas," I said.

"Perhaps you're thinking of the vulva."

"Perhaps. I often do."

"The uvula is the little tissue hanging down from the middle of your soft palate. If you'd had a stroke, it wouldn't move in a straight line."

"You think I had a stroke?"

"I'm ruling it out before I schedule a brain scan."

She poked and prodded some more, jabbing little pins into my arms and feet, as if I were a voodoo doll. I kept worrying about the time. I'd missed the flight back to Miami. Now the goal was to make the red-eye leaving LAX tonight. So many worries. Marvin Fishbein likely selling me out on the campaign finance fraud. The indictment, already in Strychnine's sweaty palms. And just how was I going to get the dirt on the lady prosecutor in time to quash it?

Melissa Gold leaned over the bed, placed a hand on each side of my face, and gently held me a moment. At first I thought she was going to kiss me. Well, a man always hopes.

"Your face appears symmetric," she said in her purely professional voice. "Same amount of wrinkles on either side of your forehead."

"Wrinkles! They have Botox in this joint?"

She used a thumb to trace a line down my face, just alongside my nose. "Nasolabial folds are equal."

"Labial folds? Men have those, too?"

"The vertical lines that come down either side of your nose to your mouth. If you'd had a stroke, they likely wouldn't be the same length or depth."

"Okay, no stroke. Let's move on."

"Please try to relax, Jake."

"That brain scan you mentioned. Is it really necessary?"

"As you lawyers like to say, 'To a reasonable degree of medical certainty,' yes."

"Then let's do it. I need to get back to Miami."

"We'll do the scan tomorrow. At UCLA."

"I don't have time to wait. There's a legal matter at home. A ticking clock."

"What? Some brief you need to file?"

"Way bigger than that. Personal issue."

She waited for a more detailed answer. So far I'd been open with her, far more than was my custom. But how would she react if I told her there was a big, fat indictment with my name on it, ready to be unsealed? How would I even say it?

"Next Friday look for my perp walk on the evening news. Yeah, the big guy in the gray suit, hands cuffed behind his back."

I could tell Melissa I was innocent, but would she believe me?

Tired of waiting, she asked point blank, "Want to tell me about the personal issue? The ticking clock?"

"The wheels of justice—or rather *injustice*—are rolling like a runaway train. I need to derail the damn thing in the next six days."

She didn't skewer me for being so vague. Instead she said gently, "I hope you'll learn to trust me as we get to know each other."

"As we get to know each other."

I liked the way that sounded. As opposed to last night at dinner when she speculated why I seemed to be so open with her.

"Maybe because you know that we'll never see each other again."

A good lawyer listens carefully to the witness. Any change of tone or expression can be meaningful. The eyes can turn warm or cold. The mouth can harden into the blade of a sword or melt into a playful invitation. Right now Melissa Gold was reflecting interest and intimacy and care. And here I was, flat on my back, like an invalid, not the manly oak I liked to think I was. Okay, a manly oak with feelings.

"I do trust you," I said. "And I will be more forthcoming. It's a process, but I'm getting there."

Her smile was laced with the warmth of the midday sun. The day was looking up. I hadn't had a stroke. My headache was practically gone. I was feeling good about doing the brain scan. A clean reading could put all these fears to rest. And my lady physician might be interested in more than the movement of my uvula. In turn, I wanted to get to know her, too.

With those pleasant thoughts swirling in my mind, the door to my hospital room opened and Steve Solomon hustled in.

I must have been groggy, because I was happy to see him. It didn't occur to me that Solomon would do to my promising morning what the Garner twins did to Thurston's Jacuzzi . . . fill it with crud.

-37-

World's Worst Best Friend

Solomon tossed a bouquet of purple lilies—wilted and dry—onto my hospital bed. "Sorry I'm so late, Jake. How you doing?"

"Terrific. I have the best doctor in California. Where's Victoria?"

"Bringing the rental around. We've got a flight to catch."

"Sorry I can't join you."

"Damn, I'll miss you busting my balls for six hours."

"If all goes well, Mr. Solomon," Melissa said, "you'll have your friend back in a couple of days."

"Outstanding," Solomon said. "Say, Jake, I've been on the phone with Ray Pincher."

"Why?"

"The esteemed State Attorney was trying to reach you last night. When he couldn't, he tracked us down."

"Yeah?"

"Jeez, Jake. Why didn't you tell Vic and me you'd been indicted?"

Oh, shit on a stick! The one thing I hadn't told Melissa.

"Not now, Solomon," I warned.

"Indicted?" Melissa's eyes went wide. "For what, Jake?"

"Nothing. I mean, something. But I'm innocent. I'll explain."

"Jake, why didn't you tell me?" she persisted.

"I was going to. Really. But I was hoping I'd have it all cleared up first."

"Bribing a juror," Solomon said casually.

"Shut up, Solomon," I said.

"Bribery?" Melissa said. "That's serious, isn't it?"

"Actually, not a biggie," said Solomon, the world's worst best friend. "Clarence Darrow was charged with bribing a juror and probably did it. But the jury acquitted him. And Jake's got me as a lawyer. We'll get a big, fat NG."

"Without bribing anyone?" Melissa asked.

"Intriguing concept." Solomon had missed her sarcastic tone. "Bribing a juror in a bribing-a-juror trial. Want to hear my theory of defense?"

"No!" If I hadn't been in a hospital bed, I would have slugged him. "Stow it, Solomon."

"I wish you had told me, Jake." Melissa's voice was heavy with disappointment.

"I'm sorry," I said. "I'll tell you everything later."

"Brain damage!" Solomon sounded excited, maybe even happy. "CTE. We'll break new legal ground."

"I'll break your jaw!"

"Hell, it might even be real, which always makes for a better defense, right, Jake?"

"I mean it, Solomon. Shut up."

"You gave us the theory for Carla's case, and I can use it to defend you. How's that for symmetry. Or is it serendipity?"

"I don't need your help. I don't want your help."

"It's simple. Clean. Elegant. Dr. Gold can be our expert."

"This is going way too fast for me," Melissa said.

By now Solomon had fallen in love with his own voice. "Here's my closing argument. 'Whatever Mr. Lassiter did, he didn't know he was doing it. He's bonkers. Out of his mind. Hell, he might even be dying.'"

"Could I use the same defense if I kill you, Solomon?"

"Jeez, I didn't even ask you. Did you bribe that juror?"

With no weapon handy, I threw my pillow at him. He caught it and kept talking. Something about jury selection and how he wanted people with grievous diseases in their family history. I looked toward Melissa. She avoided my gaze, turned, and left the hospital room.

-38-

Hello Obit, Get Me Rewrite

The hospital on the UCLA campus was named after Ronald Reagan. Who died of complications from Alzheimer's.

Whose symptoms are eerily similar to those of chronic traumatic encephalopathy.

At the moment I wanted to win one for the Gipper.

I was in an imaging lab awaiting my brain scan. I wore one of those hospital gowns where your bare butt sticks out the rear. It's humbling. So was the ride to get here yesterday after checking out of Cottage Hospital in Santa Barbara. Melissa Gold did the driving. I'm from a generation where men drove the fast cars, shot the wild game, and branded the burly steers. I'm not used to yielding the steering wheel to a woman or baring my butt for hospital technicians.

I'm obsolete. Warranty expired. So sue me.

Yesterday, after Solomon had declared me a criminal defendant—albeit a legally insane one—Melissa had disappeared for a couple of hours. When she'd returned to my hospital room, she said she had walked to a nearby park and sat on a bench under an oak tree, thinking about her life. She believed that I had come into her life for a reason, though she didn't know what it was. She decided that I needed help but was too damn stubborn to get it, and maybe that was fate's motive in bringing us together.

"I'm going to help you," she said, "whether you like it or not."

"I like it," I replied.

On the drive to Los Angeles, I'd told Melissa everything. I wish I had done it sooner. She listened patiently and restrained herself from scolding me. She asked all the right questions, meaning they were sharper than those pins she used to check my nervous system response.

"You say you didn't bribe that juror," she said as we drove along the ocean near the coastal town of Ventura.

"I swear that's the truth."

"But you admit unethical contact with him?"

Ouch. The doctor as cross-examiner.

"Yes. Speaking with a juror outside the courtroom is flat wrong. No excuses."

"Have you ever done that before? Tried to curry favor with a juror."

"Nope."

"Why do you suppose you did it this time for a client you didn't like and you hoped would be found guilty?"

The question rocked me, and I didn't have an answer. "I don't know. Seems irrational, doesn't it?"

"It's the product of the cognitive dissonance we talked about at the restaurant. You have an irreconcilable conflict between your duties as a lawyer and your ideals."

We both stayed silent for a few moments. Outside the car windows, a train was barreling along, the Pacific Surfliner, also headed toward Los Angeles. We were making better time in Melissa's Lexus.

"Yesterday you mentioned that you thought about killing your client," she said. "Did you really plan to go through with it, or was it just a fantasy?"

I wanted to lie. I wanted to say it was just a harmless daydream. But in my experience, you don't lie to your doctor or a woman who interests you—in this case, both. If you prevaricate, prepare to die two different forms of death.

"I planned it. Thought it out. Then when I had the chance to shove Thurston off his balcony, I didn't do it."

Sounding as if I wanted a gold star for exercising admirable restraint.

"Why didn't you?"

"Maybe I don't have the guts. Maybe I just chickened out."

She thought that over a moment. "Be introspective, Jake. Was it lack of guts? Or did your notions of right and wrong, or for lack of a better term, your morality, keep you from killing the man?"

"Lately I've been having moments of intense anger. On that balcony with Thurston, I wasn't thinking about right or wrong. I wasn't thinking at all. I was just on fire."

"On fire," she repeated as if I'd said something important or troubling.

"And I can't promise it won't happen again."

"It's as if the wires of your impulse control mechanism burned out, and that concerns me, given what we know of your history of head injuries."

She was speaking in a neutral professional tone, the way they must teach them in med school. As opposed to saying, "The reason you're behaving like a psychopath is that you're dying from an incurable brain disease." But the softness of her measured words still frightened me.

Again we were both quiet. There was just the hum of tires on pavement, the brilliant blue sky, and, to our right, the ocean waves skittering toward shore.

"You think I'm ill," I said just as we hit the outskirts of Oxnard. "From a traumatic brain injury."

"I really don't know, Jake."

An RV towing a Jeep swerved from the slow lane into ours, and Melissa hit the horn.

"You haven't been diagnosed," she continued, "but as you are aware from the Carla Caruana case, irrational violent actions are often hallmarks of CTE."

"Then let's get the damn test going," I said.

* * *

With my butt peeking out of the hospital gown, I signed the required consent and disclosure forms for my encounter with positron emission tomography. The paperwork informed me that the radiation probably wouldn't kill me, but who knows? Also an accidental overdose could cause my testicles to shrivel into BBs. Okay, it didn't say precisely that, but I can read between the lines.

Melissa stayed in the waiting area outside the imaging lab. She promised that the radiologist—a colleague—would immediately decipher the findings. She brush-kissed me on the lips, and her eyes brimmed with tears but didn't shed a drop.

"I'll be fine," I told her.

"I know."

She turned around and didn't watch me walk into the imaging lab, which was kept at a temperature suitable for storing sides of beef. A technician injected a radioactive tracer into my arm, and we waited a bit for it to find my brain. Then they put me into a machine with a large doughnut hole for my head. The equipment buzzed and clicked and did its magic while I stayed as still as possible. I've had a bunch of MRIs, so the test was no big deal. Maybe that's why I felt sleepy, listening to those odd mechanical sounds.

With my eyes closed, my mind wandered. I wondered if there might have to be some changes to my obituary. I imagined a sympathetic article because of my tragic death. Perhaps with a flattering picture of me in uniform. Helmet off, sideburns and mustache on, and that cocky grin so many barmaids found semi-irresistible.

Life—or death—was looking up:

Jake Lassiter, a former Miami Dolphins linebacker and veteran trial lawyer with a reputation for courtroom theatrics, died yesterday in his sleep after a long battle with chronic traumatic encephalopathy.

Don Shula, who coached Lassiter, remembered him as "a guy who gave one hundred percent of his limited abilities. He was a heckuva hitter who would sacrifice his body as if it were somebody else's."

Thanks, Coach. Looking back, this wasn't such a bad life. Growing up barefoot and poor, but never hungry, in the Keys. Catching a mess of snapper in the Gulf in the morning, grilling them at night with Granny's homegrown okra and eggplant. Somehow, on the path to becoming just another redneck smoking Camels in a double-wide, I got a decent education and moved on. Played football for Joe Paterno and Don Shula, two legends who made me a better person off the field. And as much as I whine about the tilted scales of the justice system, I've had some thrills exonerating the innocent along the way.

Regrets? I've had a few. Unlike Sinatra, *not* too few to mention. But I didn't want to dwell on them now. My eyes grew heavy, and I was smiling as I dozed off, thinking that through it all, I stood tall and did it my way.

-39-

Of Mice and Men

I watched Melissa Gold speaking to the radiologist through a window in the lab.

Wished I could read lips.

But I can read expressions. Disappointment isn't that hard to read.

A moment later Melissa entered the room where I waited, my big-boy pants back on.

"I was afraid of this," she said.

"What? Give it to me straight."

"Oh, I shouldn't have put it that way. All I meant . . . I was hoping for more clarity, but the results are not conclusive."

"Jeez, for a second there—"

"I'm sorry. I deal with so few living patients, I'm afraid my bedside manner is lacking."

"So what is it?"

On the speakers, a calm voice announced, "Code blue, room seventeen-twelve." Someone was in cardiac arrest, and it wasn't me. Yet.

"As I told you before, the only one hundred percent certain diagnosis comes from an autopsy."

"That's where I draw the line. No autopsy."

"When we're looking at actual brain tissue through a microscope, it's far different from seeing magnetic images, which are pretty much shadows of the tissues themselves."

"I won't relent. No autopsy."

She ignored my jittery and lame attempts at humor. "First, your brain does not appear to have the distinctive tangles of tau protein that would indicate active CTE."

"'Does not appear.' You're hedging."

"As I said, it's not conclusive."

"Okay, what's the rest?"

"Walk with me," she said. "My office is in the adjacent building."

We headed out of the maze of the building, following one of those yellow lines that does not lead to the Wizard of Oz.

"You have some misshapen tau that cannot be called tangles. At least not yet."

"Misshapen? Tangles? What's the difference?"

"We've done experiments with mice, intentionally giving them concussions, then examining their brains. Before they develop full-blown brain injuries, they form misshapen tau protein. Consider it a precursor to the fibrous tangles. The misshapen tau disrupts neuron function and spreads through the brain."

"Turning tau into tangles," I said.

"Yes, with the resulting brain damage we call CTE."

"Are you telling me I have the brain of a mouse?"

"Your scan reveals misshapen tau in the folds of the frontal lobe."

"But not full-blown CTE?"

"The best we can determine, you have a precursor to the disease. We can't be certain of the progression because there's no clear line between the misshapen tau and the fibrous tangles. We're in a gray area, no pun intended."

I let that sink in. I hadn't even noticed, but we were outside, the sidewalk packed with students, all sneakers and jeans and backpacks. Many hurried along at a quick pace, probably fueled by caffeine, this generation's uppers. Few, I suspected, were pondering their own mortality. Why should they?

Me? Thoughts of death, and not a pretty one, crowded out everything else. A sudden image. My nephew, Kip, at my funeral. Who would toss the ball with him? Who would teach him the hazardous art of being a man?

Like so much of life, I thought, *my diagnosis is uncertain.* When the alarm clock awakens us, none of us knows that particular day will be our last. I was hoping for some kind of certainty—*you're dying or you're well*—but instead I got the gray area.

"I need to get home," I said. "Maybe I can take the red-eye tonight."

She didn't miss a beat. "I'm going with you, Jake."

"Why? It's not like I need an attendant."

She leveled her gaze at me. "Is that how you regard me?"

"No. I respect you as a physician, hugely. And I'm indebted to you for the diagnosis, grim as it is. I'm also a man, and I'm attracted to you. Big-time. But let's just say this doesn't seem like a great time to start a long-term relationship."

"I have something shorter term in mind."

"Okay?"

"We've been experimenting with injecting protein antibodies into mice with traumatic brain injuries. The antibodies bind to the misshapen tau, which is then destroyed by the body's mechanism for clearing waste. It stops tangles of tau from ever forming."

"Mice again!"

"It's not approved for humans."

"Which is why I'm a prime candidate?"

"Not approved as a course of treatment, but if you'll sign the consent forms, basically agreeing that this might kill you, we can do it on an experimental basis."

"Sounds like a great deal."

"There are no protocols, no templates, no prior studies I can rely on. I'll inject you once a day with very small doses of the antibody and monitor you. Every four weeks, we'll scan your brain. And we'll be quick to modify procedures, depending how you respond. You'll be relying on my instincts more than anything else."

"I trust your instincts, and like I said before, I trust you."

We stopped just outside the entrance to her office building. She reached up and placed her hands on either side of my face, just as she had done when testing me for neurological deficits. But this time she kissed me. And I kissed her back. Soft and slow, oblivious to the flow of people on the sidewalk.

"We'll see," Dr. Melissa Gold said. "We'll see how good my instincts are."

PART FOUR

"So much of the time we are just lost. We say please, God, tell us what is right, tell us what is true. There is no justice. The rich win, the poor are powerless. We doubt ourselves. We doubt our beliefs. We doubt our institutions. And we doubt the law."

—Closing argument delivered by Paul Newman in *The Verdict*, script by David Mamet, adapted from Barry Reed's novel

-40-

The Everlastingness

On Monday morning in soggy, sweaty Miami, Melissa injected my butt with the magic elixir. The unapproved, experimental, only-to-be-used-on-mice antibodies intended to stop CTE in its tracks. In the afternoon she took my vital signs and a blood sample. Then she spoke on the phone with a neurologist she knew from the convention circuit. He was a big deal at the University of Miami School of Medicine and could arrange for a series of brain scans. Plus he had a brain study of his own he wanted to discuss with Melissa. She seemed excited—brains and nervous systems did that to her—but she didn't want to say more until she met with the guy later in the week.

Of course, later in the week, I could be booked into county jail. Friday was the first day to file for the election. The day Ray Pincher always filed. The day Stacy Strickstein planned to smear him by arresting little old jury-briber me. Yeah, the same guy who supposedly solicited illegal cash campaign contributions for Pincher.

A leads to B, which leads to C, which lands me in jail and Pincher out of a job and maybe under indictment, too.

It was such a wickedly clever plan, I almost admired it. I still had no plan to derail Strickstein, and the clock was ticking ever faster.

Visitors came to the little coral rock bunker on Poinciana. Social calls maybe. Or to pay their respects to a dying man. They didn't say.

Victoria Lord and Steve Solomon dropped by, bringing a Key lime pie with a graham cracker crust and whipped cream. Victoria asked how Melissa and I were getting along. There was a lilt to her voice, as if asking if there was any monkey business after the medical business. Alas, no. I had invited Melissa to use the spare room, but she politely declined and was staying at a hotel in Coral Gables.

Solomon said he needed a written report attesting to my brain damage. It would help him defend me in the bribery case. I told him I didn't want his help. He persisted, prattling on, claiming we would make legal history.

As if that were a good thing.

"You remember the mafioso Vincent Gigante?" Solomon said, "They called him the Oddfather."

"Sure. He was a boxer before he became a gangster. When he got old, he wandered around lower Manhattan in his bathrobe, mumbling to himself."

"That's him. His lawyers claimed he had dementia, a slick move to dodge a racketeering charge. So I figured you'd show up at your arraignment in an old Dolphins jersey, calling out defensive signals."

"Didn't Gigante die in prison?" I asked.

"Details! Always the petty details with you."

Solomon and Lord hustled off to their office to prepare for the summary judgment hearing in the *Caruana* case, which was coming up tomorrow. I hadn't yet done my preparation, either. It's not easy to plan how to fall on your sword gracefully.

Doc Charlie Riggs parked his muddy pickup in the driveway, toddled inside, and talked medicine with Melissa for an hour. Then he pulled me aside and said, "She's a keeper, Jake." The last time he'd said that, he was referring to a giant grouper he'd pulled from the waters off Lower Matecumbe Key.

"A keeper," I said. "As a doctor or a woman?"

"Are you blind? Both!"

"No progress on the woman part, but I have faith in her doctoring."

He winked at me. "Use your famous charm on her."

Yeah, right.

Melissa Gold wasn't a Miami Dolphin cheerleader, and I wasn't the cocky mustachioed guy in the old team photo I hoped would run with my obituary. Time weakens the body and also the spirit. And the cocksure yet inane belief that a smile, a hello, and a cocktail will open the door to a woman's heart as well as her apartment. I had lost a hefty slice of my confidence along with my brain cells.

* * *

Around dinnertime, with Doc Riggs napping in the hammock out back, Melissa and I sat at the kitchen counter as Granny buzzed with excitement at having a visitor in the house.

"We had a doc down in Islamorada made house calls," Granny said. "Or was it Key Largo? Can't remember. I may have a case of water on the brain."

"More likely moonshine in your belly," I said.

"Hush, Jacob! Anyways, Dr. Gold, I'm pleased you come all the way from California to have supper with us."

Pronouncing it *Cal-ee-foyne-I-ay.*

"I'm happy to be here, Ms. Lassiter," Melissa said.

"Call me Granny. Or Jane, if you're more comfortable with it."

"Your name is Jane?" I said.

"Hush up!" Granny turned back to Melissa. "I'm just pleased to see Jacob bring home a gal who's not a shady lady, a trashy hussy, or what do you call it, a femme fatale."

Pronouncing it *fem-ee fat-towel*.

"Melissa is my doctor, Granny," I clarified.

"Better than that gal who shot her husband," she persisted.

"*Allegedly* shot her husband."

"Nothing *alleged* about the bullet hole between his eyes."

"Okay, Granny. What's for supper?" Trying to change the subject.

"What's it look like?" She pointed to the kitchen sink, where a three-foot-long carcass of an iguana lay belly-up, its tongue sticking out.

"Ah, jeez, Granny."

"Doctor, why do you suppose no gals ever stuck?"

"I'm not sure I know what you mean," Melissa said.

"Stuck with Jacob. He ain't bad-looking. Got a sit-down job with air-conditioning, so he don't stink up the house. Got victuals on the table and a roof over his head. But he falls like a ton of turds for the fractured ones."

"Fractured?" Melissa said.

"Granny, I'll slice the veggies," I offered. Anything to get her off the subject of my miserable personal life, as seen through her eyes. "Is that pot boiling yet?"

"The birds with the broken wings," Granny went on. "Like he's gonna fix all their problems and, meanwhile, they got nothing to give him. They're just users, some downright wicked. Once their wings are fixed, poof! They fly away. Except for the ones who go to prison."

"Ah, jeez, Granny."

But she wasn't done. "A parade of faded beauty queens, gold diggers, and strippers who just need a helping hand to straighten out their lives."

"Is that true, Jake?" Melissa asked. "You're not attracted to women of substance? You go for the needy ones?"

"Ancient history. I made mistakes in my youth."

"Jacob's youth must have lasted till his hair started turning gray," Granny added.

"But now I know what I've missed," I said in my own defense. "The mutual commitment between equals. The sharing. The everlastingness, if that's a word."

"It's a word, Jake," Melissa said. "A very good word."

"Dr. Gold, I hope you brought your appetite with you." Granny plopped the iguana carcass, skin and all, into the boiling water. The lizard was so long, Granny had to use a spatula to push it into a circle, where it looked as if it were eating its own tail.

Melissa's eyes widened and her mouth dropped open, but she managed not to scream or even gasp. Professional training, I supposed. She watched as the churning water propelled the dead iguana around the pot in endless circles.

"Found this big bugger sunning himself in the driveway," Granny said. "Brained him with a frying pan. Doctor, you like fresh iguana?"

"Never tried it." Melissa shot me a sideways glance. "What's it taste like?"

"Not like chicken." I continued slicing potatoes and carrots for the stew. "More like a chewy piece of rawhide."

Granny reached into the boiling pot with a pair of tongs. The skin of the dead reptile slid off like a pair of baggy pants.

"I'm not actually that hungry," Melissa said. "Jet lag probably."

"Me neither," I said. "We'll grab a bite later."

Thankfully Doc Riggs helped Granny devour the iguana stew. Then they headed for a walk down Le Jeune to the Gables Waterway. I figured they intended to play kissy face—and heaven knows what else—in the little park along the canal.

Relieved of the requirement of eating roadkill reptile, I took Melissa out for stone crabs at Captain's Tavern, an old fish joint on Dixie

Highway, then drove to her hotel in the Gables. We took the elevator to the ninth floor, and I walked her to her room.

Standing outside the door, we kissed. A long, slow, deep kiss. And then another. And one more.

"Jake, would you—"

She stopped, so I finished her sentence. "Like to come in? Sure."

"I was going to say, 'Would you forgive me for not inviting you in?'"

"Ah, I misread the situation."

"No you didn't. I just need to take my time . For now, let's just keep it professional. And anything else, we'll move slowly. Is that okay?"

"No problem." That wasn't entirely honest, and, wanting to be true to my new philosophy of openness, I quickly amended. "Okay, a small problem. I'm finding myself thinking about you at all times of day and night. Especially night."

"Slowly, Jake. Okay?"

I considered my options, of which there was only one. "Okay," I said.

We kissed again, and she closed the door.

* * *

I was heading south on Ponce de Leon when my cell rang. Of course, it would be Melissa, telling me to hang a U-turn and dash straight to her room.

"Hey there, beautiful," I said cheerily.

"Jake? That you?"

A man's voice.

"Yeah, who's this?"

"Marv Fishbein. Jake, I'm sorry, fellow, but I'm gonna have to drop the dime on you."

"Even if you could find a pay phone Marv, it would cost you fifty cents."

"Not funny, Jake. That prosecutor offered me a deal, and that means flipping on you."

"Marv, come to my house. Now. I'll be on the porch in the back with a bottle of Jack Daniel's. Let's talk it over."

"I'll give you the courtesy, Jake. But my mind's made up. I can't do time. I got no choice. I gotta pin it all on you."

-41-

Just Say It!

A male peacock with an eight-foot train of turquoise-and-green feathers waddled across my backyard, screeching in the direction of a female, who was rooting around in Granny's bed of pink begonias. It was mating season, and the screech was the equivalent of a millennial guy offering champagne to a millennial gal at the Fontainebleau's trendy nightclub, Liv.

I was sitting in an Adirondack chair on the back porch, the night air thick with honeysuckle and whiskey, the former from the lavender bougainvillea, the latter from my tumbler of Jack Daniel's. I was barefoot, wearing sweatpants and a tattered Penn State football jersey, number fifty-eight. A late thunderstorm had managed to cool the temperatures, and the evening was almost tolerable.

My headache, dormant through much of the day, had returned, a steady beat of *ka-boom, ka-boom, ka-boom-boom*. My temples throbbed in time with the drum and bugle corps that must have taken up residence in my ear canals.

Just before midnight I heard a rustling at the side of the house, and in a moment, there was Marv Fishbein, pride of Harman and Fox, still in his lawyer's blue suit, white shirt, and burgundy tie, knotted just below his double chin.

Fishbein mumbled an embarrassed hello and took the chair next to me. Wordlessly I poured him a drink. I didn't ask if he desired ice because I didn't have any. If he wanted whiskey, he'd have to drink it neat. I am not the perfect host, particularly when my guest is threatening to put me in prison.

"I'm sorry about this, Jake," Fishbein said. "I got arrested for DUI, and my big, stupid mouth got us in trouble."

"Got *you* in trouble."

"Stacy Strickstein has been leaning on me hard to give you up."

"What broke first, your back or your vagina?"

"Ease up, Jake. It may all work out. I've been talking to Strickstein."

"Without a lawyer?"

"I am a lawyer."

"No, Marv. You're a rainmaker who hustles clients at the Bankers Club. You're a golfer who can't break a hundred. And a million years ago when you *were* a lawyer, you busted unions on behalf of companies that fired women for getting pregnant."

"Point taken. But before the night is out, you're gonna thank me. Hell, you're gonna owe me."

"I'm listening."

"On the way over here, Strickstein called me with an offer. I couldn't believe it, but we can save both our asses."

"I'm still listening."

"Easy peasy, Jake. All you gotta do is say under oath what you did."

"What did I do?"

"You know. You can say it to me."

"You first, Marv."

"You asked me to bundle cash for Ray Pincher's campaign."

"Cash? Really?"

"And you said Pincher promised to deliver the courthouse bond issue to the firm."

"Two problems, Marv. I didn't say either of those things."

"You don't have to be coy with me, Jake. Just say it, and I'll confirm the conversation. I'll admit delivering the cash in return for the bond work. Strickstein will give us both immunity and indict Ray Pincher. That's the sweet deal I worked out."

I stayed quiet.

"It is, after all, what happened."

Putting that clunky footnote on what he'd just said.

"Just say it, Jake. Just say it to me."

"Your needle is stuck, Marv."

"What?"

"You remember vinyl, Marv? Records. Turntables. Hi-fi."

"Sure."

"You're a record with a stuck needle. How many times are you gonna go, 'Just say it'?"

"I don't catch your point."

"You're no good at this, Marv. I'd say you're the gang that couldn't shoot straight, but really you can't even load the gun."

"Don't know what you mean, Jake. All you gotta do—"

"I know. 'Just say it.'"

I unfolded myself from the chair, stretched my back muscles, and towered over Fishbein, who was still seated. "Why you wearing a suit coat tonight?"

"I like being dressed."

"Aren't you warm?"

"Not that bad tonight."

"Oh, it's gonna get a lot hotter before you leave."

I grabbed him by the lapels and pulled him to his feet. He was heavy, but a bowl of Jell-O would have given more resistance.

"Hey! Jake, what the hell?"

"Face it. Serpico you're not."

I patted him down. Nothing in the armpits or the small of the back. Ran my hands up and down his legs. Nothing. Smacked his balls with the back of my hand out of frustration.

"Ouch! Jesus, Jake!"

"Where is it? Where's the wire, Marv?"

"I don't know what you're talking about."

From somewhere in the bougainvillea, a peacock screeched.

"Take off your jacket," I ordered.

He did, and I examined the buttons. No mics, no cameras. Then I noticed his belt.

Brown imitation leather. Not so spiffy with his Italian light-wool blue suit. I unsnapped the belt and pulled it out of the pants' loops. Solid silver-plated buckle. On close examination, it wasn't solid at all. There was a tiny lens on the outside and a compartment perhaps one-quarter-inch thick on the inside. I clicked a small button, and an SD card popped out.

"Any transmitter?" I asked.

He shook his head, looking ashamed. "It only records."

"So Stacy Strychnine isn't in a van parked over on Loquat, listening to us."

"No. I'm supposed to deliver the belt to her office in the morning."

"Have you given her a statement yet? Anything implicating either of us?"

"No. Despite what I told you, I hired a lawyer. I'm not stupid. My lawyer asked what she was looking for. The stuff I told you, that was it exactly, except for the deal."

"You get immunity, and I go to jail along with Pincher, right?"

His stricken look gave away the answer. "I'm sorry, Jake. I was desperate. Pincher is her main target. You're secondary but still a target. She's got it in for you, but it's my fault. I was salivating over that bond issue. So I bundled cash from my partners plus friends like Cye Frick."

"The insurance company guy? You put him at risk, too."

"And others. Strickstein wants to sweat them out of me. But most of all, she wants you. I was supposed to trick you into confessing to something you didn't do. Convince you she didn't care if you were dirty, as long as you flipped on Pincher." He dropped his head into his hands. "And I caved. Dear God, I'm ashamed of myself."

The anger was welling up inside of me, a ball of molten lava in my chest. I wrapped the ugly brown belt around my right fist. Measured the distance to Marv Fishbein's chin, readied a punch that would leave him eating through a straw. Felt the blood pounding in my ears, the headache cleaving my skull. Through the fog my brain was telling me that Fishbein's shattered jaw would relieve the pain.

Tears welled in his eyes. "Jake! Jake, are you gonna whack me? Feed my bones to the gators in the Glades?"

I dropped my fist and laughed. Realized that I couldn't hit this poor schmuck. Remembered what Melissa told me about my illness and bouts of violence. I had aimed the punch at the wrong target. It was Strickstein and Thurston and that lying juror and my pal Pincher and the whole damn system that had let me down.

"Marv, there's a seven a.m. flight to Nassau. Be on it."

"The Bahamas? Why?"

"So Strychnine doesn't have you brought to her office, where she'll browbeat you into saying—and signing—whatever shit she makes up."

"You think I'm weak, don't you?"

"We're all weak in our own way. Just spend a few days on the beach. Don't answer your cell unless it's me. I'll let you know when it's safe to come home."

"What are you gonna do?"

"The only way to beat this is to destroy Strychnine."

"You can do that, Jake?"

"It's her or me, Marv. By high noon on Friday, one of us is coming out on the other side, and one of us is as good as dead."

-42-

One-Way Ticket to Palookaville

I should have been going after the lying juror.

I should have been working to clear my name.

I should have been digging up dirt on Stacy Strickstein.

But I had to be in court at 1:30 p.m.

Life, John Lennon famously said, is what happens to you while you're making other plans. Now that I think of it, Lennon, that wizard of words and music, probably wasn't the first. There's an old Yiddish proverb, "Man plans and God laughs." Probably every culture has a virtually identical aphorism.

With those notions swirling in my addled brain, I walked into a sixth-floor courtroom of the downtown courthouse, prepared to do as little as possible in defense of Biscayne Life Insurance Company. I gave a tight, professional nod to Steve Solomon and Victoria Lord, who were unpacking their briefcases at the plaintiff's table. Then I sneakily smiled at Dr. Melissa Gold, who sat in the first row of the gallery behind them. She was a spectator, the sole occupant of the rooting section for the plaintiff.

Cyrus Frick, my client's general counsel, sat in a pew in the second row of the gallery, sweaty and anxious. "Jesus, Lassiter! There you are. Hearing's in three minutes."

I plopped down beside him. "Judge Duckworth always runs late. Especially after lunch."

"Drinking problem?" He licked his lips.

"No, she has an English bulldog named Bruno she keeps in chambers. Walks him at midday."

"You know your way around the courthouse, Lassiter. I like that."

"As the old saying goes, a good lawyer knows the law. A great lawyer knows the judge. Or in this case, the judge's pooch."

He chuckled a little more than absolutely necessary. The man was wired tight. Maybe he'd missed his usual three-martini lunch.

"Where's your file?" Frick asked. "You don't even have a briefcase."

"Don't need one." I pointed to my head. "It's all in here."

"Oh, dear Lord."

There would be no testimony today. At a summary judgment hearing, all that matters is the written record. The sole question for the judge: Do the affidavits and depositions create any issues of fact so that the case should go to trial? The motion filed by the insurance company before I hopped aboard argued that there were no such issues, and everybody should go home. Or, in the language of Ye Olde Common Law, the "Defendant shall go hence without day."

I wanted to lose the motion but not so flagrantly as to be disbarred. I didn't want to be Marlon Brando's Terry Malloy, who could have been a contender instead of punching a one-way ticket to Palookaville.

My mind raced as the seconds ticked away to the hearing. Dr. Gold would probably diagnose me with a case of cognitive dissonance, billiard balls ricocheting inside my head, denting my skull, as I argued with myself:

"Hey, Lassiter old pal, you really planning to take a dive? Ain't like you."

"I'll carry my sword into battle. I just might not swing it."

"Speaking of swinging swords, you want to sleep with the lady doctor."

"True but irrelevant."

"You should be ashamed. Playing footsie with the opposition's expert."

"I've got a higher calling than just winning."

"There is no higher calling. The Florida Supreme Court was right about you. You're not cut out to be a lawyer."

"Truth. Justice. Redemption. That's my credo."

"Who you trying to fool? I know you. In fact, I am you."

"Shut up, me."

"You can't do your job because you might have the same disease as Carla Caruana, and you feel for her kids."

"Hey, I'm only human."

"Ha! Your greatest failing as a lawyer. Carla Caruana is the enemy. But you're feeling empathy. Her ghost has Stockholm syndromed you."

Finally the other me shut up, and I took inventory of the courtroom. The judge was not yet ensconced on her throne. Below and to the front of the bench, a court clerk was sorting files, and the court reporter was setting up her stenograph machine.

The courtroom door opened, and Frick wheeled around. A city cop peeked in and then departed.

"Where's Marv?" Frick said. "He should be here by now."

Ah . . . Marvelous Marv.

I'd spoken to him an hour earlier. On the lam, he was poolside at the Atlantis in the Bahamas. Accepting no calls except mine.

"Marv can't make it," I said.

"Why the hell not?"

"He needed some R and R."

"Now?"

Just then the bailiff, a retired sheriff's deputy with a bowling-ball paunch, entered the courtroom through a rear door behind the bench. "All rise!" he commanded, and Judge Melvia Duckworth hurried in, black robes flowing. She was an African-American woman in her late fifties who had served as a captain in the US Army, handling courts-martial as a JAG lawyer. She could be stern but was always fair and, unlike most of our judges, had a playful sense of humor. More important, she had never jailed me for contempt, as so many of her brethren had. Today she wore a filigreed jabot at her neck. It was shocking pink rather than the snowy white that most female judges favored, making them look like Methodist bishops.

The clerk cleared her throat and announced, "The estate of Carla Caruana versus Biscayne Life Insurance Company. Defendant's motion for summary judgment."

I bounced up, passed through the swinging gate, winked at Melissa Gold, and stood at attention as if ready to break into the national anthem. Cyrus Frick followed me. He had filed the original defense papers and was now listed as cocounsel.

"Is the plaintiff ready?" Judge Duckworth asked.

"We are, Your Honor," Solomon and Lord chanted in unison. Sometimes the kids are so darned cute.

"Is the defendant ready?"

"Ready. Willing. And able," I said.

"First time I've seen you representing an insurance company, Mr. Lassiter," the judge said. "Have you moved downtown and joined the power elite?"

"Shaping up to be a brief excursion, Your Honor."

"And who's that nervous-looking fellow next to you?"

Frick buttoned his suit coat. "Cyrus Frick, Esquire." He cleared his throat and in a deep voice, intoned, "General counsel of Biscayne Life Insurance Company."

"You make that sound like chairman of the Joint Chiefs. Welcome to court, Mr. General Counsel."

The judge opened the slim pleadings binder. "Give me a moment to skim the paperwork. As you were, soldiers."

We remained standing, though our postures relaxed a bit. Except for our little group, the courtroom was empty. The ancient air-conditioning cranked away noisily, costing taxpayers a bundle and turning the courtroom into a meat locker. At least no one would fall asleep. After several moments, the judge said, "I see Mr. Frick wrote a rather extraordinary denial of coverage letter. 'Perhaps the little dears are better off without their pill-popping, muscle-brained, tattoo-parlored, cage-fighting holy terror of a mother.'"

"I can explain that, Your Honor," Frick said.

"Don't bother."

"An unfortunate combination of alcohol and prescription drugs—"

"Stow that along with your rucksack, Mr. Frick!"

Cyrus Frick opened his mouth, then wisely closed it before emitting so much as a squeak.

"At ease, all of you," the judge ordered, sounding very much like the army officer she once was. "In fact, take a load off and sit down."

We all took our seats, and the judge continued reading quietly. Another few moments passed, and she said, "The issue on summary judgment appears to have changed. Originally the question was when the suicide occurred. Now it's whether there was a suicide at all. Is that correct?"

"Yes, Your Honor," Victoria said.

"On the money," I chimed in.

"In a deposition," the judge said, "Dr. Melissa Gold, a neuropathologist, asserts that an autopsy of Ms. Caruana reveals traumatic brain injury to such a degree as to deprive her of the ability to consciously form the intent to commit suicide. Is that the plaintiff's case?"

"In a nutshell, Your Honor," Victoria Lord said.

Judge Duckworth turned to me and issued an order. "Mr. Lassiter, on your feet. It's your motion. Argue it!"

-43-

Fight or Flight

I stood and stretched my neck, which was too thick for my dress shirt. I shot a look at Melissa Gold, who gave me a little smile. I wanted her to be proud of me. I wanted to do justice.

"May it please the court," I began, just as lawyers have done for a few hundred years. Then I paused. I had been ready to be pummeled and then take a knee. But something odd happened. From the time I was nine years old, playing tackle football with no pads or helmets on a field strewn with cracked seashells, I'd always wanted to win. Desperately. Sometimes viciously.

To win!

Isn't that the purpose of every game? Now my competitive instincts kicked in, just as they had in the Thurston trial. My conscious brain wanted to lose, but my subconscious wouldn't let that happen. *Yes, Melissa Gold, that damn cognitive dissonance.*

"Mr. Lassiter?" the judge prodded me. "Would you be kind enough to report for duty?"

"Yes, Your Honor," I said. But I didn't seem to be able to begin my argument.

I thought about Jake LaMotta, the middleweight brawler immortalized by Robert De Niro in *Raging Bull*. The mob had ordered LaMotta to take a dive against Billy Fox, and LaMotta readily agreed, even placing a bet on his opponent. Yet when he came out in that first round, he landed some sharp jabs that turned Fox's eyes glassy.

The primordial instinct kicking in? What else could it be?

Coming to his senses, probably afraid the mob would kneecap him, LaMotta basically quit fighting in the fourth round. His intent to lose was so laughably obvious the boxing commission suspended and fined him. The Florida Supreme Court would hammer me even harder.

"Mr. Lassiter, if it's not too much trouble, argue your damn motion." The judge sounded irritated.

The same genetic code—fight or flight—had me in grips. Like LaMotta, I was a slugger, too.

"Your Honor, Ms. Caruana took every step necessary to commit suicide—the ingestion of excessive alcohol with a lethal dose of drugs—prior to midnight on the three hundred and sixty-fifth day of the policy. This was not an accident. As evidence of her intent, there is the suicide note. Therefore, if the court rules this was a suicide, the motion must be granted, and the case is over."

So far I was playing the game by the book.

"Agreed, Mr. Lassiter. The court rejects plaintiff's original notion that the suicide did not occur until death the following morning. But what about the argument that Ms. Caruana lacked the mental capacity to form the intent to commit suicide? That's the meat and potatoes here."

"For the plaintiff to survive our motion, Mr. Solomon and Ms. Lord must win two issues. Fail on either one, the motion must be granted."

I was still throwing jabs without landing anything that stung.

"First, Your Honor must rule that the law recognizes the disease Dr. Gold calls chronic traumatic encephalopathy."

"And why wouldn't I, Mr. Lassiter?" the judge asked.

"No such disease appeared in the medical literature until Dr. Bennet Omalu's article in *Neurosurgery* in 2005. It was controversial then, admittedly accepted by most today."

"Most, Mr. Lassiter?"

"Jerry Jones, owner of the Dallas Cowboys, disputes its existence."

"And his medical qualifications are what?"

"He's had a face-lift."

"Thank you for your candor, Counselor. The court recognizes the existence of the disease. What's the second issue the plaintiff must win?"

"The harder one. That the disease destroyed Ms. Caruana's mental capacity."

Notwithstanding the crack about Jerry Jones, I was still doing the job for which I'd been paid. Whoring for the insurance company.

"I've read Dr. Gold's deposition," the judge said. "Does the defense have any testimony from physicians to contradict her testimony?"

"Your Honor, I made no attempt to hire the quacks the NFL paid off to dispute the solid research done by Dr. Gold and her colleagues."

"Biting the hand that used to feed you, Mr. Lassiter?"

"Just being truthful with the court."

Even an insurance company harlot can occasionally be candid. It helps establish credibility so your more outlandish arguments won't be laughed out of court.

"Appreciated," the judge said. "But you've just been digging foxholes. Where's your artillery, Mr. Lassiter? What's your argument on the medical issue?"

"I'm getting there, Your Honor."

"Let's hear it. Just why should I rule that there is a no jury issue as to Ms. Caruana's mental capacity and your client is entitled to summary judgment?"

Ah, so it comes down to this. Sure, I'd been flicking jabs, but now I either had to throw a left hook with some power behind it or trip over my shoelaces and fall to the canvas. I knew what I wanted to do. I just didn't know if I could do it.

-44-

What Is Justice?

Judge Duckworth waited patiently for my argument. I stood next to the defense table. Two feet to my left, Cyrus Frick was perched on the edge of his seat, a vulture on a power line.

At the plaintiff's table, Victoria was her usual self. Posture perfect, hands folded in front of her. Next to her Solomon was slouched in his heavy chair, a sardonic grin in place. Behind them, in the first row of the gallery, Melissa's head was cocked at an angle. She was studying me as if I were a fairly interesting subject in a scientific experiment. She seemed to be wondering just what I was going to do.

Me, too.

For several seconds, the only sounds were the wheezes and clanks of the AC. Finally I turned toward the bench and said, "What is justice, Your Honor?"

"In my courtroom, whatever the hell I say it is," the judge shot back.

"Your Honor, I was speaking rhetorically."

"Ah. Sorry to interrupt your flow. Feel free to start over."

"What is justice? Is it the exclusion of a person's rights? Is it the sleight of hand that lawyers sneak into contracts? And where do we find justice? In the boardrooms of banks and hedge funds and insurance companies? Or in a mother's heart?"

"Lassiter!" Frick tugged at my coat sleeve. "What are you doing?"

"Let go of me," I whispered, "or I will knock all the bleached teeth out of your filthy mouth."

"What!"

"And then I'll see that you're indicted for slipping cash to Ray Pincher's reelection campaign."

His jaw dropped open, and he let go of my sleeve.

"Marv told me everything," I said. "If you don't keep your trap shut, you're going down."

It was partly true. Marv had told me about Frick's cash contributions. But I wasn't going to rat out Frick or anyone else. I just figured he had a spine as stiff as a slice of flan, and my threat would keep him quiet.

So yeah, I had finally decided.

I'm going with my heart and my innate sense of justice, and damn the consequences.

I turned toward the bench and repeated my refrain. "What is justice? Is it the cold, stern unforgiving language of legislators and lawyers? Or is it empathy?"

"Empathy, Mr. Lassiter?" The judge raised her eyebrows.

"It's become a big word in my life."

"I'm happy for you. But could you tie that term to the issues on summary judgment?"

"Please bear with me, Your Honor. One morning after taking over this case, I was making breakfast for my nephew, Kip. Scrambled eggs with ketchup and sliced mangoes. I had just watched a video put together by the insurance company investigators in this case."

"That's work product!" Frick hissed at me.

239

I leaned close to him. "Indictment! You and Fishbein can share a cell. Or you can shut up now."

Frick clammed up, and I continued. "The video included a television interview with Carla Caruana. She slurred some words, and her eyes were unfocused. Everyone thought she had a drug and alcohol problem. But she'd recently suffered the latest of several concussions. She had post-concussion syndrome. And we now know, something far worse, chronic traumatic encephalopathy, which would have killed her sooner or later. The video contained scenes from Carla's most recent fight. She took a kick to the face that dislocated her jaw. The camera froze on that shot. Jaw misaligned, sweat flying off the strands of her ponytail, eyes squeezed shut in pain. Now, I'm thinking about Carla as I'm making breakfast for my nephew in the comfort of my kitchen, sun streaming through the windows, the tangy aroma of mangoes in the air."

"Mr. Lassiter, I'm having difficulty seeing the relevance of all this," the judge said.

"I promise to tie it up, Your Honor. The interview was conducted two days before Carla Caruana bought the life insurance. Knowing that, watching her, seeing her love for her children, I thought I could read her mind. She knew her job was terribly dangerous. Consider the term itself. *Cage fighting.* It even sounds lethal. Gladiators battling to the death. But cage fighting was the only way she had to support her children. The father of her children had deserted her. She was the sole support, the sole family, for Elizabeth and Joshua.

"She already sensed the frailty of her battered body and bruised brain. On this particular morning, she was likely nursing a wicked headache that would plague her until her death. She feared for her children, should anything happen to her. So she bought the life insurance policy, believing my client would protect her children financially if she was gone. She did what I would have done for my nephew, what any of us would have done for our loved ones.

Should the court not feel empathy for this woman and her children? Should Biscayne Life Insurance Company not feel empathy? Under the law, a corporation is a person. Today both Mr. Frick and I are the flesh-and-blood embodiments of that corporation. Should we not feel empathy?"

Judge Duckworth raised the palm of her hand to stop me. "Mr. Lassiter, have you gotten turned around again? Are you running to the wrong end zone?"

"I don't think so, Your Honor."

"Might I remind you that you represent the insurance company?"

At the defense table, Frick squirmed in his seat but kept as silent as a mourner.

"Alas, Your Honor, I do."

"Yet your argument, if it can be called that, seems to be a stream of consciousness about the decedent's hard life and good intentions."

"I'm adopting a style of litigation called humanistic lawyering."

"Frankly, I've never heard of it."

"Honestly, I just made it up."

"No wonder. Humanistic lawyering is an oxymoron, in conflict with the adversary system." The judge sighed and swiveled a full 360 degrees in her high-backed chair. When she stopped spinning and faced me again, she said, "I always enjoy having you in my courtroom, Mr. Lassiter. Most lawyers pad in here on kittens' feet, meowing and hoping to be petted. You burst through that door like a brass band. You even wake up my bailiff. But today? I don't know what to say. I would hate to see you hit with a malpractice suit or worse."

"I'll take my chances, Your Honor."

"As you are well aware, Mr. Lassiter, the Ethical Rules require a lawyer to zealously represent his client. Should I quote the provision?"

"I know it by heart, Your Honor. 'Zealous advocacy is not inconsistent with justice.' I've always thought that was such an odd

PAUL LEVINE

phrase. It doesn't say that zealous advocacy is consistent with justice, does it?"

"But until today, you didn't need to be reminded which side you're on. What's happened to you?"

"I started asking myself the question, 'What is justice?' I was hoping to learn the answer today."

The judge shook her head at me, a teacher pestered by a quarrelsome student. "The courtroom is no more the place to find justice than the battlefield is the place to find peace. We resolve disputes here. That's all we do. Now, please concisely state the best reason you know that I should grant your motion for summary judgment."

"As long as we're talking about the Ethical Rules, I'll have to rely on number four-dash-three-point-one."

"Let's hear it, Counselor."

"It states that a lawyer shall not assert a position 'unless there is a basis for doing so that is not frivolous.' I can't controvert Dr. Gold's testimony because anything I say would be frivolous. CTE is the black lung of football. It's the NFL's industrial disease, and Dr. Gold's findings are irrefutable."

"Junk science!" Cyrus Frick leapt to his feet, unable to contain himself. I'd miscalculated. Not even the threat of indictment could keep him bottled up. "The connection between head trauma and CTE is the handiwork of ambulance chasers, publicity hounds, and the sleaziest elements of the plaintiffs' bar! I ask Your Honor to strike Dr. Gold's deposition in its entirety and sanction Mr. Lassiter for his malfeasance, malpractice and . . ."

"Malapropisms?" I suggested.

"He's a menace!" Frick declared. "I demand you sanction him!"

"You demand!" Judge Duckworth seemed to levitate a few inches off her chair. "Mr. Frick. Did you say you *demand*?"

"For God's sake! What kind of freak show are you running here, Judge?"

Judge Duckworth banged her gavel, an explosion that echoed through the mostly empty courtroom. "Stand down, Mr. Frick! Or would you like to visit the brig?"

"No, ma'am." Frick slunk back to his chair and seemed to shrivel into a smaller self.

"Mr. Frick, you don't demand anything in my courtroom. You ask. You plead. You beseech. Second, don't use the Lord's name as part of your argument. She won't help you. Third, you will address me as 'Your Honor,' not 'Judge.' Am I clear?"

"Yes, Your Honor," he squeaked.

"Good. For the moment, we'll put aside Mr. Lassiter's conduct. As cocounsel you have the right to be heard. Now, can you point to anything in the record to contradict Dr. Gold's deposition testimony?"

Frick stood up rather cautiously, as if afraid to become a larger target. "I'm not prepared for that. Mr. Lassiter's negligence prevents me from making a cogent argument. We move for a continuance, and I hereby ask Your Honor to remove Mr. Lassiter from the case."

"Too late for all that. You hired Lassiter. He's your soup sandwich, and you're stuck with him through today's hearing. Fire him tomorrow if you wish. Now, sit down."

Again Frick folded himself into the second chair at the defense table.

The judge still held her gavel. She aimed it at me and said, "Mr. Lassiter, wrap up your argument, such as it is."

"In summary," I said, "to grant our motion, Your Honor would have to rule that all the science is wrong. You would have to declare that Dr. Bennet Omalu's studies are wrong. Dr. Ann McKee and Dr. Robert Stern's studies at Boston University are wrong. The University of Toronto's studies of cage fighters are wrong. Dr. Gold's research findings are wrong. All the peer-reviewed articles in respected journals are wrong, and Mr. Frick is right. In other words, Your Honor would have to rule that the Earth is flat. In conclusion, I respectfully ask that you deny our motion for summary judgment."

The judge stayed silent a moment, scribbling a note on a legal pad. Then she said, "Thank you, Mr. Lassiter. I hope this is not the last time you appear in my courtroom." She cleared her throat. "Given the state of the record and the argument, I have no choice but to deny the defense motion. Before I set the case for trial, has the plaintiff cross-moved for summary judgment on liability?"

Whoops.

Solomon and Lord shot looks at each other.

"No, Your Honor," Solomon said. "We didn't anticipate the possibility that you might—"

Victoria Lord bounced to her feet and stood as still as a tree, spine straight, hands on her hips. In body language terms, she was Amy Cuddy in power pose, a look that commanded our attention. Victoria was not satisfied with just surviving the defense motion. Now, picking up the judge's cue, she sought victory. "Your Honor, the plaintiff moves, *ore tenus*, for summary judgment on liability. We have a valid insurance policy with no remaining impediments to coverage. The question now isn't who wins, but rather how much?"

The judge turned toward me. "Mr. Lassiter, any objection?"

"None I can argue without blushing."

"Son of a bitch," Frick fumed under his breath.

"Very well. The court enters summary judgment on liability in favor of plaintiff on the policy and also rules that the denial of coverage was in bad faith, as defined by Florida law. See my assistant for a trial date on damages. Mr. Frick, do you understand the posture of the proceedings or are you again suffering from an unfortunate combination of alcohol and prescription drugs?"

"I see the handwriting on the courtroom wall," he said glumly.

"A jury will assess damages on bad faith after reading your denial of coverage letter and listening to your explanation, should you wish to give one. My advice is that you ought to bring your client's checkbook to the trial, or perhaps sooner. I don't usually press lawyers to settle, but if you asked me, I'd say that a multiple of ten times the policy might be a good place to start."

I was always lousy at math, but those digits popped up in my brain's calculator. Five million bucks.

Cyrus Frick was already on his feet, heading for the courtroom door. At the defense table, Steve Solomon and Victoria Lord hugged each other. Melissa Gold winked and smiled at me. Losing in the name of justice was sweeter than winning for the sake of winning. I felt something fundamental about me had changed, but just now I didn't precisely know where it would take me.

PART FIVE

"He who fights with monsters should look to it that he himself does not become a monster. And if you gaze long into an abyss, the abyss also gazes into you."

—Friedrich Nietzsche, *Beyond Good and Evil*

-45-

I Bring Pain, Bloodstains on What Remains

I spent the next two days having needles stuck into my butt and blood drawn from my arm, courtesy of Dr. Melissa Gold. The medical procedures reminded me—not that I had forgotten—just how precarious our lives are.

A thread, I thought.

We are all dangling by a thread.

I still had not come up with a plan to bring down Strickstein and save my own hide.

On Thursday morning, I drank my coffee and tried to hatch a plan. Two cups of java, and still no plan. The *Miami Herald* had a small story buried deep inside . . . well, not that deep, the A section ran only eighteen pages, including ads for septic tank cleaning. The story was about the forthcoming local elections. There was speculation that "hard-charging prosecutor Stacy Strickstein" would challenge her boss Raymond Pincher for the state attorney job. First day to file papers to run was tomorrow.

Tomorrow!

The day my indictment would be unsealed, and I would be arrested. Full speed ahead for Strychnine's corruption probe. She would chop block me at the knees and clothesline Ray Pincher and crawl over our bodies to the top of the Justice Building.

My cell rang. George Gonzalez at Fisher Island Security.

Oh, crap. Now what?

"Clyde Garner is back on the property," Gonzalez said.

"How did that happen?"

"No one recognized him at the ferry station."

"Why the hell not?"

"We told the staff to be on the lookout for a truck with a Garner Tree Farm sign, but he drove onto the ferry in a pickup without any signage."

"Insidiously clever disguise," I said.

"Minimum-wage security on the perimeter," Gonzales said, sighing. "You think you could reach him, talk him into getting the hell out of here?"

"I can try. Did you call Thunder Thurston?"

"No choice. I alerted both Mr. Thurston and Mr. Drexler."

"And?"

"They both said they're armed."

Of course they were.

"And said something to the effect, 'Tell the old man to bring it on.'"

Of course they did.

They would be armed and trigger-happy. And drinking champagne, their breakfast juice. Cocaine was not out of the realm of possibility. I hung up, wondering how the hell this day would end without bloodshed.

* * *

Clyde Garner's cell phone went straight to voice mail, as I'd figured it would. So I saddled up and, with my brand-new canvas top yanked down on this warm, moist morning, I aimed my old Eldo north on Dixie Highway. Took the flyover to the MacArthur Causeway to the Fisher Island ferry station. Once off the boat, I drove straight to Thurston's high-rise tower.

Three security cars were parked out front, blue lights spinning. Two uniformed guards who should have been home collecting Social Security flanked the entrance to the building. Walking briskly, I nodded as if I knew them and they must certainly know me, and one opened the door and waved me inside. Fortunately for Fisher island residents, I was not a suicide bomber.

I punched in the private elevator code, and in a moment I was stepping into Thurston's penthouse, where I was greeted with girlish squeaks and squeals. Four young women were playing volleyball on the sand court in the living room again, two to a side. Just as before, one team wore bikini tops, the other bottoms. Alongside the usual ice buckets with Cristal and the silver tray with the mountain of cocaine.

A gunshot startled me.

And then another.

The volleyball players were unperturbed. A lanky bare-breasted woman attacked the net, leapt high, and spiked the ball, which may or may not have nicked the end line.

"Kill!" she yelled.

"Out!" one of her opponents yelled back.

Arguing ensued.

I made my way past the court to the open door to the balcony. Outside the morning was bright and soggy hot, but with a whisper of wind from the ocean. On the marble tile: a cooler filled with champagne. Five empty bottles nearby.

Thunder Thurston held a twelve-gauge shotgun, Jelly Bean Drexler a Glock nine-millimeter handgun. They stood at the railing, barefoot and bare-chested, wearing only shorts, aiming in the general vicinity of three terns headed toward the ocean.

There was a *ka-boom*, followed by a *bang*.

Shotgun blast, pistol shot.

No feathers were ruffled.

"Damn!" Thurston said.

"Shit!" Jelly Bean said.

I stepped onto the balcony, and Thurston wheeled around, shotgun pointed at my head.

"Whoa! Whoa!" I shouted.

"Shit, Lassiter. I thought you might be that old cracker, come to shoot me in the back."

"No worries, Thunder. There's a crack SWAT team surrounding the building."

He laughed. "Yeah, that's why we're armed."

"What's with the baggy khakis, Lassiter? You look like that asshole Michigan coach."

Thurston was right. Wrinkled chinos and a long-sleeve blue shirt. The Jim Harbaugh goofball look. "Only thing in my vast wardrobe that was clean," I said.

"Butt ugly."

"What you doing here, Lassiter?" Jelly Bean Drexler demanded, slurring his words. *Lash-i-ter.*

"Trying to make sure nobody gets hurt."

Drexler leaned over to grab a bottle of Cristal from the cooler. Either it was his bulk or his blood alcohol, but he stumbled and grabbed the railing to keep from falling. "I got my homie covered. Go home shitbag." *Shirt-bag.*

"Thunder," I said, "you might want to think about disarming your buddy."

"Screw you, benchwarmer," Drexler said.

"Jell, chill on the Cristal, okay?" Thurston said.

But Drexler was working his fat fingers to uncork a fresh bottle. He aimed the neck of the bottle at me but staggered just as his thumb popped the cork, which rocketed straight at Thurston and bounced off his forehead.

"Shit! Jell! That stung like a son of a bitch. Sober the hell up!"

"Ah'm fine, T."

Thurston's anger passed quickly. He grunted and said, "I gotta go inside and piss."

"We got a balcony," Drexler said.

"Downstairs neighbor complains."

"Piss on him, bro." Drexler laughed at his own stupid joke, his massive stomach jiggling.

"Gonna get one of the hos to bring you coffee," Thurston said, "then chase them out. Squawking like a flock of geese, distracting my aim."

"Cuban coffee!" Jelly Bean yelled after him.

Thurston entered the condo, hollering at the young women playing volleyball. The only words I could make out were "café Cubano" and "your skinny asses out of here." As soon as Thurston disappeared from view, Drexler hoisted the newly opened champagne bottle to his lips and chugged nearly half of it.

Just as he burped, my cell phone rang, and I fished it out of my back pocket.

"Put the cell down," Drexler ordered. *Shell down.*

"Why?"

The phone rang again.

"Put it back in your ugly pants!" He aimed the nine millimeter at me. "House rules. Balcony is for shooting, drinking, and screwing."

"And pissing," I reminded him helpfully.

"It's a no-phone zone."

"Says you."

"You want, I take the phone away and shove it up your ass."

I waved the ringing phone back and forth in front of his face. "Why don't you try?"

With his free hand, he swatted at the phone, but I flipped it from one hand to the other. "Jelly Belly," I taunted him. "Your fast twitch muscle fibers are a lot like your brain. Very, very slow."

The phone stopped ringing.

Drexler scowled and tossed his Glock into the cooler with the champagne. "Gonna crush your phone in my bare hands, shitbag, then do the same to your head."

"What? What did you say?"

"You heard me."

Yes, I had. I also remembered the grand jury testimony that Ray Pincher had given to me. Manuel Gutierrez testifying about the bribe.

Q: What happened when Mr. Lassiter came in the house?

A: He takes his cell phone, the burner, and crushes it in his bare hands. He's very strong. And he says, "Shitbag, this is your head if you tell anybody about our deal."

"It was you, Drexler! You bribed Manuel Gutierrez."

A cackle gurgled up from inside his enormous belly. "You just figure that out? Who's slow now?"

"Why, Drexler? Why the hell did you do it?"

He took another pull on the champagne. "'Cause T is my bro. I couldn't let him go down."

"But why the hell did Gutierrez say it was me? You put him up to that?"

"No way. I just told him what would happen if he punked on me."

"The cash with my fingerprints. How did you get it?"

"Your lazy-ass courier left it at the front desk in the lobby."

"Nice," I said. "You stole from your bro."

"Best twenty-five K of T's money he never knew got spent."

"You didn't tell him?"

"Not till after the verdict. I did my job, and you did yours, Lassiter. Just let it go."

"I can't. Thanks to you, I'm under indictment."

"I got nothing to do with that. It's the prosecutor railroading you."

"Right. And if Strickstein had introduced all the evidence, Thunder would have been convicted, and none of this would have happened."

"What evidence?"

"His texts to you. 'Bitch touch my chedda, feel my Beretta.'"

Drexler gurgled up another laugh and said, "I bring pain, blood-stains on what remains."

"Exactly."

"You think Thunder sent that gangsta rap to me?"

"Are you saying he didn't?"

"Notorious B.I.G., that's *my* man. *My* rap. Thunder's into Michael Jackson, Prince, all that crossover shit 'cause he think he's white."

"So you texted Thunder. Makes no difference. His defense, Stand Your Ground, was pure fiction."

"You right about that part. But you missing the bigger picture."

"Which is what?"

Again a laugh burbled up, and his cheeks waggled. "Because, you stupid-ass lawyer in ugly pants, Thunder didn't shoot Eva. I did."

-46-

Understanding Muck City

A brunette about six feet tall sashayed onto the balcony, delivering a pot of Cuban coffee, a bowl of sugar, and three espresso cups with tiny spoons on a silver tray. She wore a smile and a gold bikini top and no bottom. She had a Brazilian wax job.

Yeah, I looked. So sue me. I'm a guy.

"Hasta luego," she singsonged and slipped back inside.

A moment later Thurston emerged onto the balcony, just as Jelly Bean Drexler was filling his cup with two-thirds sugar and one-third *café Cubano*.

"Got a request, Thunder," I said. "Next time you're charged with a murder you didn't commit, tell your lawyer the truth."

He shot a look at Drexler, who was guzzling—not sipping—what could only be described as *azúcar con café*. If there were any justice in the world—and there's not—he would contract diabetes in the next ten minutes.

"Jell, what shit you been talking?"

"Lassiter be chill 'cause he know what happen to him otherwise."

Thurston grumbled something to Drexler that sounded like, "Always cleaning up your messes." Then he turned to me. "Lassiter, it's true that Jell shot Eva, but it was my own damn fault."

"Saved you millions in a divorce," Drexler said, with pride in his voice and a smile that creased his fat cheeks. I wanted to knock all his teeth out.

"Eva hated Jell and all his badassery," Thunder said. "Always saying he's stealing. He's an embarrassment. He's a gangsta gonna bring me down."

"So basically she told the truth," I said.

"Eva grew up on that big tree farm, never went to bed hungry. Never understood Muck City. Never understood me and Jell, our history. When we were kids, if one of us had enough money for a Coke, we'd split it."

"And if all our pockets were empty, we'd steal it," Drexler said.

"We were so poor, the Haitian cutters looked down on us."

"True dat," Drexler agreed.

"I could have forced them to make peace," Thunder said. "But I never did. Just sat back laughing as they cursed each other out. That last night they got into it, Jell was hitting the Colt 45 and Hennessy like some dumb-ass thug."

"I was wrecked," Drexler said.

"Eva grabbed that little kitchen knife and was screaming at Jell, 'That's the last time you call me a cracker ho, you fat black bastard.'"

"Offended my body image and my racial pride." Drexler smirked at me. "T's nine was sitting on the kitchen counter. I grabbed it and opened up on her. Five rounds."

"So you were never in fear for your life?" I asked Drexler.

"From that itty-bitty thing?"

"If Eva was waving the knife at you, how'd Thunder get cut?"

"How you think?"

"Not hard to connect the dots. Once Thunder decided to cover for you, he knew he'd have a better defense if he took a little slice out of his gut."

Drexler shrugged. "Tired of talking. Let's lock and load." He picked up his Glock and started jamming nine-millimeter shells into the magazine. Thunder, with more dexterous fingers, inserted twelve-gauge shotgun shells into the loading flap on the underbelly of his Mossberg 500.

"You took a helluva risk, Thunder," I said. "Taking blame, relying on Stand Your Ground."

"Newspaper said I was the third most popular athlete in the history of Miami behind Dan Marino and Dwyane Wade. Everybody in town has seen my commercials, and when I'm interviewed on TV, I'm respectful. Got no tats. I come out of the locker room in a shirt and tie. I got no crew, hardly any posse except Jell. I'm not—"

"A big fat black bastard." Drexler shook with laughter.

"Plus we had a deal, Jell and me. If I got convicted, he'd confess, overturn the whole deal."

"It doesn't actually work that way," I said.

"Drone!" Drexler wheeled toward the railing and fired off several rounds with the Glock, hitting nothing.

Thunder studied me a moment, cradling the shotgun. "We done with this subject, Lassiter. And that ain't a question."

He had lapsed into his Muck City diction. If that was supposed to scare me, it didn't work. Facing a possibly fatal disease tends to strip away your fears. The knowledge—and uncertainty—of my condition stuck with me every waking moment. I was ill. I had a "precursor" to CTE, according to the very smart Dr. Melissa Gold. At any time, a new brain scan could drop the word *precursor* in favor of *full-blown*, and my imaginary obituary would become real.

Want to shoot me, Thunder? Well, that's a quicker way to go.

I dug my knuckles into my forehead. The gunshots had kicked up my tinnitus. A heavy metal band was clanging inside my head,

Motörhead banging away with "Bomber." I squinted my eyes closed, and when I opened them, my vision was blurry.

"Just tell me one thing, Thunder. How did you buy off Stacy Strickstein?"

"Got nothing to say about that."

"She was seen with you right here after the trial."

"So what if she was?"

"Prosecutors don't make house calls on acquitted defendants. I figure you paid her to protect Jelly Bean and to frame me on the bribery charge."

"Why would I do such a crazy ass thing?"

"Because he's your badass dawg. Your fam. Your bro."

"Drop the gangsta rap. Ain't working for you, Lassiter."

"What about it, Thunder? How much did you pay Strickstein?"

"Got nothing to say. And there's nothing you or nobody else can prove."

"Drone!" Jelly Bean hollered again. "Damn thing's circling the building."

Both men swung their weapons—Thunder's shotgun and Jelly Bean's handgun—over the railing and started firing at the drone, a white contraption with four small propellers. It looked about mosquito-size as it rounded the building, out of harm's way.

"Damn! Gotta be TMZ or Gawker," Thunder said. "Bastard was hovering outside my bathroom window the other day. Everybody want a piece of the Thunder."

"Birds!" Drexler again, firing at a flock of gulls. So far neither the bird community nor the drone population had suffered any decline.

My cell rang with the Penn State fight song, and when I answered, a male voice said, "Get the hell off the balcony, Lassiter. You're in my line of fire."

"What? Who's this?"

"I got Thurston in my scope," Clyde Garner said, "but if I'm eight inches off, I'm gonna blow a hole through your throat."

-47-

Silent Scream

No phones on the balcony!" Thurston yelled. "Take it inside."
Gladly.

I entered the condo, cleared of seminude volleyball players, and whispered into the cell, "Garner, where are you?"

"Snuggled under a pink bougainvillea. Needs fertilizer, something with iron in it."

"You're outside the condo tower?"

"Seventy-five meters from the base of the building. Got Thurston right in the crosshairs."

"Don't do this, Garner."

My tinnitus was roaring, and my headache had returned. It felt like one of Garner's steel-bladed garden rakes was digging deep into my skull.

"Haven't calculated wind speed," he continued. "And I'd have to do the math to figure my distance to the balcony."

"Are you listening to me?"

"The hypotenuse length squared equals the sum of the square of the length of the other two sides. They taught us that in sniper school. Bastard's moving a bit. Gonna wait till he stands still. I got all day."

"Put the rifle down, Garner."

I appreciated the irony. I was trying to save the life of the man I had planned to kill. But things had changed. Thurston might be a jerk, but he wasn't a murderer. Vigilante justice goes astray when you kill the wrong guy.

"Used to be deadly at eight hundred meters," Garner said. "But my M40 seems a helluva lot heavier than it was back in 'Nam."

I heard two gunshots and nearly dropped the phone. Realized it was Thurston and Drexler shooting at birds or drones or cruise ships, for all I knew. "Listen to me, Garner. Thurston didn't kill Eva."

"Bullshit!"

"Jelly Bean Drexler did. Thurston played me. Played the court. Played the jury."

"If I could make manure out of all the shit that comes from your mouth—"

"I'm not lying! Drexler killed Eva."

"I see him right now. Fat turd on the balcony. Big target."

"Garner, no!"

"You sure he's the one who pulled the trigger?"

"He admitted it. But please—"

"Should I blow out his aorta or his femoral artery?"

"They're waiting for you at the ferry station. You'll never make it off the island."

"I don't care."

"Eva wouldn't want this."

"Aiming for his femoral artery. Let the bastard watch himself bleed out, knowing he's gonna die."

A brave man would have rushed onto the balcony and pulled Drexler inside. A moral man would have summoned the arguments to keep Clyde Garner from avenging his daughter's death. But I am a foolish man, plagued by moral ambiguities. Part of me—a large part— wanted Garner to pull that trigger. Wanted to hear Drexler scream, maybe even watch a fountain of blood drench him as he lay dying. But I didn't want Clyde Garner to spend the rest of his life tending a potato patch at Raiford Prison.

"Hold your fire, Garner. I'm coming out."

"At your own risk, Lassiter."

I hustled onto the balcony. Looked over the railing, scanned the pool deck, the jogging path, the stand of palm trees, and a patch of pink bougainvillea. Saw the glint of Garner's scope in the glare of the sun.

"There!" Thurston pointed at a pair of red-tailed hawks that drifted lazily in the updrafts near the building. With their five-foot wingspans, they were a juicy target.

Ka-boom!

Thurston blew one bird out of the air with a shotgun blast. "Got him! Got him! I got him!"

The next several seconds passed quickly.

Thurston pumped the shotgun and swung the barrel toward the other hawk, now beating its wings to flee. Another blast, this one missing.

Drexler fired three rounds with his Glock at the same bird.

Miss. Miss. Miss.

If Drexler saw me move behind him, he didn't show it. I took a deep breath and exhaled a long blast. This would be like lifting a refrigerator three feet off the ground.

How will I ever get the leverage?

As the hawk neared the far corner of the building, Drexler leaned over the railing, half his massive stomach folded over the outside. Then he went onto tippy-toes.

Now! It has to be now!

I was never an offensive lineman, but I dropped into a three-point stance just behind him. Intended to drive block forward and add upward thrust. My feet at shoulder width, keeping my ass down, I fired out and up with all the power my legs and back could muster.

I lifted his feet off the marble tile a few inches, but his enormous butt crushed my right shoulder, and the vertebrae of my lower back crunched together. Damn, that was a high railing!

"Hey . . . what the fuck?" Drexler's voice soft, more puzzled than afraid.

For a split second, we were stuck there. My left knee shook and nearly buckled. Drexler's torso wobbled backward. I was losing my grip. If he fell, it wouldn't be over the railing. It would be on top of me.

"The hell you doing?" He showed no fear, didn't grasp the concept. Maybe he thought it was some locker room prank.

A few feet away, another shotgun blast. Thurston was looking toward open water, his ears doubtlessly ringing.

I managed a choppy step with my right foot, then my left, and surged upward and forward.

The tipping point!

Drexler toppled over the railing headfirst, arms flailing, mouth open. A silent scream. His eyes wide with unspeakable fear.

I glanced at Thurston, who was still peering toward the ocean, hoping for more prey.

We both heard the thunderclap. A 350-pound sack of cement hitting the travertine marble pool deck with a sickening splat. A sonic boom at this distance, an explosion of flesh and vessels, bones and organs in one cataclysmic second.

Then a woman's scream. A sunbather in a chaise leapt to her feet. She screeched a high-pitched wail and backed away from the body. A workman in a landscaper's uniform dropped his leaf blower and stood in place, paralyzed.

"Jesus! Jell! Jell!" Thurston turned the shotgun on me. "What'd you do?"

"Nothing! I was watching you shoot. He leaned over too far."

"No! Nooooooo!" Thurston wailed now.

"I reached out for him," I said. "But even if I'd gotten hold, no way I could pull him back."

"My poor mama."

I figured he meant "his" poor mama. Meaning Drexler's.

"My poor, poor mama." Rocking back and forth, pain rising from him like smoke from a furnace. "I told our mama I'd always take care of Jell," he said.

Our mama?

"You're brothers?" I asked.

"Half brothers. Different worthless fathers."

"Jell's my bro."

That's what Thurston had said when he fired me. I didn't realize he meant it literally.

"Brothers," I said. "For real."

"Straight-up real."

"I didn't know. I'm sorry, Thunder." And I was. For his loss. But I told myself if I hadn't done it, Clyde Garner would have. And the poor, grieving father of Eva Thurston would have been caught. Premeditated first-degree murder by hiding in wait. Death penalty eligible. Minimum penalty, mandatory life without parole.

I was waiting for it to hit me, some emotional shock wave because of what I had done.

Killed a man.

Sneakily. Stealthily. Not very damn heroically.

But I felt nothing. Except . . . surprise. First, that I did it at all. Second, that I felt no guilt. No shame. No remorse. No fear.

Maybe my brain had been fried by too many concussions. Maybe my moral center had been knocked off-kilter.

"Jell, you were always a screwup." Thurston talking to his dead brother now. "I was always the one to rescue you."

"You did everything you could for him," I said. "Your entire life. Nobody could ever say different."

"I let him down." Thurston's eyes brimmed with tears. "Let our mama down." He studied me a moment, shotgun still in his hands. "If I thought you pushed him over . . ."

We stood frozen there a moment. I searched my brain for a plausible story of an accident, some evidence that couldn't be questioned. Instead bits and pieces of a new death notice orbited my brain, all involving my own fall from the balcony. An article with the phrase "bizarre double homicide high atop a luxury condominium." I chased the thoughts.

"Thunder, even if I wanted to, there's no way I could have lifted Drexler off his feet. I'm too old, too broken down."

He seemed to accept it. Lowered the shotgun, looked down at the pool patio, where half a dozen people surrounded the body, a uniformed security guard pointing toward our balcony. Then Thunder Thurston began to sob.

-48-

Tricky Cop Questions

I had George Barrios on speed dial. The chief homicide detective of Miami Beach answered on the first ring. "The body still warm, shyster?"

Cop humor. Or very good instincts.

I told Barrios I had just witnessed a fatal fall, which was semitrue. He told me not to leave and not to touch anything. I already knew that.

The Miami Beach cop shop on Washington Avenue is only a little more than a mile from Fisher Island . . . as the crow flies. But Detective Barrios wasn't a crow. He had to drive south to congested Fifth Street, then fight his way onto the clogged MacArthur Causeway to the ferry station. And wait for the ferry.

I had told him to commandeer a police boat at the Miami Beach marina for a pleasant five-minute ride to the island, but he gets seasick on tiny boats. He said he'd see me in thirty minutes, at best.

Next I called State Attorney Ray Pincher. He was in his office in the Justice Building on the mainland. An even longer drive.

I spent a few minutes consoling Thurston, telling him several times that he was the best brother any thug could have. Okay, I didn't say exactly that, being a sensitive guy and all. I did advise him to clean up the piles of cocaine strewn around the apartment, and that kept him busy for a while.

My headache had miraculously subsided, but maybe I just couldn't feel it because my left knee was throbbing. I had twisted it with the final push that sent Drexler overboard. My knees do not respond well to any torque. I would need anti-inflammatories and maybe a painkiller before the day was out.

The crime scene techs were already on the pool deck by the time Barrios and a female plainclothes detective got off the elevator that opened into the condo's foyer. The female detective took Thurston into his den for questioning. That left me with Barrios in the living room. Standard procedure, separating the witnesses.

Barrios was within spitting distance of retirement age but still thick through the chest and flat of waist. He wore a lavender guayabera with white embroidered stitching. His shaved head was suntanned the color of café con leche. He looked at the sand volleyball court and said, "Some people got more money than they know how to waste."

Then I led him onto the balcony for my show-and-tell.

Show everything. Tell as little as possible.

"Why are you limping, Jake?" he asked as we stepped into the afternoon sun and ocean breeze.

"Tweaked my knee getting into the car this morning."

He studied my face with that skeptical detective look. "You oughta be more careful."

He took out his little cop notebook, counted the half dozen empty champagne bottles scattered on the tile, and scribbled something.

"Make sure they do a tox scan," I said. "You'll want Drexler's blood alcohol reading."

"No shit? I never would have thought of that." He peered down at the pool deck, where the medical examiner's crew was taking photos of the body and otherwise puttering around. "This Rashan Drexler. Would you say he was a friend?"

"I would say he was giant sack of protoplasm without a purpose."

"Are you always this grief stricken when you see someone die a horrible death?"

"Is that a tricky cop question?"

"You know me, Jake. Just asking in my polite way if you threw him off the balcony."

"It would have taken a forklift."

"So that's a no."

"No, sir."

"Did you have a beef with him?"

"No beef. No pork."

"Even though Thurston fired you and hired him as his agent?"

"Ooh, you are a good detective. Is this where I'm supposed to start crying and confess?"

"If you want."

"I figured Drexler would screw up the negotiations and Thurston would come running back to me, so, no, I had no problem with the guy."

"And your client, Mr. All-Pro? He didn't shove him, either?"

"Nope. He loved the guy."

"That's a pretty high balustrade," Barrios said, using the fancy word for *railing*.

It wasn't a question, so I chose not to answer. He whipped out a tape measure, crouched down, spread it out, then whistled. "Forty-six inches high, more than the building code requires. How the hell does a man fall over that?"

"Drexler was about six foot five. You might plug that into your computer."

"Would you say he had a high center of gravity? Like an NBA center?"

I shook my head. "His weight was in his midsection. Kind of like a septic tank."

"I'm gonna have to get a human factors engineer out here," Barrios said, "show me how somebody falls over that railing."

"My tax dollars at work," I said.

"Any chance Drexler committed suicide?"

"I don't think he ever planned that far ahead."

"That balustrade," he said yet again. "How the hell does somebody fall over it?"

"Life is full of mysteries," I said.

"There are four manners of death," Barrios said, as if I didn't know. "Natural, suicide, homicide, and accident. And you're sure it was an accident?"

"Drexler was inebriated and leaning over a railing two hundred fifty feet off the ground, trying to shoot birds out of the sky. I'd say you could close your notebook, but do what you have to."

He eyed me and kept quiet. Trying to see if I'd break eye contact or maybe start shaking and confess all manner of homicides, including one on the grassy knoll in Dallas.

"Anything else, George?"

"Nah. Just wondering why you don't spiff up your wardrobe. Those baggy khakis don't do you any favors."

I felt movement behind us. Just then Ray Pincher came onto the balcony, but he wasn't alone. Stacy Strickstein was tagging along.

-49-

All Fall Down

Detective Barrios said his hellos to the two prosecutors and good-bye to me. He wanted to go down to the pool deck and get a close-up look at the body.

"That's it, George?" I asked. "Aren't you going to say, 'Lassiter, I wouldn't leave town if I were you'?"

"Hell, no. I've been wanting you to leave town for years."

We've had this conversation before.

"An accidental death, and here we have the county's two top prosecutors," I said after Barrios left the balcony.

"You called me," Pincher said.

"And you don't get to decide if it's an accident," Strickstein said. "I'm chief homicide prosecutor."

"Chief, how do you handle that, when you spend all that time firing up the grand jury to railroad innocent people?" I asked.

"I won't dignify that with an answer," Strickstein said.

I hadn't seen her since she left the courtroom, glaring at me, after the Thurston jury returned its verdict. In the interim she still hadn't learned to smile. Strickstein was in her late forties and wore a perpetual scowl along with her no-nonsense charcoal pin-striped business suit.

"Sorry, Jake," Pincher said, "but this is Stacy's jurisdiction."

I didn't say anything because I was busy hitching up my baggy khakis.

"What's with those ugly-ass pants?" Pincher asked.

"I wear mostly blue. Blue suits. Blue jeans. Blue shirts. Not browns or khakis, but I found these in the back of my closet."

"More than I needed to know, Jake." Pincher peered over the balcony railing, or should I say balustrade. On the pool deck, two coroner techs were huddled over the messy remains of Jelly Bean Drexler. Maybe trying to figure out if they needed a stretcher or a vacuum cleaner.

"Turns out these old khakis are my only pants that go with a brown belt," I said.

"Okay, already. I wasn't asking to inventory your wardrobe."

I unbuckled the belt and slipped it out of the pants' loops. "This belt."

"Who cares?" Pincher said.

Stacy Strickstein cared. I watched her face. Her jaw fell slack, and her face reddened.

"I borrowed it," I said cheerfully. "Want to know who gave it to me?"

"That's government property!" Strickstein reached for the belt, but I pulled it away.

"Marvin Fishbein, the worst undercover informant since Jonah Hill in *21 Jump Street*."

"What the hell's going on?" Pincher asked, truly puzzled.

"So much. Oh, so much, isn't there, Strickstein?"

She stayed quiet, but her jaw muscles quivered. In Government Cut, a cruise ship with probably three thousand tourists aboard steamed toward open water. A week of prepackaged fun and midnight buffets awaited.

I turned the belt over and opened the compartment behind the buckle. "To make chain of custody clear, Ray, I'm handing you a disc with several separate conversations. First is Marv Fishbein, who says Strickstein tried to get him to lie under oath and trick me into doing the same."

"Ridiculous!" Strickstein said. "Mr. Fishbein will soon be indicted for campaign finance fraud, so his credibility is nil."

At the mention of campaign fraud, Pincher's eyes widened.

"We'll get back to that," I said. "Also on the tape, Jelly Bean Drexler. Just before his unfortunate fall, he admitted to killing Eva Garner."

"What the hell?" Pincher said. "Why did Thurston say he did it?"

"Because Jelly Bean was not the third favorite athlete in the history of Miami. And Thurston decided he couldn't let his bestie go to prison. A bestie who happened to be his half brother."

"No harm, no foul," Pincher said. "Thurston was acquitted and Drexler's dead. Except . . ."

"Except Thurston committed perjury by claiming under oath he killed his wife," I said.

Pincher shook his head. "What a legal conundrum."

Across the narrow cut, in South Pointe Park, I could see several young people playing Frisbee football. An older guy on a recumbent bicycle pedaled past them. On the grass sunbathers spread out on beach towels. Everyone there was having more fun than the three of us.

"Ray, I've only scratched the surface," I said. "Drexler also admitted he's the one who bribed the juror."

"I don't believe it!" Stacy Strickstein's face had turned the color of a ripe plum.

"You'll get a chance to hear him say it. The dead man speaks only the truth."

Pincher wiped a hand across his face as if to clear his vision. "Jesus, Jake. First you represent a guy who claims he shot his wife in self-defense, only he never shot her at all. Now you got his best friend saying he's the killer. Not only that, he bribed a juror. What the hell has happened to our justice system?"

"I've been asking myself the same thing for years."

Thirty yards off the balcony, a single red-tailed hawk floated in the breeze. I wondered if it was the same one that lost its buddy to Thurston's shotgun. I felt sorry for the dead hawk, but not for the dead Drexler.

"So why would the juror ID you on the bribery?" Pincher asked.

"You're gonna have to get that out of him, but I have a theory."

"Which will be as fanciful as the rest of this," Strickstein said.

"Gutierrez was scared to death of Drexler, who'd threatened to kill him if he squealed. So I'm guessing he was pissing his pants when he gave Strickstein his statement. He probably told her he's afraid to testify in open court."

"Ray, are you listening to this?" Strickstein said. "'Guessing'? 'Probably'? Where's the evidence?"

"Hear him out, Stacy."

"I'm betting that Strickstein told Gutierrez that Drexler worked for me. After all, I'm defending the case. She'd already found the video with me talking to Gutierrez outside of court. She tells him that was unethical of me, which it was. He's accepted a bribe, and he's scared. He'll do anything it takes to get immunity. He picks up her cues and says the dirty lawyer bribed him."

"And what's my motive for suborning perjury?" Strickstein asked, sounding haughty and offended.

"Power and money."

"Meaning what?"

The hawk flew closer to the balcony. Was it watching us with accusing eyes? I entertained a paranoid thought. The hawk not only saw Thurston kill its fellow raptor but saw me shove Drexler to his death. I had a vague recollection of a Perry Mason novel, *The Case of the Perjured*

Parrot. Didn't the bird witness a murder and keep squawking about it? I hoped Detective Barrios never interviewed the hawk.

"Do you have an answer or not?" Strickstein demanded.

"Indicting me tars my pal Ray with corruption so you can steal the election," I said. "That's the power. The money is the two hundred grand you extorted from Thurston."

"Absurd! Why would Thurston pay me anything?"

"To have Gutierrez nail me and protect Drexler. And one other thing. To take a dive in Thurston's murder trial."

"You bastard! I'll sue you for slander."

"Jesus, Jake. Can you prove even a little of this?" Pincher said.

"Proving it is your job, Ray, but I can point you in the right direction."

"Go ahead. Point."

"Go back and look at Strickstein's subpoena for Thurston's cell records. Either she put in the wrong phone number or a misspelled name or a bad time frame, because she couldn't get his texts. She never even sought Drexler's records, and it turns out he's the one who made the threats."

"Any mistakes—if they were made at all—would have been innocent typographical errors," Strickstein said. "I was prepping a murder trial, not proofing my assistant's work."

"I don't get it, Jake," Pincher said. "Why would Drexler have to bribe a juror when Thurston paid Strickstein to dump the trial?"

"At first I thought they were just buying insurance. But that's not it. What Thurston and Drexler had—to quote the captain in *Cool Hand Luke*—was a failure to communicate. Thurston didn't tell Drexler he'd bribed Strickstein, and Drexler never said a word about the jury bribery until after the trial."

Looking distraught, Pincher turned to Strickstein, "Why Stacy, why?"

She didn't answer, so I did. "Strickstein knew you'd been soliciting cash for your campaign. She felt she had to do the same thing. Only difference is, you didn't suborn perjury in return for the money."

"No, he just promised a bond issue," Strickstein fired back.

"For the record, I deny that," Pincher said, not very convincingly.

"Two hundred thousand!" Strickstein fumed. "Where's the evidence?"

Pincher said, "Jake do you have Thurston on tape saying Stacy squeezed him for money?"

"Unfortunately not in so many words. In fact, not in any words."

"Ha! I knew it." Strickstein thrust both hands in the air. She must have thought she scored a touchdown. "All speculation and calumny and innuendo."

"On tape Thurston admitted that Strickstein came to see him after the acquittal. I pressed too hard for details, and he clammed up. Honestly, that's all I have."

"So you have nothing!" Strickstein's Prada pumps did a little hippity-hop, her own victory dance.

"Not all sweaters come ready-made," I said. "Sometimes, you have to knit them."

"Could you try not to talk in riddles?" Pincher said.

"Sometimes cases have to be pieced together. Strickstein, what were you doing in Thurston's condo?"

She wouldn't look at me. "Ray, I don't have to answer this shyster's questions."

"True enough. Jake, what do you suggest my office should do?" Pincher asked.

"Subpoena Thurston's corporate account maintained at Harman and Fox. It will show the day before Strickstein's visit, Thurston withdrew two hundred K in cash. The firm has the receipt plus IRS Form 8300 for cash transactions above ten grand. The next day Strickstein visited Thurston's condo. She was empty-handed going in and came out carrying a small duffel. Clyde Garner saw her, and the security cameras will confirm it. I think that raises an inference she walked out of the condo with a bag filled with cash."

"That's not enough, Jake," Pincher said. "You can't theorize cash in a duffel bag."

"It's enough to subpoena Thurston and ask him to account for the cash once he withdrew it. When he won't be able to, offer him immunity, and he'll tell you it went to Strickstein. That's my educated guess."

"There's no basis for bringing in Thurston," Strickstein said. "Tapes of Lassiter's conversations with Drexler and Thurston were illegally obtained. Lassiter wasn't acting on behalf of law enforcement, so he needed their consent to the taping, which he clearly didn't have."

"She's right," Pincher said, a bit sadly. "The recordings are inadmissible."

"Inadmissible in *court*," I said, "but admissible on page one of the *Miami Herald*."

"It's a crime to tape-record someone without their consent," Strickstein said. "You publicize this, you'll be indicted."

"We all will!" I said. "That's the beauty of it."

"I fail to see anything remotely beautiful," Pincher said, looking as downcast as I've ever seen him.

"Think about it, Ray. If this gets out, we all fall down. Which is why everything has to be settled. Right now. Right here. One day before the filing date for the election. One day before my indictment gets unsealed. Either we all go home, or we all go to jail."

-50-

The Dark Side of Me

At 5:00 p.m. I was deep in my recliner at home, an ice pack on my left knee, a tumbler of Jack Daniel's in my right hand. Receiving visitors.

Victoria Lord and Steve Solomon arrived first. I told them my version of Drexler's fall, and neither one seemed to doubt me. Told them, too, about my meeting with Pincher and Strickstein.

"We had a global settlement," I said.

"So you're not being charged with bribery?" Solomon asked.

"You sound disappointed," I said.

"I had my CTE defense nailed down. I could have made legal history."

"Sorry to spoil your fun, Solomon, but the indictment disappeared before it was unsealed. Poof!"

"That's wonderful," Victoria said.

"Glad someone's happy."

"What about the campaign finance fraud investigation?" Solomon asked.

"Poof! Poof! Pincher won't investigate Strickstein, and she won't investigate him."

Victoria said, "What about Ms. Strickstein suborning perjury in front of the grand jury?"

"Triple poof. With my indictment vanishing into thin air, that's gone, too. Some circus, huh?"

"With dancing elephants," Solomon said.

"The election got sorted out, too," I said.

"Sorted out?" Victoria asked. "Is that a euphemism for a dirty deal?"

"A sweet deal. Strickstein won't run against Sugar Ray. In fact, she's got a new job, a new civic duty, you might say."

"Anything above dogcatcher would be immoral," Solomon said.

"Pincher made a call, and she's going to be chief homicide prosecutor in Liberty County in the Panhandle," I said.

"My dad used to take me camping up there. It's mostly park land," Solomon said. "How many homicides can there be?"

"Almost none. A few illegal campfire cases, maybe some deer poaching."

I sipped at my Jack Daniel's, and Victoria said, "I think I need a drink, too, Jake. I'm happy this turned out well for you, but there's something repugnant about all this deal making."

"Hey, we're watching sausage being made here," I said. "No one said it would smell like roses."

She poured herself a Jack, and Solomon said, "You left something out, Jake. Thurston committed perjury in the murder trial."

"With the tape inadmissible, there's no way to prove that," I said, "and Pincher doesn't have the stomach for it, anyway."

"Marv Fishbein and Cyrus Frick?" Victoria said. "I assume they're in the clear, too."

"There's no campaign finance investigation, so, yeah, they're fine."

"It's no wonder you've lost faith in the justice system," Victoria said.

"Best darned system in the world," I said, "with the possible exception of trial by combat."

"You saved Fishbein's ass," Solomon said. "He oughta give you a raise."

"Actually, he fired me by text about an hour ago. Said it was the only way he could keep Biscayne Insurance as a client."

"That's too bad," Victoria said, just as Solomon said, "That's great!"

"It's fine," I told them. "I can fly solo again."

"No!" Solomon said. "Join us. You get top billing. Lassiter, Solomon and Lord. The Three Musketeers."

"Not if I have to wear a frilly shirt."

"Jake, I'd love it if you'd join us," Victoria said.

"But you can't share in the Caruana settlement," Solomon jumped in quickly. "That would be unethical."

"I don't want a dime," I said. "As far as a partnership is concerned, let's talk after I get my personal life in order."

"You don't have a personal life," Solomon said.

Victoria gave him a scolding look. "Jake means his health issues."

As if on cue, Dr. Melissa Gold walked into the study and said, "Am I interrupting anything?"

I allowed as how she wasn't. Melissa was wearing one of those clinging wrap dresses that look so good on tall, slender women. It had a belt that tied at the hip, and the color might have been called rust or plum or maybe something fancier, but it looked terrific with her reddish-brown hair.

Victoria and Solomon gave hearty hellos to Melissa with much kissing of cheeks and good-byes to me, minus the smooching.

"I'm glad you two are leaving," I said. "I've gotta drop my pants now."

"Really?" Victoria said.

"Missed my injection this morning."

"With his big butt," Solomon said to Melissa, "no chance you'll miss the target."

I eased out of my recliner and walked my two pals to the door. I was looking forward to one-on-one time with Melissa, even if a large-gauge needle was involved.

Victoria had already exited when Solomon stopped, turned to me, and whispered, "Did Detective Barrios buy that bullshit story about Drexler falling, Jake?"

"It's not bull."

"Jakie, this is me you're talking to."

"Meaning what?"

"Why are we best friends?"

"Because it's the only way I can hang around Victoria."

"Sure, there's that. But it's because we're so much alike."

I groaned. "This is where I shoot myself."

From the driveway Victoria called out, "Hey boys! What's going on?"

"In a second, Vic." Solomon moved so close I could feel his breath in my ear. "I'm your dark side. I'm you when the sun is down and there are no witnesses. I'm the Lassiter you fight against but in times of crisis, you always revert to."

"Thanks for the analysis, Solomon. Now I don't need a shrink."

"You haven't asked me how I'm dead-solid certain you tossed that fat piece of crud off the balcony."

"Go ahead. Tell me."

"Because, Jake, my friend, it's just what I would have done."

-51-

The Truth

With Solomon and Lord gone, Melissa Gold delivered the medical news.

"We have preliminary results on the first several rounds of injections," she said.

"And?"

"The antibodies seem to be working. Some of the misshapen tau has disappeared."

"Some?"

"It's difficult to quantify, but it could be as much as fifteen percent. That surprised me."

"In a good way."

"Of course. But I don't want you to think that this is determinative. First, we don't know if the tau will continue to dissipate. Second, we can't be sure that once misshapen tau forms, it's even possible to prevent full-blown CTE. Our research is really in its infancy."

Uncertainty reigns. Still . . .

"I choose to accept today's news as positive," I said.

"As you should. It's an excellent start. Now, didn't I hear you promise to drop your trousers?"

"And my Nittany Lion boxer shorts."

"Do it. And bend over, please."

I took my medicine like a big boy. Didn't even ask for a lollipop.

She asked how I was feeling. I told her my headaches had diminished a bit, though Tchaikovsky still insisted on banging timpani in my ears.

A few minutes later, we were standing on the back porch, listening to peacocks screech in the neighbor's yard. I asked how her day went, and she gave me a sly little smile. "I have big news."

"Me, too. But you first."

She took a breath and seemed to be thinking about just where to start. Finally she said, "I met with a neurologist at University of Miami Hospital today. Dr. Albert Hoch, an old friend I've known from conferences. He took an early stand against the NFL's incomplete head-injury reporting and has been active in concussion studies. So I told him about you. He actually remembered you from your playing days."

"If he bet on the Dolphins, I probably cost him some money."

"Dr. Hoch has identified four former players who are in virtually the same situation as you. Misshapen tau that doesn't really have a name. For now, we're calling it pre-CTE."

"Four ex-Dolphins?"

"Two Dolphins plus one from Tampa Bay and one from Jacksonville." She gave a look of slight embarrassment. "I had no idea you had three NFL teams in Florida."

"And none very good."

"Dr. Hoch says there are hundreds of retired players living in Florida. I guess they like the weather."

"And no state income tax. So, what's your news?"

Another big breath. Then she said, "Dr. Hoch has a grant to create a CTE study at the University of Miami. He wants to start with the five of you. He has the funding to expand it to dozens more with extensive monitoring and testing and the experimental use of different protein antibodies until one is found that will arrest or possibly reverse the disease. He can do so much more than I can do alone. Isn't that exciting?"

"I'm not sure. Are you lateraling me to this guy?"

She seemed tense, her shoulders rigid. "That's what I wanted to talk to you about."

"Am I losing you already?" I didn't like the way I sounded. Needy. And I hate needy.

Her eyes flicked away. Maybe she was looking at the red blossoms on the bottlebrush tree. Or maybe just buying time.

C'mon Melissa! What are you thinking? What are you doing?

Summoning the courage to dump me? Not that it would take so much.

"We need to have a frank conversation about the future," she said.

"Isn't that what diplomats say when they've just threatened to use nuclear weapons? 'We just had a frank conversation with North Korea.'"

"What I mean is being totally open and honest with each other about where we stand."

Here it comes. If she says, "We'll still be friends," I'll need a bottle of whiskey.

"Sure thing, Melissa. Shoot."

"Dr. Hoch asked me to run the study with him. It would require my moving here and taking a sabbatical from UCLA for at least three years, and I wanted to ask you . . ."

She let it hang there.

Ask me what? Think! Think, Jake! Don't make her say it.

Oh, that!

"Yes!" I said. "Yes, I want you to. I want you to move here. And not just to stick needles in me."

She exhaled and smiled. "I was so hoping you'd say that."

She moved a step closer, and so did I. We kissed. I slipped my arms around her, and we kissed again. Slower. Deeper. Longer. She fit perfectly in my arms, a tidy package of a woman, and I felt a stirring, physical and otherwise. There was just something about her, and whatever it was, she moved me.

After the fifth or sixth kiss, we came up for air.

"And how was your day?" she asked, her face flushed.

"Ah, well, it was eventful," I said.

"Tell me."

"Like you said, it's important that if we're going to be spending a lot of time together, we've got to be totally open and honest with each other."

"Of course I'll be. I always am."

"Not you I'm worried about," I said. "I need to tell you everything. Hide nothing. No lying, not even white lies."

"Is that a problem for you?"

"Not anymore."

"Good. In Los Angeles, I've known men who lie about their age, their hair implants, and their marital status."

"I'm going to be real with you. Always."

"I appreciate that, Jake. Now, you said today was eventful. What did you do?"

"Today," I said, "I gave justice a little shove in the ass."

-52-

Aristotle, I Am Not

We sat on the back porch. A gentle breeze carried the whistle of Metrorail, which competed for attention with the cries of male peacocks in heat. Melissa did not share my enthusiasm for sour mash whiskey, so she mixed a couple of Moscow Mules, a mixture of vodka, ginger beer, and lime juice. It was a spicy combo that tickled the throat on the way down.

With a white sliver of moon peeking through the bottlebrush tree, I told Melissa everything.

Yeah, everything. From the beginning. Things she already knew and things she didn't.

How I wanted to lose the Thurston murder trial but won. How I planned to kill him but never did. How I got framed for bribing a juror and nearly framed for campaign finance fraud. And the biggie: how earlier today I pushed Drexler to his death.

That last one got her attention. She blinked twice but otherwise betrayed no emotion, waiting for me to finish my tale. I told her that all of us—Ray Pincher, Stacy Strickstein, Marvin Fishbein, Cyrus Frick,

Thunder Thurston, and little old me—had gotten away with crimes ranging from perjury to murder.

It was a lot for me to dish out and for her to take in.

When I finished she said, "Were you in a rage when you committed this act? Wait. I shouldn't sugarcoat. When you committed this *murder*."

"No rage. No fury. No irresistible impulse. No cop-outs."

"When you looked over the railing and saw the man falling to his death, did you feel you were gazing into the abyss?"

"Or was the abyss gazing into me?"

She nodded, perhaps pleased that I wasn't totally unschooled. I took Philosophy 101 at Penn State. They made us read Nietzsche, which was cool because I was going through my nihilism stage, pretty much a sophomore's rite of passage.

"What are you suggesting?" I said. "That when I fought the monster, I became one?"

"I'm asking you to consider the damage to your own being. Do you feel guilt or shame?"

I shook my head. "My primary motivation was to protect Clyde Garner. After what he'd been through, I couldn't stand the thought of him dying in prison. If anything, I'm glad about what I did."

She took a long hard pull on her ginger-spiced vodka. Then she said, "I'm curious about your ethical beliefs. You wanted to protect Mr. Garner, so you committed a murder. And you feel fine with it. How do you justify that, morally?"

"Melissa, I don't know how else to say it. I did what I thought was right at the time."

From somewhere in the bushes, a bullfrog burped. On the porch, a green lizard about the size of my pinky poked up through the wooden slats. Its head darted left and right, didn't like what it saw, and disappeared between the boards.

"Determining what's right and wrong by the way you feel at the time is called moral subjectivism, and it's a flawed philosophy."

"I'm a flawed man."

"We're all flawed, so that won't cut it, Jake."

Her voice had taken on an edge. My policy of complete honesty did not come without repercussions.

"Okay, what line of philosophy do you follow?" I asked. Anything to get away from my moral and philosophical failings.

"I try to act with honesty, courage, and justice. Some call it virtue ethics."

I kept quiet, but truth be told, I couldn't see myself waking up each morning, looking in the mirror, and saying "Can't wait to act with honesty, courage, and justice today."

She continued. "When we act with virtue, we live a fulfilled, contented life. Aristotle called it *eudaimonia*. Is your life fulfilled and contented, Jake?"

"I lean more toward the dissatisfied and angry side of the spectrum."

Another frog croaked in the yard, two of them now in unison.

"Would you like to change that about yourself?" Melissa asked.

I knew she meant well. This was a woman's quest to improve a man, not unlike Victoria's conversation with me on the flight to Los Angeles. God bless women; they can't help it. I knew the question about changing myself was coming from a place of caring, but I felt as if a Seventh-day Adventist was shoving pamphlets at me.

The new honest me should have said: "I'm too old to change, and given the chance to rewind the clock, I'd probably make all the same mistakes. As for today, I'd do it again. I'd shove that bastard over the railing every time."

Aristotle, I am not. Aristotle, I never will be.

But the old savvy me knew she was tossing me a rope as I sank into the quicksand. My affection for Melissa had grown. I wanted to be with her, and I knew she wanted to be with me. Maybe not forever. But for now.

Which is why I had to amend the promise. I would be 99 percent honest. I would be honest every time, except when the bold, stark truth would toss a hand grenade into our relationship.

"I'm going to try that virtue thing," I said. "I'm going to emulate Aristotle. I'm going to try *eudaimonia*, even though it sounds like something that requires penicillin. In short, Melissa, I'm going to be more like you."

-53-

Mendocino Thunderhump

Granny gathered her nets, a Coleman lantern, and a Thermos. Night shrimping with Doc Riggs, or so she claimed.

Nephew Kip grabbed his sleeping bag, hopped on his bicycle. He'd be camping out with a couple of buddies down in Pinecrest. Allegedly. Maybe that was all true. Even so, they omitted their motive. They just wanted to leave the house to Melissa and me. Oh, they are tricky, these people I love.

I cooked gigantic slabs of porterhouse steaks on the gas grill in the backyard. Baked potatoes, corn on the cob. Ample quantities of beer. Melissa had a hearty appetite for someone so slender, and I do like a woman who attacks a steak like a ravenous wolf.

Earlier she had smiled when I promised to improve my deeply flawed self, or at least try damn hard. She said that was exactly what she had hoped to hear.

Now, after dinner, sitting close on the living room sofa, Melissa asked me to play some country music because she knew I liked it and wanted to hear some of the classics. We listened to Kenny Rogers sing about his lady and Waylon Jennings, in a voice as rich as Tennessee bourbon, praise his good-hearted woman. Then George Jones sang "Golden Ring," which is unabashedly about getting hitched.

In a matter of moments, there was a whole lot of kissing going on. At a pause in the action, she reached into her purse and pulled out a small plastic bag. "Would you like a glazed pecan?" she asked.

It struck me as an odd question. Given the circumstances, I mean. I politely declined, making clear I have nothing against pecans, glazed, salted, or otherwise.

"Gummy bear?" she said.

Again I declined.

"But you don't mind if I do?" she asked sweetly.

"Of course not."

She popped a gummy bear into her mouth, which did not seem to interfere with her ability to maintain long, slow kisses. Again and again.

My coral rock house is small. It's thirteen paces from living room to bedroom, but on a first encounter, it can seem like a million miles. Which was why it was helpful that Melissa stood, took me by the hand, and nodded in the general direction of the darkened room with the king-size bed and thankfully clean sheets.

"Are you sure you don't want a gummy bear?" she asked.

"No, thanks. You're sweet enough for me." Clearly my most dumb-ass, cornball bedroom remark in a long history of goofy come-ons.

"Suit yourself," she said. "Can you put some music on in here?"

"More country?"

"Music to strip by."

"Ah. What would that be, exactly?"

"So many from which to choose." She started dancing, her hips sliding seductively. "How about 'Bailando' by Enrique Iglesias." She sang it: *"Yo te miro, se me corta, la respiración."*

"You take *my* breath away," I said, "but I don't have the CD, and it would probably take me an hour to figure out have to download it."

She cocked her head, and her tongue licked her upper lip. "How about 'Loca' by Shakira? The merengue beat just makes me want to take off my clothes."

Who knew?

"And I'm crazy but you like it," she sang, hips and shoulders swiveling to a beat only she could hear.

As she danced, she twirled the belt on her clingy wrap dress, then gave it a pull and shimmied, letting the dress fall to the floor. Her bra and panties were black, lacy, and see-through shear. She was a woman who planned ahead.

The bra came off first, and she kept dancing and singing, "Loca, loca, loca."

The panties were next.

"Jake, you're way behind. Drop your trousers. No needles this time."

I did as instructed. Joined her dancing to the best of my aching knee's ability. When I moved close, I noticed her eyes were bloodshot, her pupils enlarged. "You're stoned!"

"Mm-hmm," she agreed.

"Glazed pecans? Gummy bears?"

"Marijuana infused. For medicinal purposes only. I'm a doctor."

"From California," I said, "where everything is legal."

"Dispensaries on nearly every corner. The pecans are glazed with a sativa called Mendocino Thunderhump."

"Sounds like a Roller Derby team. What's your medical condition, anyway?"

"Insomnia," she said. "But not tonight. Not for me and not for you."

In a few moments, we were in bed. Naked and alive. The scent of evening jasmine drifted through an open window. A lot of me was touching a lot of her, and she wasn't complaining. In a moment there was even more of me.

We made love gently at first, and then more urgently. There was much *oohing* from her and *aahing* from me. Her sounds grew louder, the pitch higher, until they became wails of unrestrained pleasure. My breaths came heavier, hoarse animalistic growls of need. Her heat stirred me. My passion inflamed her. Wrapped around me, she was uninhibited and free, tossing her head, hair flying.

Afterward we were both silent, and I held her for a few minutes before feeling a stirring that she must have felt, too.

"Dance with me again," she said.

We did and it lasted longer with even greater peaks. Later, eyes heavy, I knew she had been right. There would be no insomnia tonight. Just as I was dozing off, I heard her say, "Jake, dear, you've whetted my appetite."

"For more? You want more?"

"For ice cream. Do you have any Ben & Jerry's Chubby Hubby?"

-54-

You Can't Play Half-Speed or Half-Assed

In the morning, I sliced a papaya and a mango, scrambled eight eggs, fried nine strips of bacon, and toasted four slices of multigrain bread, which I served with guava jam. And a pot of coffee.

Jake Lassiter, your host for the morning after.

Melissa and I talked and ate and smooched and made plans for dinner . . . and breakfast tomorrow, too. She hustled off to meet Dr. Hoch at the hospital. There were forms to fill out, equipment to order, meetings to be had.

A few minutes later, I heard Kip banging through the front door, having bicycled home from his one-night campout.

"Shouldn't you be in school?" I asked.

"Forgot my books last night."

"Did you have breakfast?"

"Not hungry."

I offered to give him a ride, but he said he would pedal to Biscayne-Tuttle. It wasn't far. He gathered up his backpack and headed for the door, his ninety-second visit nearly over. I insisted that he eat a tangerine and take a banana and a bottled protein drink with him.

I was peeling the tangerine when he said, "Coach Coates says if I keep practicing hard, I might get some snaps at backup wide receiver."

"Great," I said, but that's not what I thought. Receivers take so damn much punishment after they catch—or miss—the ball. Kip was tall and gangly and hadn't yet filled out in the chest and shoulders. His running stride was all moving parts, flying knees and awkward elbows. Not fluid, but the kid had a lot of quick, as the coaches say. I've been tossing a football with him in Peacock Park for years, so he had good hands, too. But with all the news about head injuries, I was starting to regret ever encouraging him to play the game.

When Kip was twelve, I painted numbers on half a dozen footballs for the concentration drill. I'd throw looping soft passes in his direction, and he had to yell out the painted number before he caught the ball. More often than not, he'd get the number and make the catch with me yelling, "Thumbs in! Catch the ball thumbs in."

Now, while chomping on the tangerine slices, Kip said, "Oh, Uncle Jake. I didn't tell you. Jorge Lambiet got a stinger yesterday when he tackled Lukowski. Jorge's arm was hanging there like a dead piece of meat."

Oh, man. This parenthood business—even the pinch-hitting variety—was fraught with fears. There was something I'd wanted to say to him for a while, and now I finally let it go. "You know, Kip, you don't have to play football just because I did."

"I love to play!"

"There are other sports."

"Like what?"

"Biscayne-Tuttle has a bowling team."

"I'm not a nerd, Uncle Jake."

"All I'm saying, be careful."

"Playing football? How?"

I was stumped, and before I could come up with an answer, Kip said, "When you played in high school, you got a frozen elbow in practice. You told me you put your arm in a vise in wood shop and a teammate used a mallet to pound the elbow straight."

"Did I also tell you I bawled my eyes out all night? And now the elbow creaks like a rusty gate every time I hoist a beer?"

"Me and you are Lassiters," he said, ungrammatically but accurately. "We can handle the pain."

Jeez, I don't want a carbon copy of me. I wanted someone better.

"Most injuries occur in practice. You know that, right, Kip?"

"So?"

"Next time you scrimmage, let's say you're at wide receiver, running a slant across the middle against the first team defense."

Thinking of little Mark Duper, my teammate on the Dolphins. Fearless then, brain damaged now.

"The pass is a little high and a little long," I continued. "Suppose you sense a defensive back coming at you hard and fast. You can hear him snorting like a Thoroughbred on the back stretch, and he's gonna clean your clock. What do you do?"

"I lay out for the ball and take the hit. What else can I do?"

"Short-arm it. It's only practice."

"What? 'You can't play half-speed or half-assed. In football or in life.' That's what you told me."

"Maybe I was wrong."

I had taught Kip what I had been told. Once you strap on the pads and buckle your chin strap, you go full speed. Deliver a shock! Hit somebody! But that seemed damn stupid now.

"What's going on, Uncle Jake? You've been acting weird lately."

"Seems everything I once believed is now open to question."

"Not football!"

"I wish high schools would switch to flag football. It can be fun without tackling."

"Jeez, Uncle Jake. You want to pussify the game."

"Don't talk like that, Kip. It's disrespectful to women."

"Okay, but what's going on?"

"When you reach my age, Kip, there may not be professional football."

"No Super Bowl? That would be like a ginormous tragedy."

"Huge men in knickers and plastic hats hurling themselves at one another? What's the point?"

"The Super Bowl!" Kip said.

"That's for the car companies and breweries to hawk their products. I wouldn't shed a tear if the sport went away. But seeing our heroes lose their bodies and their minds? That's the damn shame of it, Kip. That's the tragedy."

·55·

Planting a Tree

Five minutes after Kip bicycled off to school, I was still in the kitchen, reading the morning paper. I had nowhere to go.

A voice mail from the Harman and Fox office manager had informed me not to cross the threshold of those sacred grounds. Trusty assistants would box up my "personal effects" and deliver them by courier.

I was reading about the latest Burmese python hunt in the Everglades—ninety-five caught, fifteen thousand to go—when the phone rang. Coach Johnnie Duncan calling from Atlanta. I had last seen him in court, where he testified to Thunder Thurston's good character. On his way out of the courtroom, he'd hugged Thurston—a strong man-to-man hug that the jury seemed to appreciate.

"I heard about Jelly Bean Drexler," he said. "Horrible."

"It surely was," I agreed.

"From the time he was ten years old, he couldn't stay out of trouble."

"But Thurston was always loyal to him, wasn't he?"

The coach was silent a moment. Then he said, "I apologize for not calling to congratulate you after Marcus was acquitted."

"That's not what you should apologize for, Coach."

"Not following you, Lassiter."

"You knew, didn't you? You knew Drexler killed Eva."

He didn't answer.

"I accused Thurston of lying to you," I said. "He denied it. Told me you were the best man he ever knew, and he'd never deceive you. I think he was telling the truth."

"And I never lied to you, Lassiter. I told you Marcus Thurston was innocent, and he was. In the end, justice was done, wasn't it?"

"It took a helluva serpentine path getting here. Not the way the system is supposed to work."

"I'm just a simple football coach, Lassiter. *X*s and *O*s on a blackboard. I'm gonna let you deal with the bigger issues."

We said our good-byes, and I sat there for several minutes. Then I heard heavy gears grind and brakes squeal in my driveway.

I headed outside and found an open-bed truck with a giant palm tree tied down and covered with wet tarps. Clyde Garner stepped down from the high cab, and his twin sons, Slade and Brick, slid out the passenger door. This time I could tell one from the other thanks to name patches on the coveralls. In total, three barrel-chested men in work clothes and muddy boots.

"What's this, Garner?" I gestured toward the truck.

He took off a pair of dirt-caked gloves, grabbed my right hand, and shook it with his own calloused paw. His grip could have crushed walnuts. When he let go, Brick bear-hugged me, lifting me off the driveway and putting me down so his twin could do the same. I would check for broken ribs later.

"The Garner family owes you, Lassiter," Clyde Garner said.

"No, you don't."

"There's no way to repay you for what you did. But as a token of our love for Eva, we brought you a royal palm. Not just any tree. Her favorite. I planted it outside Eva's bedroom window the day she was born."

"I don't know what to say, Clyde."

He untied the end of a rope that lashed the tree to the truck bed. Ran his hand across the bark, as gently as if he were touching his daughter's face. His pain was palpable. "Look at it now. Nearly sixty feet tall. Stood there all those years like it was guarding my little girl, protecting her from harm." He wiped a tear with the back of his hand. "Turned out nothing could protect her, not even the family that loved her."

Lost for words, I clasped an arm around his shoulder.

"You're the one who did justice by her," he said. Now his tears began to flow. "Me and the boys are gonna plant this right outside your window. When you look out, think of my family and how grateful we are to you."

"I'll think of Eva," I said. "Every day."

"As we do," Clyde Garner said.

"Backhoe and crane are on the way," Brick said.

"Got to get it into the ground quick 'cause of transplant shock," Slade said.

Brick grabbed a bucket of soil from the truck bed and toted it to his father.

Clyde Garner dipped his bare hand into the bucket and let the moist, black dirt run through his fingers. "We shook this soil off the root ball. When the tree's in the hole, we're each gonna grab a couple handfuls and pour them in, and we want you to join us. A family ceremony. I'll recite the Lord's Prayer, and we'll have a moment of silence to think our private thoughts."

"I'd be honored," I said.

"Good, 'cause you're family now, and I don't mean a distant cousin. Anybody ever messes with you, they're gonna have to deal with me and my boys."

The twins started untying the ropes that lashed down the giant tree. Just as their father had done, their hands glided softly across the trunk.

"Yesterday when you talked me out of taking that shot," Garner said, "you didn't just save me. But my boys, too."

"I don't understand."

"They were with me, Lassiter."

"I was in the truck," Brick said. "Getaway driver."

"I was flying the drone," Slade said. "Creating the distraction."

"That was you?" I said. "Buzzing the balcony? Thurston thought it was TMZ or Gawker."

"It's our Phantom 4 drone with 4K video," Slade said.

"We use it to take inventory of the trees for tax purposes," his father said.

"Figured if we flew close to Thurston's condo, he'd come out and start shooting. I'd seen him do it to somebody else's drone the day I was over there. My plan was to shoot him once he came out to the railing."

"But getting your sons involved," I said, shaking my head. "They would have been indicted as coconspirators or accessories."

"Like I said, you saved them. Another reason I'm eternally grateful to you."

Slade stuck his head back into the truck cab and emerged with an iPad. "You wanna see?" he asked me. "I got a close-up of the bastard's face when he was falling. Freeze-framed it. Never seen a man so scared, knowing he was seconds away from just being pulverized."

"Oh, shit! You recorded it? You have it on video?"

Your Honor, the state wishes to mark as Exhibit A a videotape of Mr. Lassiter pushing Mr. Drexler to his death.

"Pretty much the whole thing," Slade said. "Phantom was hovering about forty feet off the balcony. Had the sun behind it, a good angle. Caught you crouching down behind Drexler and firing up. You still got some powerful legs to toss that ton of shit over the railing."

"Except you damn near fell over backward." Brick said, chuckling.

"We watched the video ten or twelve times last night," Slade said.

"More like twenty," his father said. "I hope you don't think less of me, Lassiter, but I loved every second of it. Afterward I got my first good night's sleep since Eva was killed."

"This video could be a problem," I said. "For me, I mean."

"No worries. Burned the disc last night, and we'll delete the iPad file as soon as you watch it."

"I don't need to see it." I looked around, as if Detective Barrios might pop out of the bushes. "Could you delete it now?"

"No problem," Slade said. I watched as he erased the file.

Garner cleared his throat and nodded in Brick's direction. Looking embarrassed, Brick said, "Me and my brother want to apologize for smacking you around down at the farm. We had the wrong idea about you."

Clyde Garner chimed in. "That goes double for me. Sorry about those names I called you."

"Shyster, sleazebag, and bloodsucker," I said. "Hey, I earned every one."

"No, that's not you, Lassiter."

"Maybe not now," I said.

Everyone was quiet a moment. Then Clyde said, "Say, Lassiter, you have a lady?"

"I think so. I hope so."

"Maybe bring her down to the farm Sunday. We're roasting a pig on a spit. Corn pudding, fresh-picked tomatoes. Homegrown potatoes. Lots of beer. After supper I might play a little fiddle music. We'll make you feel welcome."

"You already have, Clyde. You're my family, too."

-56-

Redemption

About a minute after the Garners drove off, a black Chrysler with government plates and a tinted windshield pulled into my driveway. I was watering my new royal palm with a garden hose. The tree was deep in its newly dug hole, wood struts supporting it until the root ball spread its wings.

Ray Pincher got out of the Chrysler and walked over to me.

"Sugar Ray. Business or pleasure?" I said, hosing down the tree at the roots.

"Not sure. Was that Clyde Garner I just saw pulling onto Douglas Road?"

"And his boys."

Pincher eyed the palm tree. "You buy that from the Garners?"

"Gift."

"I thought they hated you."

"Not anymore. People change."

"You or them?"

"They're good people. As are you, Ray." I grinned at him. "Coffee?"

He shook his head. "Just wanted to tell you something face-to-face."

"Why? Because you don't know if your phone is bugged or because you just like my handsome mug?"

He didn't answer, so I kept watering the tree.

"C'mon, Farmer Jake. Let's walk and talk."

I turned off the faucet, dried my hands on my Dolphins jersey, and we headed west on Poinciana. For a guy who wanted to talk, Pincher didn't say much. Not a word until we hung a left on Braganza and headed toward El Prado. Like much of the south end of Coconut Grove, my neighborhood is heavy with vegetation. Live oaks. Bougainvillea. Palms. Shrubs of a hundred varieties.

"A man shouldn't be judged by the worst act of his life," he said at last.

"Hey, that's what defense lawyers say, not prosecutors."

"You know what I mean, Jake."

Actually, I didn't. I wasn't sure if he was talking about himself. Or me.

"I like to think I've done a lot of good in this community for a lot of years," he said.

Ah, nice. This was about him.

"You've done a helluva lot of good, Ray."

"And then one day I decide to solicit cash for my reelection. Well aware of the illegality. But perhaps oblivious to the moral toll it would take on me."

"Like you said, we shouldn't judge a man on his worst day."

"I'm giving the cash to the homeless shelter downtown. Anonymously, of course. And I'm going to volunteer there two weekends a month."

"That's great, Ray. I know it comes from your heart."

A pair of monarch butterflies fluttered out of a palm tree and flew past our heads. "What I've believed ever since I was at seminary is this: no matter how much a person has erred, there is still redemption. I'm seeking a state of grace through humanistic actions."

303

"You're on your way, Ray."

"And you, Jake? What of you?"

Whoops. So this was about me, too. I slowed, picked up a fallen palm frond from the middle of the street, and carried it to the berm, just to buy time. We turned left on El Prado, a busy street that connected Le Jeune to Douglas Road.

"I remember what you said about redemption the day you knocked me out cold in the ring," I said.

"Biblical redemption? Saul of Tarsus on the road to Damascus."

"More like Jake of Miami on the road to South Beach."

"I'm listening."

Pincher's confession had loosened my tongue. I would never admit what I did, but I wanted to unburden myself of a couple of thoughts. "Ray, for a long time, I followed a set of rules that often led to injustice. I left pain and hurt in my wake. I can't undo my mistakes, but I thought I might find a way to help the people I've hurt."

"A way that wasn't strictly by the book." Pincher was with me stride for stride.

"A way that was blatantly illegal and patently immoral," I said. "All in the name of redemption, even though my actions could not possibly be considered redemptive by a civilized society."

"Do you care what society considers redemptive?"

I thought about it. "I'm supposed to. It's probably implicit in the oath we both took as lawyers. But really I don't care. I feel redeemed, and that's gonna have to do."

"As I am not without sin, I will not cast the first stone."

"Thank you, Ray."

"I feel better having talked to you, Jake."

"Same here."

He stopped abruptly at the intersection of Utopia Court, surely the best-named street in Miami. Utopia ran in a circle with four grassy cul-de-sacs filled with trees. "Let's head back, Jake. I want to take another look at that royal palm. Helluva tree."

"Tallest one on the block."

We walked in silence another moment.

"It's good having friends."

"You and me, Ray. You bet."

"Sure, but I was thinking about you and the Garners. Good karma."

"How do you mean?"

"I pulled Clyde Garner's cell phone records from yesterday. He called you just moments before Drexler took his unfortunate fall."

"Really?"

"You answered, but then everything was muffled."

"How would you know that?"

"That disc you gave me from Fishbein's belt. Every conversation was clear before and after Garner's call. I figure you covered your belt buckle with your big, meaty hand."

"Whatever prompted you to get Garner's cell records?"

"Didn't I tell you? Security cameras at Fisher Island caught him and his boys going on and off the ferry yesterday."

"No crime in that."

He chuckled softly. "Thanks to you. What the hell were they thinking? All three of them would have spent the rest of their lives in prison."

I kept quiet, and Pincher didn't seem to mind. He knew what I was thinking, and I knew what he was thinking. Likely Detective Barrios had shared his thoughts about the unlikelihood of an accidental fall over that high railing. Just as likely, Pincher would have said, "So what? We've got no witness who says otherwise."

As we rounded the corner onto Poinciana, he said, "You gonna fertilize that tree?"

"Not for a while. Clyde said fertilizer would increase the chance of transplant shock. Tree could die, which I don't even want to think about. I'd feel I let the Garners down."

"Just water, then?"

"That's what he advised."

As we approached the tree, we both craned our necks upward, past the green crown shaft into the dense stems and fronds at the top.

"Lots of water," I said.

"It'll be fine," Pincher said. "That's one tree that's not gonna die."

Final Words

I spent the rest of the day at home, considering my options. Solomon and Lord had offered me a spot—leadoff hitter—on their team. It was enticing. But I could also fly solo again. That had its advantages.

Melissa called around 1:00 p.m., and we firmed up plans for dinner at a Cuban place in Coral Gables. Granny poked her head into my study and allowed as how I seemed "mighty mellow" today, winking as she said it. Then she padded down the corridor to take a nap, feeling pretty mellow herself after a night allegedly shrimping with Doc Riggs. Kip was at football practice, hopefully staying safe.

At about 3:00 p.m., I was looking out the window at my new royal palm when the phone rang again.

"Mr. Lassiter, this is Rudy Schulian at the *Miami Herald*."

"I already subscribe, though some days I wonder why."

"I'm a reporter, sir. An intern actually."

"An intern! In the old days, Edna Buchanan would call me for quotes."

"Actually, I'm in the obit department."

"I didn't know Rashan Drexler well enough to comment."

"Not him, sir. It's your obit."

"How's that? I think I'm still alive."

"Yes, sir. But we prewrite obits on prominent Floridians."

"Didn't know I was in that club."

"The editors say the Thunder Thurston murder trial elevated your profile."

And will follow me to the grave.

"Any chance you might run a photo with the obit?" I asked.

"Not my call, but I see several pictures in the file. Here's an old one in your Dolphins uniform. You have a big, bushy mustache."

"I know that shot. I look young and rugged."

"With due respect, sir, you look like one of those eighties porn stars."

"Well, memory plays tricks. Maybe you can delete it."

"I don't think I'm allowed to do that, sir."

"How much they paying you in this internship, Rudy?"

"Actually, nothing. I'm doing it for the experience."

"Do you get college credits?"

"No, sir. I've already graduated."

"When we're done, Rudy, you round up all the freebie interns and come see me. Do you know what a class action is?"

"Yes, sir, but I don't think I can sue my employer."

"Okay, work for free. What else do you need, kid?"

"Is it true you got the nickname Wrong Way Lassiter because you scored a touchdown for the opposing team?"

"First of all, that's not my nickname. I'm Last Chance Lassiter because I take hopeless cases and occasionally win. And, Rudy, for future reference, it's impossible to score a touchdown for the opposing team."

"But you did, Mr. Lassiter, against the Jets."

"A safety! Not a touchdown. I got turned around, ran to the wrong end zone, and got tackled for a safety."

"I see." He sounded unsure. "That's two points, right?"

"Of course! Where the hell did you go to college?"

"Sarah Lawrence."

"That explains it. What else, kid?"

"I need to confirm you've never been married."

"Yet. That could change before I'm dead. Hopefully, not the day before."

"Of course. Would you like to hear my lead? I have a rough draft."

"Fire when ready, Rudy."

"Jake Lassiter, a second-string linebacker with the Miami Dolphins and later a criminal defense lawyer with a reputation for courtroom theatrics, died—"

"Wait! I changed my mind."

"Sir?"

"I don't want to hear it. I don't want to focus on the end of my days. I want to think about life."

"I respect that, sir."

"Now, do you need a quote?"

"Well, no. My assignment is to check facts, not gather quotes."

"Let's expand the assignment. Think big."

"But I'm only an intern."

"I know. From Sarah Lawrence. Working for free. Now listen, Rudy, because you might learn something."

"Learn about what, sir?"

"About life! You want to know my philosophy?"

"I guess."

"I want to live fearlessly. I want to love mightily. I want to leave a legacy of having done more good than harm."

Over the phone line, I heard his keyboard clacking. He was taking notes.

"That's pretty good, Mr. Lassiter."

"Thanks, kid. Just when I thought I'd run into a streak of bum luck, everything turned around. Life is looking up. So take that obit and file it high in the digital clouds, as high as heaven itself. I've still got a helluva lot of living to do."

ALSO AVAILABLE

LASSITER, SOLOMON & LORD SERIES

"The pages fly by and the laughs keep coming in this irresistible South Florida romp. A delicious mix of thriller and comic crime novel."
—*Booklist* (starred review of *Bum Rap*)

BUM RAP: Defending Steve Solomon in a murder case and fighting his growing feelings for Victoria Lord, Jake Lassiter find a missing witness—a stunning Bar girl—before she's eliminated by the Russian mob.

JAKE LASSITER SERIES

"Mystery writing at its very, very best."
—Larry King, *USA TODAY*

TO SPEAK FOR THE DEAD: Linebacker-turned-lawyer Jake Lassiter begins to believe that his surgeon client is innocent of malpractice . . . but guilty of murder.

NIGHT VISION: After several women are killed by an Internet stalker, Jake is appointed a special prosecutor and heads to London and the very streets where Jack the Ripper once roamed.

FALSE DAWN: After his client confesses to a murder he didn't commit, Jake follows a bloody trail from Miami to Havana to discover the truth.

MORTAL SIN: Talk about conflicts of interest. Jake is sleeping with Gina Florio and defending her mob-connected husband in court.

RIPTIDE: Jake Lassiter chases a beautiful woman and stolen bonds from Miami to Maui.

FOOL ME TWICE: To clear his name in a murder investigation, Jake searches for buried treasure in the abandoned silver mines of Aspen, Colorado.

FLESH & BONES: Jake falls for his beautiful client even though he doubts her story. She claims to have recovered "repressed memories" of abuse . . . just before gunning down her father.

LASSITER: Jake retraces the steps of a model who went missing eighteen years earlier . . . after his one-night stand with her.

LAST CHANCE LASSITER: In this prequel novella, young Jake Lassiter has an impossible case: he represents Cadillac Johnson, an aging rhythm and blues musician who claims his greatest song was stolen by a top-of-the-charts hip-hop artist.

STATE vs. LASSITER: This time, Jake is on the wrong side of the bar. He's charged with murder! The victim? His girlfriend and banker, Pamela Baylins, who was about to report him to the authorities for allegedly stealing from clients.

SOLOMON vs. LORD SERIES

(Nominated for the Edgar, Macavity, International Thriller, and James Thurber awards)

"A cross between Moonlighting and Night Court. Courtroom drama has never been this much fun."

—FreshFiction.com

SOLOMON vs. LORD: Trial lawyer Victoria Lord, who follows every rule, and Steve Solomon, who makes up his own, bicker and banter as they defend a beautiful young woman, accused of killing her wealthy, older husband.

THE DEEP BLUE ALIBI: Solomon and Lord come together—and fly apart—defending Victoria's "Uncle Grif" on charges he killed a man with a speargun. It's a case set in the Florida Keys with side trips to coral reefs and a nudist colony where all is more—and less—than it seems.

KILL ALL THE LAWYERS: Just what did Steve Solomon do to infuriate ex-client and ex-con "Dr. Bill"? Did Solomon try to lose the case in which the TV shrink was charged in the death of a woman patient?

HABEAS PORPOISE: It starts with the kidnaping of a pair of trained dolphins and turns into a murder trial with Solomon and Lord on *opposite* sides after Victoria is appointed a special prosecutor, and fireworks follow!

313

STAND-ALONE THRILLERS

IMPACT: A Jetliner crashes in the Everglades. Is it negligence or terrorism? When the legal case gets to the Supreme Court, the defense has a unique strategy: kill anyone, even a Supreme Court justice, to win the case.

BALLISTIC: A nuclear missile, a band of terrorists, and only two people who can prevent Armageddon. A "loose nukes" thriller for the twenty-first century.

ILLEGAL: Down-and-out lawyer Jimmy (Royal) Payne tries to reunite a Mexican boy with his missing mother and becomes enmeshed in the world of human trafficking and sex slavery.

PAYDIRT: Bobby Gallagher had it all and lost it. Now, assisted by his twelve-year-old brainiac son, he tries to rig the Super Bowl, win a huge bet . . . and avoid getting killed.

ABOUT THE AUTHOR

The author of twenty novels, Paul Levine won the John D. MacDonald fiction award and was nominated for the Edgar, Macavity, International Thriller, Shamus, and James Thurber prizes. A former trial lawyer, he also wrote twenty-one episodes of the CBS military drama *JAG* and co-created the Supreme Court drama *First Monday* starring James Garner and Joe Mantegna. The critically acclaimed international bestseller *To Speak for the Dead* was his first novel and introduced readers to linebacker turned lawyer Jake Lassiter. He is also the author of the Solomon vs. Lord series, featuring bickering law partners Steve Solomon and Victoria Lord. Levine has also written several stand-alone thrillers, including *Illegal, Ballistic, Impact*, and *Paydirt*. A graduate of Penn State University and the University of Miami Law School, he divides his time between Miami and Santa Barbara, California. For more information, visit Paul Levine's Amazon author page at www.amazon.com/Paul-Levine/e/B000APPYKG/ or his website at www.paul-levine.com.